Nox Longa

Phantoms of Zibelaude Vol. 1
By Vesta Clark

Preface:

The tale of this story's conception is perhaps as engaging as what you will find within its pages. As with many interesting stories, it began at the opera where the talented artist, Kristen Margiotta, was displaying several of her paintings outside the auditorium.

At the time, I was primarily absorbed in writing fan fiction, though I had begun to conceptualize entirely new stories in worlds of my own making, and this set the stage as it were for new developments.

Margiotta's work featured gothic-style characters who inhabited spaces which were both threatening and abstract. The innocent-looking characters appeared nearly swallowed up by their environments, or with some threat looming over them which spelled impending doom... but for some reason it seemed they were mainly annoyed by the threats and not intimidated.

Even as I gazed at these paintings, I began to feel dizzy as the abstract patterns were distorted just enough that they seemed to drag my eyes into an alternate dimension, and my mind along with it.

After wandering up and down the hall, gazing at the paintings in admiration and awe, I vividly recall turning to my friend and commenting, "If I keep looking at art like this, my stories will get much darker..."

I was slightly gleeful at the idea that these new images and characters and themes were swimming around in my head. I'd never toyed with the idea of steampunk before, but there it was. Not only that, but I had a growing love of the works of Edgar Allan Poe, and it helped germinate the idea into what I titled jokingly, *Scarie Creepie*.

My aim was to name every character after another one in some work or another of Edgar Allan Poe's, though since then I've decided to veer out of that method. I still maintain at least half of my Poe references from that original draft, and I've added a few more.

What I offer you is the coming of age of this tale, which has fermented over the years from a giggling pseudo-Goth's doodles into something complex and much more self aware than it previously was.

Chapter 1: Midnight in Amontillado

The Kingdom of Zibelaude was experiencing a silver age. Nearly everyone was aware of a decline from gold, but it alarmed none of them even as they knew that it was quickly approaching something more akin to a brass age. For other kingdoms, it would perhaps have been a golden age, and with that the citizens were content.

Once, Zibelaude had been a prosperous portion of the Nespolan Empire, and now in this new era of freedom, Zibelaude led the world in industrialization and flights of exploration. A great deal of the kingdom's wealth was owing to its royal family's commitment to fostering the people's ambitions, and the way it split up each portion of the kingdom between the king's sons each generation.

One of these states was the bustling town of Amontillado, and its surrounding villages were alive with factories. Bolstered by their hold over the factories, the citizens of Amontillado were dripping with wealth… at least *most* of them were.

Each bell in all Amontillado chimed the hour in grim unison, alerting all those availing themselves of the opulent nightlife that midnight had at last arrived. As was the people's wont, they raised a cheer and drank deeply of their peppermint sherry.

None of them were out celebrating anything in particular; rather they had made it local custom to fiddle away each night in carnal frivolities.

The city itself had suffered from its people's general lackadaisical attitude, from the sagging infrastructure that had never recovered from an earthquake years previous to the cemetery groaning with the remains of pickled livers and opiate fiends. Of course, this was not the only reason most mausoleums were overstocked and more and more ground had to be consecrated by the local clergy—of late there had been an incident involving the Ravens who lived upon the hill.

While there were actual ravens which nested upon the hill outside town which sat on the border between the world of the living and the graves of the dead, this was not the only murder which nested on the old house. The local doctors, Mabel and Cecil Babcock, had found it lucrative to accumulate more cases than perfectly necessary.

Cecil was an educated sort, the local apothecary as well as the fellow who with the help of his wife prepared the local men and women for burial… except that he had at some undefined point decided it was much more fun to *cause* death than to prevent it. Thus over a period of five years, healthy citizens would fall ill and into the care of the Babcocks, never to emerge on their own two feet again.

The entire time, it had seemed that they were testing experimental methods of practicing medicine, and hypochondriacs from all corners of Zibelaude had met their destinies under the Babcocks' roof.

After Duke Julian had been forced to open up an investigation into the Babcocks despite his years of resistance, the people had uncovered the horrible truth, mutilated corpses of the dead were found in the basement passages of the house, and many aggrieved family members had been forced by their sorrow to flee the city. Now that the Babcocks had been hanged for their crimes, a new apothecary had been ordered from one of the other provinces in the kingdom—nobody knew or cared which one. All that mattered was that the person in question knew medicine, was willing to bury people, and didn't intend to kill anyone.

In fact, among the few who even knew that the new apothecary would arrive was one Richard Ambrose Phaal, who shuffled through the party attempting to blend in with the other revelers. He could not afford to mimic the opulent Amontillado fashions outright, but he had still done his best.

Despite the fact that his clothing was not as sumptuous as the pinstripe silks and checkered satins which surrounded him, he had done his best to sew a jacket with a similar pleated capelet out of brown and gray throwaway wool. Sure, his overcoat was rough-spun, but it was still spangled with brass buttons that had little lion faces stamped onto them, in imitation of the widespread fashion of etching fanciful images onto buttons.

His boots had once been worn by a high-powered barrister, who had paced the floor of the courthouse on many a day, and because of this, they were of fine construction. However, their soles were no longer solidly fixed in place, and the leather had begun to peel and flake. Of course, that was how he'd been able to afford them in the first place. He still polished them carefully, hoping to make the best of what he'd been able to afford, though another man may have been ashamed to stoop to such a low standard.

Richard wore this imitation of upper class garb with such pride that it may as well have been an officer's coat bedecked with medals commemorating years of heroic prowess. He was a young man newly minted with the motto, "naught beyond my means," which he hoped one day would adorn a coat of arms. Hopefully by then he would meet someone who could translate it into Latin, for he lacked the confidence to hazard the translation himself.

He no longer lived with his parents, and had not since he left for boarding school in his tender years. They were of the middling sort, and he was well aware they had quite a task already with his spinster elder sister, Hyacinth. Once he had graduated University, he was at the hard work of establishing himself as a fresh-faced solicitor in a town where reputation was as delicate as porcelain and as dearly attained.

It was for this set of circumstances that he ascended the flight of stairs to Bacchanal Hall, the most celebrated venue in the entire town outside Duke Julian's castle, Usher Abbey, which had been converted into his luxurious abode when he had displaced an order of monks.

Nobody who was anybody knew where those fellows had gone any more than they knew who was responsible for lighting the gas lamps each night, such that the fact that it was still called the Abbey was the sole reminder of its consecrated past.

Richard gazed at the cackling drunkards who surrounded him, ladies overflowing with cascades of silk, men tottering under top hats adorned with what appeared to be the entire anatomy of a clock, and everyone with wine spilling out of their hands

Richard would have to work a lifetime to drink one sip of.

He recognized many of the faces which had forgone or misplaced their masks, but he was looking for one in particular. He found her amidst a gaggle of her ten closest friends, seated beside a voluminous bouquet of roses and swirls of wire peppered with gold dust. As he approached, he hoped he would not offend them with his lowly presence.

By now everyone knew where he lived, and that was a count against his reputation. The accommodations he'd been able to rent were midway up the town's central clock tower, and they'd been within his reach since his little apartment was located in one of the many buildings still sagging from an earthquake which had rocked the town the moment Duke Julian had ridden into town in his bejeweled landau.

It wasn't even bad enough that he had to live in one of the least stable buildings in the town, whether or not the townsfolk had taken a liking to the tilted architecture which had accidentally become characteristic of the whole town. No, he had to share this clock tower with only one more resident, who was even more of a social pariah than he was.

Braxton Coy may have been a wunderkind, but unfortunately he was not the fashionable kind. His inventions were spectacularly effective at making sure the fashionably tilted buildings did not fully sink into the ground, yet he got so inordinately sooty in the process that no society-conscious person would dare admit they'd come into contact with him.

Even at this disadvantage, Richard managed to put one foot ahead of the other to approach the gorgeous and widely celebrated Lenore Roget. Her cascade of blonde ringlets framed her face under her cocked miniature top hat and she sat festooned in pink and green silk, pinstriped to the toes, shining with the soft lights arranged in her petticoats.

Richard cleared his throat as he attempted to summon the courage to say something to her. He may even have done it if he hadn't been interrupted by an ominous noise from behind him.

Screams broke out which had nothing to do with laughter, and he whirled around to see partygoers dropping their glasses of wine and backing away from one sector of the room.

Richard took that as a sign that he needed to see what everyone was so overworked about, and when he had pushed his way through the crowd, he saw a shadowy, misty figure in the corner of the mirrored hall, arms outstretched in ominous silence.

While there were some men trying to batter at the figure with their canes, Richard saw that none of them were able to reach whatever they were looking at. His instincts told him that there was some wire apparatus and perhaps steam jets perpetuating an illusion, but the shouts of "ghost!" were pervasive.

A stampede of revelers made a rush for the doors before the ghost had even done anything to anyone. A stunned Richard began to think that it was some elaborate performance to make the party more enjoyable and the greater danger rested with the stampede of petticoats and waving canes.

Except for the cries which switched from horror to agony, he would have held onto that opinion.

Were those gunshots?

Alarm rang in his ears, but Richard was not afraid for his own fate. He turned to see the flustered Lenore backed into a corner with her friends all clinging together, trying to avoid the tide of fleeing party-goers.

Richard ran toward her with a hand outstretched. "I'll get you out of here!" he promised breathlessly.

She stared at him as several of her friends babbled in incoherent screams. Her eyes were wide with cerulean terror, but she slowly reached out her lace-swathed hand for his.

Though Richard knew his hands were sweating, but he hoped she couldn't feel it through the barrier of his plain gray gloves. There was only one hole in them, anyway. He closed his hand around hers and led her through the tidal wave of shrieking runners.

With his eyes locked on the door straight ahead of them, Richard felt the drag of the several ladies clinging together as he led them along. It was as if he was wandering along the ocean floor, and he realized it was partially due to the mist filling the room.

He could hear people in the far end of the room choking, but didn't spare a glance. He knew the sight of what was going on would only terrify him more, so he refused to allow himself to get distracted.

That was exactly what Lenore's friends were doing, however. Through the pounding in his ears he could hear Lenore calling out for them to come back, but instead they were running to the windows and attempting to batter their way through them.

One girl got herself shot in the back for her trouble, and she slumped down to the ground as a crimson puddle collected around her.

Lenore screamed but Richard couldn't let her share her friend's fate.

"She may still be alive," he told her, swinging her around so she was in front of him and they could see eye to eye. "We need to get out of here or nobody will be able to help her!"

Lenore's eyes were so wide it looked as if they might fall right out of her skull, but he didn't wait for her to catch on, they simply had to run.

Since he was a gentleman, Richard didn't toss her over his shoulder, and since he wasn't particularly athletic, he didn't carry her, at all. Instead he wrapped one arm around her waist and bolted for the door.

As he ran it felt as if something bit his arm, and he imagined it might be a wild dog or a giant spider, but he didn't dare look back and check. Both ideas were ridiculous, anyway. Why did the door ahead of them appear to be melting?

Gritting his teeth in obstinate determination, Richard made that one final dash to the door and shoved it closed behind himself and Lenore. In so doing, he successfully blocked a bullet which winked at him through the oak door which stopped it short.

"My friends!" Lenore cried, and attempted to claw the door open.

"It's better to check from outside," Richard panted, assessing the crowd between them and the exit, which was clogging up the stairwell with a mass of screaming bodies.

There had to be an alternative route to escape!

With his arm firmly locked around Lenore, he sidestepped the flow of fleeing citizens. The further they were driven against the banister, Richard knew there was a risk that they might be pushed over to their deaths.

"What do we do?" Lenore squealed in his ear.

Richard's vision was beginning to betray him, but he knew Lenore still relied on him, so he'd have to do something quickly. As he cast about for something to steady himself, he felt a velvet curtain under his fingers. Even if it did fail them, it was better to try than to allow themselves to be thrown off the edge with no recourse.

He gripped the curtain with all his waning strength and tossed the edge of it over the edge of the banister. There was a fair amount of fabric that hung down, but it wasn't quite enough.

"Here!" Lenore took a pin from her hat and cut through the velvet until she and Richard were able to tie one edge to the banister and then slide down to the atrium.

While there was still a crowd fighting its way out the door, not all of them were fast enough to dodge the bullets coming from the top of the stairs.

Richard and Lenore ducked and slid carefully through the door until they were out in the midnight air, watching the people stream out of what had previously been the event of the evening, and was now something closer to the event of the decade.

Understandably, Richard watched Lenore flutter over to stand by the windows and see if her friends had made it, but that was all he was able to really take note of before he went careening to the grass below.

All he needed was a brief rest...

Chapter 2: Case Report Inconclusive

A harpsichord's delicate, intricate refrain pervaded the dark, candlelit halls of Palazzo di L'Espanaye, whose ancient walls had housed some of the kingdom's most prestigious denizens. This was a sprawling mansion which had centuries ago been built upon the crest of a hill, several hours' journey from Amontillado.

On this particular occasion, the halls had been spruced up to accommodate the arrival of the king to grace the last remaining great matriarch of the L'Espanaye family. This woman, Lady Monique of the Red Tower, was the most masterful of the noble poker champions, and today, she was putting her talents to the test yet again.

"Then we have an agreement, Your Highness?" asked the stately woman from across the table. She produced a Queen of Diamonds and won herself yet another tower of red gaming chips.

The king nodded thoughtfully, watching her as she meticulously stacked all the red chips she'd won with an amused smile. "This *is* a momentous decision, Red Tower," he said affectionately as he applied her nickname to her as an honorific.

"I promise I've found you the perfect agent for the job, Your Majesty. You'll not regret investing in this venture."

The harpsichord playing continued unabated, but there was a greater gravity to the notes which followed, as the player was listening intently for the king's reply.

"I cannot but feel that you've done all the thinking for me, already," said the king.

"I find it is the best policy to serve one's friends a fully-baked cake, rather than the batter."

The king and his attendants all laughed, and the harpsichord player pressed the keys in a sprightlier manner, anticipating the outcome she had hoped for.

Sure enough, the king said, "I believe I shall partake of this cake you've baked me, Mistress L'Espanaye, let me facilitate your endeavors to the fullest. Send all requests to my seneschal, and I will see them fulfilled."

Monique grinned at the harpsichordist, who nodded solemnly in return. "It's been a pleasure defeating you again, Your Majesty," said the woman with a grin, stacking the red chips she'd won from the king admiringly.

"It was a pleasure being bested by one so skilled, Red Tower," the king replied indulgently. "All that remains is to keep your niece in Amontillado with my son."

"Easily done, Your Highness." The woman smiled again as a servant presented her with her hat. She waved coquettishly to the captain of the guard, and was out the door.

"Percival," the king said, rising from the table.

The captain of the guard bowed, walking up to the king. "Your highness?"

"Please arrange for my dear friend to be escorted home properly."

Captain Percival nodded. "As you wish, Highness."

The king put on a long brown coat with a caplet attached. "Be friendly with her. She needs constant entertainment."

Captain Percival nodded once more. "Will you be wanting anything more, Highness?"

The king paused a moment. "Yes. On your way out, tell someone that I owe Red Tower another thousand sovereigns, and let our detective here have the case files."

The harpsichordist took the papers offered her by the captain, and then took her leave of the meeting. The less she said in the presence of the king, the better, as he may later be called upon to reveal something of what had transpired. She climbed into the cab which had been arranged to her before she broke the seal on the documents for the first time.

After several hours on the road, she concluded that none of the records out of Amontillado were quite as conclusive as she would have liked. Of course, had any of the officials in Amontillado known a pen from a tea kettle, Moretta would be out of a job.

She flipped through the photographs, but again it seemed as if someone had forgotten to clean the camera lens before shooting the images she'd been given. What she knew for sure was that her predecessors had made such a display that the townspeople were downright traumatized. Perhaps the photographer hadn't been capable of keeping their hands from shaking.

The pictures couldn't have been taken on a tripod since the angle wouldn't have been possible while using one. Even the moment it would take to use one of the new cameras couldn't have passed without jittering. The poor specialist!

She peered out the window of her cab and furrowed her brows. From what she'd heard, Amontillado was a brilliant moonlight jewel, but this wasn't exactly what she'd expected to find.

The gas-lit streets were silent save for the sounds of Richard making his way along them. Had there been a missive that told them to expect the new GP? Moretta flipped the straight-edge fringe out of her eyes and stared. Why would anyone celebrate a new town doctor like that? She was getting in hours later than she'd expected, so it wasn't as if there would be people who had the attention span to remain waiting for her to arrive.

She caught her first sight of her new abode through the mists and knew that it was much smaller than she'd expected. How much lab space was she actually going to have?

Once her cab was actually within the confines of the town's wall, Moretta realized the streets were much too choked to admit her in the cab. Thus she paid off her driver and set off on foot.

She had never seen such an array of bizarre clothing, so that consumed her thoughts most of the way down the main street of the town.

There were some women whose petticoats were stained with blood, and others who Moretta found getting fires on their skirts extinguished.

"What's happening here?" she asked one of the men extinguishing the flames. "Is this what the streets always look like at this time of night?"

Instead of an answer, Moretta received an elbow to the face, at which point she realized nobody had noticed her.

Well, this was fun. She pressed a hand to her face, and wobbled further down the street, dodging several shrieking citizens on her way. There was no point asking what had happened, not when they were too engaged in shrieking nonsense about ghosts and Bacchanals at one another to spare her a thought.

With trudging steps, Moretta reached the top of the hill, despite the congestion in her way. "I'm the doctor!" she called to the people trying to get into what was now her house by wrenching the door off of its hinges. "Let me by, I have the key!"

At last, those words sank in, and the three men backed away from the door to let her by.

"Why did it take you so long?" one of them demanded of her.

"None of the airships were willing to land on a broken airstrip," Moretta grumbled. "Maybe someone should repave that, hmm?" With those words she finally opened the door to the house.

A musty cloud of odor assaulted her for her trouble, and she stood back to cough.

"Get all the patients in!" one of the men shouted, and Moretta was nearly bowled over by those who were trying to get into her house past her.

"Wait!" she shouted. "Wait! I'll treat you out here, this air will surely harm you! Let me just go find some supplies!"

All she had with her, after all, was her doctor's bag and her keys. The rest of her luggage would have to be delivered tomorrow, thanks to this abominable crowd!

She darted into the house, and turned the gas on. There were several floor lamps and wall sconces which illuminated the drawing room, which she saw doubled as a parlor. Its bottle green wallpaper was only visible in places due to the portrait photographs which glared at her from the walls.

She set her pet carrying bag down on the faded pink couch and opened it fully, so that her little friend could hop out. "There you go, Renata," she crooned softly. "How does my baby girl like her new home?" she stroked the silken black fur from the crest of Renata's head between her ears, and then down her back to her tail.

Renata purred, and rubbed her head against Moretta's cheek.

"I know it smells something awful in here, but we'll make the best of it."

Renata began to bathe herself, so Moretta decided she was doing well enough to be left alone.

There was still a grand expanse of house to be explored, after all, not least because of the veritable mob waiting for her outside. She started with the closet across from the couch.

What she found when she entered and pulled the string to light the lamp were floor boards which appeared to be etched out for a trapdoor. "What were you *doing*?" she whispered to herself, but she wouldn't have the time to search a passage.

There at least had to be a façade of reasonable business practice, right?

"Do you need some help?"

Moretta turned to see that there was a young man leaning in the doorway clutching at his arm. Was it the lighting that washed him out? No, the faint golden glow of the lamps would over-saturate his face, instead... "I think it's I who's supposed to help you," she said, and guided him to the couch, where she unfortunately displaced Renata.

The good-natured cat did not hiss or bite, but she did jump onto the fellow's chest and peer into his eyes with her curiosity.

"What are you looking for?" the fellow asked as Moretta flitted about the room opening every drawer and cabinet until she finally opened the door into a kitchen.

"Doctor things!" she called back to him as people began to file into the parlor against her wishes.

She was really too distracted to bother scolding any of them, but inside she cringed at the thought of having to attack the blood stains some of the people would leave behind before she located any bandages.

"I've been here while it was in operation," said one of the ladies who had invaded the house, and she brushed past Moretta to open another door at the end of the parlor. "Come in here! It's an examination room!" she cried, and a flood of townsfolk followed after her.

"Wait! I can only tend one patient at a time!" Moretta protested, but her pleading went entirely unheeded... except by the young man she'd laid out on her couch.

He sat up and smiled woozily at her. "I can help," he said, though if Moretta was convinced of anything it was how erroneous an impression that was. He tried to stand and she waved her hands at him to stop.

"You've obviously had a long trek up here, you need rest," she said, and turned to concern herself with the way the examination room she hadn't even had time to find was being ransacked by the townspeople.

It became apparent that they had all utterly given up on actually getting professional treatment. In the madness they were throwing bandages and rubbing alcohol at one another and they were in a frenzy to treat their own wounds as well as those of one another.

"Stop!" Moretta cried. "You may do something wrong! There's a procedure for everything!"

When had she last raised her voice?

None of them took heed, even when Renata darted into the examination room and hissed at several of them. Instead, Renata came running into Moretta's arms after a few townsfolk had tried to stomp her lights out.

"If that's all they want to do, I might as well go upstairs," Moretta muttered to Renata. She would have done so, as well, if she hadn't caught sight of the fellow on the couch and empathized with him.

She knelt beside this fellow and opened her bag again. "Let me see," she said quietly.

The fellow pulled off his shabby brown coat, and showed her that there was a scrape wound just above his elbow. It wouldn't have been so serious if not for the fact that there was a discolored halo around the wound.

"A poisoned knife?" she asked.

"I don't think so," he rubbed at his brow. "There was someone shooting people…"

Moretta's brow rose in dismay, but she kept her lips tightly shut. There was no need to add to the bluster in the next room, she would just have to be quiet and think over what could have happened.

"So do you think you could have been grazed by a bullet?" she asked.

"Oh… yes, that could've happened," he grimaced. "There were people who may still be alive back there…"

"I can't do anything for them if I don't know where they are or what's wrong with them," Moretta responded, "but I *can* help you. Now, hold still, this is going to sting a bit."

Or a lot, but she couldn't do more than soften his expectations. She pressed alcohol-infused gauze against his wound, and he shook in spite of her trying to hold him still.

"What's your name?" she asked softly as she attempted to maintain his calm.

"Richard… I'm Richard Ambrose Phaal."

"What a peculiar surname," she said, clutching that thread in the hopes that it would lead her to a conversation to distract him.

"Right, it's… peculiar to this town…" he grunted through his teeth. "The Phaals have always been in the town… my grandfather was the owner of the fist button factory in town."

"That's lovely," she said as she attacked the wound with more alcohol, but finally began to sew the wound closed. If she could only decide what kind of poison this was, she could also find the antidote…

"Are you almost done?" Richard asked though it was clearly a strain on him to ask.

"Nearly... how are you feeling? I'm terribly sorry to ask, but you see, I need to ask about your symptoms so I can determine which antidote to use."

She was about to look through the little catalog in her bag before she saw Renata with one vial in her teeth, giving her an expectant look.

"I can't just take your word on that," Moretta told the cat, almost scolding.

Undaunted, Renata tipped the vial into Moretta's hand and she looked at the label. With a sigh, Moretta had to admit that Renata had very likely picked the right antidote. This particular vial contained a high-strength concentration of Mithradatic Panacea.

"Outdone by my feline assistant yet again," Moretta sighed as she took a syringe from its sanitary pouch and withdrew a measure of the Panacea from the vial into the syringe.

"Do you... often take advice from your cat?" Richard asked warily.

"I don't know hardly what she's got going on behind those eyes, but she's rarely ever wrong," Moretta shrugged. She administered the shot despite Richard trembling in fear, but there was no time to try and calm him down.

"What's... your name?" Richard asked as the Panacea went flowing into his veins.

Moretta paused, and pretended it was due to her preoccupation with cleaning his wound and bandaging him up. It was the first time she would have to introduce herself as her alias, and the moment required a certain degree of gravity.

"My name is Berenice," she said softly, and looked Richard in the eye with a gentle smile. "I'm pleased to make your acquaintance."

Richard returned her smile, and she wondered if the lights were failing or burning more brightly than before. It was an incredible fluttering in her heart which told her the truth.

She shied away from him and looked toward the treatment room to see what had become of the invading mob. They were now slowly, even lethargically, trailing their way back through her parlor. "Well?" she asked of them.

None of them had an answer for her, and she wondered how she was ever to set up a local practice if nobody bothered to ask her professional opinion.

"The people here don't like Ravens," Richard whispered to her as the others filed out the door and closed it, leaving them alone.

"I'm not a raven," Moretta contended with a frown, and sat beside Richard so Renata could curl up in her lap. The warmth of the purring cat managed to calm some of her flighty imaginings.

"No, see what I mean is, they're used to the doctors being criminal abusers," Richard said, and reached over to stroke Renata's head along with Moretta.

"What does that have to do with ravens?" Moretta asked, watching Renata stretch out so both she and Richard would have room to pet her.

"It's what we call them," Richard explained, letting Renata play with his fingers and lightly nibble on his fingertips. "Ravens, I mean. We call them that because they live off the dead."

Moretta pursed her lips and looked at Richard, who was too engaged with Renata's little game to look back at her. "Is that what everyone already thinks of me?" she asked. "I already know what my predecessors were doing... at least to some extent..."

"I know you must be a bit overwhelmed with this place," Richard said sheepishly. "Even I'm a bit overwhelmed with it... I was even looking forward to someone new coming to town who wouldn't know about... me."

"What's the matter with you?" Moretta sputtered an instant after asking this question and waved a hand. "I mean, why would there be a problem if someone knew about you?"

"It's just that... I'm not really at the place I want to be, professionally. I'm a solicitor, but nobody wants to solicit me."

"And I'm a doctor... or a Raven... that nobody is asking for treatment," she sighed and leaned back against the couch. "I'd say we're even. Let's not worry about what one another might think, I'm prepared to speak to you with extreme candor, if that would be acceptable."

"I don't see why it wouldn't be," he shrugged, and gave her a grin. "Besides, don't I have to stay here until I heal?"

"I don't' think so, what I gave you is an ancient antitoxin developed by none other than the Poison King, Mithradates."

Richard stared at her in dismay. "Who?"

"Well, you see he was one of Rome's most worthy enemies, after Hannibal, and drove Romans out of the East for a time, but… He was also very clever. His own people considered him a hero for saving them from the oppressive Romans and whatnot… He used an awful lot of poisons in his strategies, and that's why we call him the Poison King… I've got a book about him if you'd like to borrow it… it was an excellent read in the cab."

"I'd like that… sounds interesting enough."

"I left it in the cab," she blushed, and looked down at Renata, who was giving her a skeptical look. "My luggage gets here tomorrow, so I'll give it to you when I've finished it."

"You don't have any of your things with you?"

"Well, I was able to bring two bags… one of them is Renata's little home, actually. So she gets to sleep in her own bed."

"But what about you? You've never even seen this whole place, have you?"

"No… honestly at this point I'm considering just sleeping on the couch. I'd rather not poke around this place too much at night."

"I understand… people think the house is haunted."

"Because of the graves out back and the murdering inside?"

"That's right… they think restless spirits may still live here."

"Well, then, it's a good thing I know how to deal with restless spirits, isn't it?"

"I wouldn't taunt them…" Richard grimaced.

"I'm not taunting them. Ghosts are just people, like an orange is still an orange after it's been peeled. They retain much of their native natures, most of them are perfectly ordinary. It's the frightened or the annoyed ones that just need to be treated like frightened and annoyed individuals."

"Who taught you a thing like that?"

"Actually I mostly learned by experience." Having said so, she watched Richard uneasily sidle away from her, and couldn't blame him. She got to her feet with Renata clutched close to her chest. "I should look at my examination room… you know, it's rather late, and I don't want to send you home, so why don't I make some tea?"

"I don't think I should impose," Richard got to his own unsteady feet. "You should probably clean out the kitchen. I think whatever's left over here is probably poisonous."

Moretta paused, and glanced at the kitchen. "They had to live off something, right?"

"Sure, but they've been gone for awhile, so their food is probably unsanitary now."

Moretta's nose twitched and she saw Renata's whiskers do the same. "Would you mind terribly if I asked you to help me go to market tomorrow? I'll have to wait for my luggage to arrive, too, and that'll be at the local post office."

"Oh, sure! I know where those places are!"

"In the meantime, feel free to avail yourself of my couch. It's the least I can do."

Richard was becoming rather spry, she noted, as he followed her to the kitchen. "And I'll help you look around and get acquainted with your new home. Where did you live, before?"

"I've been at university for some time… I went to the Capitoline Nursing School."That was possibly too much factual information, but Moretta decided it was easier to tell some of the truth than lie all the time. Besides, she was almost certain she could trust Richard.

He took her by the arm and led her to the examination room, but they both stopped in the doorway. "Was he here all along?" Richard asked as they stared at the man stretched along the examination table.

"I… doubt it… he looks as if he were newly dropped here… I'll deal with it in the morning." She closed the door firmly between herself and the mystery cadaver. "I may never sleep again if I don't start now."

Chapter 3: A Murderous Miasma

His nightmare did not end when Richard awoke. Laughter echoed off the green wall paper which surrounded him, and he thought he could see malicious eyes gazing down at him.

"You think you're safe here?" the familiar face of Mabel Babcock mocked him from the shadows, leering closer to impose more on his field of vision. "Don't you remember what happened last time?"

Wasn't he supposed to be awake?

He heard footsteps coming down from the floor above, and his heart seized in his chest.

"The raven is coming down for breakfast…" Mabel Babcock chuckled much too close to his ear, and she pinched his arm until he screamed.

The footsteps sped up, and he imagined it was Cecil, rushing down to chain him up again.

"Richard!" he heard a female voice call to him just before the woman who called herself Berenice appeared on the landing of the steps.

"Raven!" he croaked back.

She stared at him, with her lopsided ringlet pigtails and dove gray lacy nightgown reminding him that this was something utterly *real*. She was beyond the apparition of the gleeful murderess, her rounded pale face devoid of any sign that she also saw Mrs. Babcock.

Renata the cat, however, took the steps three at a time and hissed in Richard's direction.

He thought at first that she was angry he had intruded on her feline domain, until Mrs. Babcock turned away from him to look the cat in the eyes.

"What is it, *princess*?" the apparition demanded in a sneer.

Renata hissed again, her tail fluffing up so much it alarmed her mistress, who knelt beside her. "What's the matter, pretty kitty?" she asked in a soothing voice which distressingly had no noticeable effect on Renata.

"There's... witch..." Richard forced out, though it was difficult as he seemed to be suffering from some unseen force putting pressure on his chest.

This of all things got a reaction out of Renata, who seemed deeply offended, only to dart across the room caterwauling at not Richard, but Mrs. Babcock.

In moments, the apparition had faded entirely, and Renata sat cleaning herself.

"What's the matter?" the new Raven asked, kneeling beside Renata and hesitantly offering her a hand. The cat hopped into her mistress's waiting arms, and Richard finally found the strength to sit upright.

"I saw the former doctor's wife," he explained. "She had a sort of treatment she'd give people who came here... the cleansing cure..."

The raven gave him a very solemn look, and brought Renata to sit next to him again, petting the cat's fur slowly. "Did you see her just now?"

"I did... I saw her here just as she was the last time I visited... I was feeling poorly, so my parents suggested I spend some of my summer holiday from school up here letting the Babcocks take care of me."

"Were you among the witnesses?" Raven asked softly, her gentle question managing to shield him from some of the horror he knew he ought to feel.

"I was… you can probably find my statement in the Sentinel's back issues."

"Noted… they made a point of redacting the witness's names. I'm sure I read something you said, I was sure to read everything I could."

"Well, needless to say, when she purged my system… she didn't really put much in to replace it… I remember chilled cucumber broth, and tomato juice… she said disease was a byproduct of food…"

"And I'll wager she was rather healthy herself, and did not practice the diet on herself."

"You're right about that…" he sighed. "It's actually humiliating. I'm sure I should have known better right away, but everyone assured me that Mrs. Babcock knew just what she was doing and I wasn't to doubt her."

"Surely the survivors of her ministrations sounded the alarm?"

"We did… I was better off than most, but I didn't even free myself."

"There's no shame in that, she got away with it for so long because she was an expert at what she did."

"That's what everyone said, we just didn't know what she was actually doing… she *enjoyed* watching us slowly dying."

"Which is why you're still having nightmares, isn't it? That's nothing to be ashamed of… we all have our darkness."

Renata *meowed* as if she was agreeing, but of course, she was a cat, so there was no way she could know what had been said.

"That's right, Renata," the raven said, and kissed the cat's head.

"Does Renata have innate darkness about her, too?" Richard asked, half joking.

"Yes, but she's never told me where it started," the raven said quietly.

"Oh... would she be able to tell you?"

"If she really wanted to, certainly, she could. She's a very communicative feline."

"I see... well, um... do you want to check on that fellow on the examination table and see if you can figure out anything about him?"

Moretta bit her lip. "I suppose I ought to, but let's get something to eat soon, I haven't had anything for hours and I was up most of the night."

"I completely understand," Richard picked up his jacket and slowly eased it on despite his wound. "Any instructions for this bandage, Raven?"

She appeared somewhat taken aback, but didn't correct him. He couldn't even remember what her real name was, so perhaps she'd just taken to the nickname. "Just let me go back up and get dressed. Try not to get attacked by the coffee table."

Less than a quarter hour later the two of them were wandering down to the center of town with Renata draped across Raven's shoulders.

Richard walked the line between being gentlemanly to Raven and not making it seem as if he were too involved with the outsider. It wasn't good practice to get saddled with an even more questionable reputation than what he already had.

"We should ask if anyone is missing my friend in the examination room," Raven said.

"Or you can," Richard said, grimacing at the idea of doing Raven's job. People might start thinking that he'd become her assistant, or *worse*, that he was *courting her*. Any chance he could have had with Lenore would be defenestrated, forever.

"Right… I could certainly do my job on my own, so it's not a question of that. I merely thought perhaps you would like to help me… perhaps as my solicitor?"

At that suggestion, Richard couldn't help but consider her offer. Sure, he didn't want to work as her assistant, but if she had the money to pay for him to do his *actual* job, he may be capable of cutting a more impressive figure at the next party… unless of course all parties were banned within town limits after the previous night's debacle.

"I could do that," he said at last. "Thank you for the offer, I'll consider it."

"The way I see it, neither of us are really being seen in this town, but together we may actually catch some notice."

"That's a possibility…" he gestured toward one of the market stalls which offered food. "I usually eat here; they've got cheap food that hasn't gone bad yet." He reached into his pocket, but blushed when his hands came out empty.

Noticing this, Raven opened the coin purse she kept at her side. "I'll pay for us both, and we'll go to a café," she said. "I promised my hospitality, and would have given it you at my home except that I was prevented by our unfortunate circumstances."

"I could not by any means impose," Richard pressed a hand to his chest, well aware that he'd been sweating all night. "I ought to get home, in fact, I'm a perfect wreck."

"I much doubt it," Raven shook her head so her ringlets bounced around her face. "As long as you keep your overcoat covering your wounded arm, nobody will notice that you've been through an ordeal unless they are willing to squint. By then he or she will be the rude party."

Richard reconsidered. "I suppose I could prevail upon your hospitality, then, though I will endeavor to be as light a burden on your purse strings as is possible me to be."

With such arrangements made against which Richard could find no adequate argument in resistance, Raven wandered down the street and only stopped when she had selected a café she said was well suited to their purpose.

"Surely it is too fine to afford?" Richard asked, concerned that me may well find Lenore at one of these tables. He noted Raven's scrutiny and blushed. "I would not insinuate that you are poor by any means, dear young lady."

"Your sensitivity to my degree of wealth is much appreciated," Raven smirked. "But, I assure you, I was given a generous gift of funding to get me started in town."

"That must be nice, I might have done that were my pride not so sensitive."

"See that you make wise investments in future, and have the grace to accept a friendly gift every now and again," she seated herself delicately in one of the café chairs, and smoothed her charcoal-tinted skirts across her lap, lace ruffles and all.

Richard blushed at feeling himself even gently chastised, and by a relative stranger who also happened to be an outsider. He found it was gravely onerous to find he had no rebuttal to such advice.

"Don't feel too poorly," she offered a barely perceptible smile which did not diminish her gracious demeanor. "I only offer this advice as a means to see a new friend better cared for."

The fact that she considered them friends, already, only made Richard all the more sheepish. Could she tell he was guilty over not wanting to be seen with her? Her demure features belied no sign of it, but that was no indication that she had not noticed.

After a quick breakfast, the first time he'd eaten something that wasn't beans out of a can in months, Richard was tempted to part ways with her, except that chivalry compelled him to help her bring all her belongings back to the house.

She was heavily laden with bags and boxes, and he could not stand the idea of the far more burdensome guilt he would feel if he allowed her to carry that burden unassisted.

Back at the top of the hill, Richard bid her farewell. Each of them had a great deal left to do, and he had spent far too much unaccompanied with a strange, unattached woman. He would have to remedy whatever damage may have been done to his reputation post haste, but first, he would have to return home and remedy his grimy, unkempt appearance.

Chapter 4: Post Mortem

Alone in her new home for the first time, Moretta found herself utterly without an excuse to avoid her unexpected, silent patient. The smell was even starting to get to her, despite the mustiness of the rest of the house nearly drowning out *l'odeur de la mort*.

She slowly edged the door open to peer at him. He appeared to have been laid out neatly for the express purpose of her examination, but he must have died while the crowd was making it impossible to get near him.

Moretta ground her teeth in irritation that she'd been deprived of the chance to treat him before death had stolen his breath. It was *supposedly* her profession, wasn't it?

She stood at his side as if he were still living and had summoned her to his bedside for help. "What should I have done for you?" she whispered.

His skin bore tenebrous bruises, and his fingertips were discolored, as well.

"Pardon me, my good man, I'd rather not invade your privacy any more than utterly necessary," she said, and lifted one of those stony, cold hands, so that she could examine it.

These fingers were neither pudgy nor willowy, but what they were was soft. There was not a single callus in sight, and Moretta appraised from this, added to his silken jacket festooned with embroidery, that he was an aristocrat.

Why had he just been dumped in her keeping?

Weren't important people meant to be mourned in the presence of their closest thirty family members who would all jostle for an honorable place in the will?

Perhaps her understanding of aristocracy only applied to the world outside Amontillado… or perhaps she was looking at the intended target of an assassination… She dropped the fellow's hand as if it had started moving.

"I just *got* here…" she groaned as she rubbed at her brow under the straight-edge fringe of obsidian hair. "The crazy things were supposed to happen *after* I'd gotten used to this place!"

She ought to have known better, nothing ever went smoothly concerning her life. Now that she'd entered what may be her life's most crucial stage, why should it be any different?

Considering her predecessors, had someone thought she was willing to cover up their crime? Did people really expect her to be that sort of person? She wasn't, she emphasized to herself as she peered into the fellow's face. She was quite the opposite, in fact!

"Whoever did this is going to *pay*," Moretta hissed, but the moment she said it she felt the air thicken in her nostrils, and glanced around in horror.

She hadn't gotten a good look around the room but now she watched every shadow spread and conquer more and more of the walls, the floors… It was all too familiar…

She backed away from the cadaver with a hand against her throat, muttering, "No… no, please… never again! No more of this!"

Renata hopped onto the examination table and let out a warning *meow*, which gave Moretta another start, but brought her eyes to meet the honey-gold depths of Renata's. It was as if the cat was telling her to focus, and let go of her panic.

If only it were so simple!

She thought she could see the shadows surround the fellow stretched out on the examination table, and it looked *almost* as if he breathed them in…

She was getting dizzy… she needed… needed… what was it?

Renata hopped off the table and darted out of the room.

While Moretta wondered why her one companion would so easily abandon her, she sank so she sat curled against one of the counters. This was so like… she scrunched her eyes shut and rocked herself in an attempt to drive away the memories. Her heart raced and her mind flew even swifter. This new job was supposed to be part of getting *past* all that!

She jumped as something warm and fuzzy rubbed against her arm, but she looked down and realized it was Renata with something in her teeth. The cat set it down with a sneeze and pushed it toward Moretta with one paw.

"You fetched my smelling salts for me…" Moretta crooned softly to the cat as she collected the pouch of smelling salts up to her nose and her feline ally into her lap.

The relief she experienced was only momentary, as she found herself glancing up only to find that the cadaver she'd left stretched out on his back was now sitting bolt upright, and pointing a crooked finger at her.

For the first time in years, Moretta screamed.

Renata did, as well, but her reaction was more that of a lioness than a house pet. Whereas her mistress was rendered motionless, Renata surged into action, landing on the cadaver's face with a shrill yowl and made to scratch the fellow's eyes out.

She was prevented only by the cadaver's hand closing around her lithe body and yanking her away.

"Renata!" Moretta shrieked, and shot to her feet, rushing to her pet's rescue.

Instead she was frozen once more by the sunken eyes of the fellow who was meant to be dead, dull and empty as the bottom of a well. The hand which was not holding Renata aloft rose to point one waxy finger accusingly at Moretta.

No, not accusingly, she realized, but as a warning. She had promised to avenge this fellow, and now as shadows seeped out of his gaping mouth and his eyes, he was telling her to uphold that promise.

Renata struggled for freedom, and Moretta reached out to snatch her free. "I promise!" she shouted. "To all those whose spirits echo here, I promise! But on *one condition*!"

She paused, as the whole world seemed to pause, giving her the impression that many disembodied ears were listening for what she may say next.

"All those who linger here, you must *behave yourselves*! I am to have proper privacy, and you shall not disturb me at odd hours! I swear, should you cross me and make impossible housemates of yourselves, I will have you *all* exorcised!"

With those words spoken, it was much easier to wrench Renata free of the rigor mortis, and the cadaver politely laid back down.

The air became much easier to breathe, and Moretta drank it in hungrily. "It seems we've come to an agreement. That's good. Now, I shall recommence my business!" With Renata perched on her shoulder, she did just that.

She worked for hours, attempting to identify the cause of death and seeking the fellow's identity, as well. Her first hypothesis was that she'd come across the victim of the same poison that had infected Richard, except for the fact that she found no bullet wounds on his person.

What she *did* find was an invitation to a Bacchanal, for one Count Otranto.

"Found your name!" she celebrated in a low whisper, just before she noticed something else which pointed the finger at the manner of murder.

There was a mottled yet subtle tinge to the skin on his back—which took a great deal of time to locate since she first had to turn him over—and the entry wound was so small it was nearly imperceptible. She would have missed it, entirely, if not for the fact that she had a magnifier handy.

"What do you think, Renata?" she asked, and the cat flicked her tail as she narrowed her eyes at the fellow's back. "I think we'll have to send this to Lady Monique. She will want to know there's been a deliberate assassination in Amontillado."

Chapter 5: Aspersions on Aspirations

Richard felt as if every eye was on him, save for the fact that there was in fact, *nobody* who bothered to glance his way as he returned to the clock tower. He hadn't told the Raven about Lenore, but he still wasn't sure what to say about her.

Her father had found her and swept her back to the Roget estate, and for all he knew, he'd never see her, again.

As these thoughts plagued him, he made his way up the stairs to his own flat. Each one creaked beneath his feet as an unsubtle reminder that he had not found the means by which to escape the clock tower as of yet. He was still the prisoner of his own limited means, and the cage of shame which shackled his heels to the stocks of ill fortune.

When he unlocked the door to his meager lodgings, he was once again humiliated by the very sight of it.

Even the Ravens on the hill lived better than he: after all, they were able to afford wallpaper, for one thing! He ought to have been on his way up in the world, by now. He ought to be coming home to dress himself in finery and a silken pinstripe suit like the one at Farthing's Apparel Shoppe.

Instead, he did a quick job of sewing a patch onto the elbow of his jacket, for it was all he could do, and then replaced his blood-stained shirt with another, as well as replacing all of his unmentionables.

Overhead he could hear his neighbor Braxton fiddling with something, even over the monotonous mechanism which overshadowed the both of them.

He grabbed his broom and knocked on the ceiling. When he heard Braxton pause, he shouted, "Don't burn the place down before I get back!"

"Don't worry!" Braxton called back through the floor, "I'll wait for you!"

Richard couldn't help but snicker at that, and let Braxton go about his business. The fellow would never sell a patent if he didn't get the chance to work unmolested, after all. Who was he to begrudge a man his livelihood?

With a final glance around the room, he decided it was time to go back out into the world, so he descended the stairs while forcing himself to be hopeful despite the odds ahead of him.

Once he was back outside in the fog, he quickly made his way to the Edgeware Carriage Shoppe. Perhaps it would help to get a sight of something to aspire to before he went about the rest of his day.

Upon entering the shop, he caught sight of his cousin, Hans Shaw, bustling behind the counter in a flurry of excitement. Well, this must mean he'd once again been left to care for the place and its wares as his father was off doing… whatever important people did when Richard wasn't able to comprehend it.

"Good morning, Hans," he called, finally catching his cousin's attention from the ether, "might I see the *Hercules*?"

Hans smirked at him. "Are you afraid someone looted it in the confusion last night?"

"Not at all, I just need something *good* in my field of vision as soon as humanly possible… please, Hans?"

"I'd never deny my cousin," Jerald snickered, and opened the door to the show room.

Lined up before them were row after row of beautifully-crafted carriages, coaches, and all other manner of automated transportation, even motorized bicycles.

Richard felt compelled to whistle at all that gleaming brass, and imagined the hum of their engines. If only he could afford even one of them... then he wouldn't have to walk wherever he went, and he wouldn't get nearly so much wear on his shoes.

"Are you sure you don't want to start off with a cheaper model?"Hans asked. "You could rent, for a while, and you'd be slightly less..." he cut himself off in discomfort but Richard already knew.

"Like a vagabond?" he suggested, and saw his cousin's answering silent confirmation.

"Well, not to put it in such indelicate terms, but... well, you do have a remarkably bohemian aspect to your wardrobe... and your accommodations."

"There's nothing I can do about all of those things all at once, so I'm afraid it will have to be an incremental improvement. Bohemian or not, it's the best I can do at present."

"At least you're aware of it," Hans said, and led Richard further into the showroom. "I recommend a fitting at the haberdashery, cousin. A good hat can define a man in ways that could even distract from the rest of your appearance."

Richard grimaced. "Well, I don't know for sure I'd be able to afford what one may call a 'good' hat."

"Well, like I said, you could rent a hat... though judging by where you live... how likely is it that plaster could rain down on your hat? Would you be able to care for it? A gentleman really should put more effort into his appearance than you do."

"It is not for lack of *effort* that I look the way I do," Richard said, "it's from a lack of *funds*. If for example I could get someone to offer me a great sum of money for the sake of building up my portfolio and my funds, I would be able to afford all the things you get off this carriage business."

"Which just goes to show there's more benefit in a family trade than a fancy degree," Hans said with a shrug. He was half haughty, and Richard could *feel* it rolling off him, but they were still cousins. Richard knew there was no malice in the observation.

In order to prevent becoming snappish, Richard took a deep breath and cast about until his eyes landed on the self-same vehicle he'd come in search of.

"I could probably reserve a model for you," Hans offered. "You're going to get some competition once the weather clears up and people are more willing to go out-of-doors."

"Tempting..." Richard stared at the finely-molded model of the *Hercules*.

It was primarily painted sky blue, with a metallic finish. Its wheels were tall and outfitted with tough-looking tires. He peered inside the windows to see its seats, which he'd had the opportunity to sit in only once. Those seats were leather, but the walls were velvet, and for winter weather not only could the riders bolt the windows shut, they could also avail themselves of a heating interface in the roof of the vehicle. There was even a viewing interface on the walls which would help steer, so that there was no need for a driver to sit outside the vehicle, itself. It was complete with the little silver statuette of Hercules on the crest of it, above where the *bestia* horse was meant to hook into the interface. "What model of horse would you recommend?"

"I'd say there's no model better suited than a Frisian," Hans admitted. "Powerful, noble, and programmed with enough horse power to keep you going for hours... except really this model isn't meant for the city, it's for the country."

"Who says I'll be in town forever?"

"Pardon me for not expecting a man of your means to have somewhere else to go."

"If I have enough means to afford a *Hercules*. That means I've acquired enough means to find some business in the country."

"Fair enough," Hans raised his hands and backed away with a sheepish smile. "Don't worry; I have no doubt you'll eventually save up enough money for that. It's only a matter of whether or not you accomplish that before you're within an inch of the grave."

Richard snorted. "Mark my words: I'll not be five and twenty before my fortunes turn."

"Oh, is that the new deadline? Thought you'd be raking in contracts the moment you graduated that fancy university of yours! We do things differently in Amontillado, I'm not sure if you forgot this while you were out of town."

"I haven't forgotten," Richard reassured his cousin. "I'm going to get my way in the grand Amontillado tradition of elbow rubbing and shoe scraping, don't you worry."

"I'll hold you to that, cousin. Anyhow, I'm going to have a little talk with my father, and ask him if we can offer you a family discount. You should hear what people say about you, you're starting to be something of a family embarrassment. We all thought you'd get out of this stage of life much sooner than you have."

"I'm ever so glad to hear how my family cares so dearly for me," Richard drawled.

"I'm serious," Hans said. "You have to think about how your bohemian vagrancy reflects on the rest of us. It looks as if our family is declining."

"Maybe it is," Richard gave Hans a stoic look. "Now, if you'd like to continue this line of conversation, I'll have to take my leave of you. I have far too much to do today, and I'd rather not think of myself as your embarrassment much longer than necessary."

With those words spoken, Richard was forced to take his leave. Even though he'd shown his cousin a strong face, he had been cut to his uttermost.

It had been too long since he'd seen his family, hadn't it? They'd formed an opinion on him based on rumors, and now he'd suffered the humiliation of the opinions they held of him just as they claimed to be humiliated by him. Were his own parents busy defaming him?

As his very ears burned with shame, Richard hung his head. He was on his way to another errand, but all the same he wandered whether or not he'd ever be able to lift his head, again.

Simply because Hans had suggested it, Richard could not bring himself to follow the good advice of visiting the haberdashery. Otherwise he would have been happy to go find the perfect hat that would rescue his image from the ash heap, but as it stood, no matter how correct his cousin may have been, he wasn't ready to take that advice.

Instead, he made his way toward the nearest shop offering suits, the Emporium of Fine Menswear and Miscellany. Sure, a suit may be more expensive than a hat, but he could at least apply the same strategy of renting as Hans had applied to the hat hypothesis.

Unfortunately, he was laughed out of the haberdashery before he'd even fully gotten through the door, and gotten a true smell of the bouquet of colognes worn by the customers who were actually permitted in the shop.

He considered getting a haircut, but when he passed and saw the prices in the window, he hung his head and decided to give himself another self-done trim later when he dragged himself home.

As noontide arrived, he slipped into the local courthouse to see if any petitioners had been turned away by the other lawyers and may be willing to hire him, instead. Like so many things in Amontillado, this routine was clockwork. He knew better than to waste his entire day loitering outside the courtrooms waiting to apprehend an unwitting petitioner, he'd gotten too well-practiced in the art of finding the stragglers.

Today, the courthouse was crowded with shouting petitioners of every stripe, vying for the attention of clerks and solicitors alike who simply could not handle the excess of potential clients. Despite knowing what this whole situation had arisen from and still reeling from the effects of it himself, Richard's growling stomach edged him forward.

"My good man!" he called to one of the flustered men on the outer rim of the crowd. "May I help you? I am a solicitor myself and willing to hear your complaints!"

This fellow pounced on Richard as surely as he'd been pounced upon. "Do you know what happened last night?" he demanded. "I own a share in Bacchanal Hall! I've simply been put out of business at a time when I have damaged property to repair! It isn't my fault some madman opened fire on my guests! And now, everyone blames me for it!"

Richard rubbed his hands together. "Sir, it would be my honor to represent you in demanding your rights as a citizen of Amontillado, both to run your business and to be compensated for the circumstances which were out of your control. I relish a challenge!"

He watched as his potential client's brow rose. "I will... consider it... who are you, exactly?"

The dreaded question had finally arrived. Richard drew a fortifying breath as he attempted to collect himself. "I am Richard Ambrose Phaal, and as I said I am a solicitor..."

"I've heard tell of you!" the fellow barked, and those who had been listening in on their exchange began to snicker. "Aren't you that fellow who lives up in the broken clock tower with that nutter?"

Richard ground his teeth in an attempt to save himself from further rupturing his reputation. "Yes... you may describe my living conditions in that manner were you devoid of charity..."

What had he just done?

He found out a few minutes later when once again, he was laughed out of an establishment, only *this* time, it was his place of work... or what would have been his place of work had he not been such a pauper.

"How is a man to improve himself when he is mocked for trying?" he asked the dreary clouds which overshadowed him.

"It's funny you should ask a thing like that," said a man's voice from a short distance away.

Richard turned to see that the fellow who'd spoken wore a red mask and a voluminous velvet black cloak. "What... sir?" he asked.

"I wonder if you would like to visit the Duke... he's looking for someone talented to help him with some ventures of his..."

"Who are you?" Richard asked warily.

"A solicitor, but of another sort," the fellow replied with a note of amusement to his voice.

As Richard scrutinized the fellow, he realized that he was wearing an Il Capitano mask, from Commedia Dell'Arte. An interesting choice, Richard mused, as in the world of Commedia plays, long-nosed, half-masked Capitano was a swaggering lout whenever he appeared, and was nearly always an outsider without true authority. Did this Capitano carry any true weight, or was he aware enough of his role to know why he wore the mask?

"Are you interested, or do you want to be a bohemian for the rest of your life?" asked Il Capitano.

"I'm certainly interested, but... I have to know what you're offering is legitimate."

He heard *Il Capitano* laugh behind the mask's frozen features, but rather than replying to Richard's suspicions, he turned to leave.

So that was how the game was played... Richard knew precisely what he had to do. There was simply no alternative to following after *Il Capitano*. Whether or not this was some manner of scam, Richard didn't care.

Chapter 6: Shadowed Secrets

Thunder told Moretta that the rain had returned for the second time that day. Why was it always storming in this place? It didn't bother her as much as it would have had she actually wanted to see the sun, but it would make getting into town dreadfully inconvenient and even impossible should it start a flood.

As she peered out her window at the rolling landscape of tall, tapered hills, she felt a dizzy spell coming on and looked away. She'd grown up moving from mansion to mansion, and yet the sight of so much open space appeared to be too much for her. She rolled her eyes to herself.

At least she was in possession of her knives, so exploring her house would be made just a little safer. She was still alone with a corpse and her cat, but what more could be done?

She caught sight of a brooding shadow swooping down to the window sill, and stared to find that it was a raven. "You're the real raven on this hill," she informed the creature who started tapping at her window. "Can't get any lonelier in here, so I might as well have a guest," she shrugged, and opened the window for the raven to come flying in.

It was drenched, of course, but she'd set up the fire in the hearth so she watched it fluff up its feathers in the firelight.

"I do endeavor to make my guests feel at home," she drawled, and gave Renata a stern look to ensure she wouldn't pounce on their new house guest.

Perhaps had she been human, Renata would have rolled her eyes, but instead she met Moretta's eyes, sneezed, and began to bathe her paw primly.

"Oh, I see how it is," Moretta snickered, but she was distracted by a noise from the raven.

It seemed to have found something distasteful on her hearth, so she investigated what the problem could be. The raven was hopping about on the hearth, and she noticed for the first time that there was a panel that stuck out on the tiles.

"Interesting…" she murmured, and glanced at the window she'd left open, noticing that there was some rain water entering the room. If the raven wanted to leave, he could do so at any time, but instead he appeared to be more intent on hopping about and sounding an alarm.

Sure, she was imposing her own interpretation on his actions, but there was something endearing about the way it hopped… someone else might have been interested in watching the same behavior from a dog. Even though this was a wild bird, she couldn't help turning him into her pet now that she'd allowed him into her home.

Still… she couldn't help but turn her attention from the raven to what he appeared to have uncovered. "This house has so many dark secrets…" she murmured. "Is this another one of them?"

Renata *meowed* as if she were not interested, but Moretta simply said, "Good thing it's my job to investigate things, not yours." Slowly, so as not to alarm the raven, she stepped closer and brushed her fingers against the panel in the hearth.

Meanwhile the raven hopped around and squawked as if she weren't moving quickly enough to suit him.

"If I find something shiny that I don't need, you can keep it," she snickered. She wedged her nails between the body of the hearth and the panel which was cut into it.

Renata darted to her side and purred, rubbing the crest of her head against Moretta's arm.

"Did I miss something?" Moretta asked.

Renata delicately made her way under Moretta's arms and clawed at the panel.

"You want to help?" Moretta asked, and watched Renata's claws scrape against the panel, and an idea sparked alive in her mind. "Oh! I haven't got something sharp enough for the job!" She scooped Renata into her arms and ignored the raven, which was warming his feathers.

She knew precisely what she'd need, it was only a matter of trying to remember which bag she'd put them in. Her eyes wandered over the regimented line of bags which she hadn't had the energy to unpack as of yet. "What do you think?" she asked Renata, setting her down gently. "You seem to have a better mind than mine."

Renata padded to the bags and pressed her paw to a few of them before *meowing* to alert her mistress that she thought she'd found the right bag.

"Let's test your skills," Moretta unzipped the seam of the bag and revealed the pale polished blackthorn wood box she'd been after. "Congratulations! My pretty kitty!" rather than focus on the box she picked Renata up and went to the jar she'd unpacked and placed on the mantle where she kept the cat treats.

While Renata celebrated her victory on the hearth, Moretta returned to her box, unpacking it on one of the end tables.

There she found those thin, delicately decorated little friends of hers. They had polished blackthorn handles, which fit snugly in her palms, meanwhile they had a different gemstone at the base of each one, and various different shades of pearl, ranging from white to black to lavender to scarlet, but her favorites were the two larger knives which had bloodstones on the bases.

These had been one of the first gifts she'd received from her parents once she expressed a desire to learn how to throw knives, and the rest of the set had come from her patroness of an aunt.

"But which one of these would be best for the job?" she asked herself, but saw Renata flick her ears as if prepared to earn herself another treat.

Under her pet's scrutiny, Moretta lifted each of the little knives out of the box in turn, until finally she settled on the one with the scarlet pearl at the base. It was a precision tool, though not one for medical practice despite its similarities to a scalpel.

Once Renata noticed Moretta had made her choice, she went about bathing herself, perched on the corner of the hearth.

"Do you think I ought to arm myself?" Moretta asked the cat, who merely cleaned her ears as if she couldn't hear. "Oh, all right, I'll do this on my own, shall I? Though not all at once..." she peered into the same bag where her box of knives had been and plucked out her leather arm guards with their little stilettos loaded into holsters at her wrists. "Good..." she sighed, "they weren't damaged *en route.*"

Beyond these, she caught sight of her portable phonograph case, and unloaded it to set it up.

"I can't believe I've gone so long without my music!" she cried.

Renata *meowed* again, and jumped off the hearth to perch on the couch and curl up as if preparing to hear music that she enjoyed as well.

Moretta selected a cylinder she found most appropriate, a selection of compositions by the Dark Horse Stampede Orchestra, and loaded it into the mechanism.

Out from the conical mouth of the phonograph, with its little rose-embossed panels rose delicate strains of harpsichord.

Moretta sat back with a sigh to soak it in, and almost felt as if she were back home instead of far away in this land where nobody knew her true name.

When the drums joined the harpsichord she swayed, imagining herself at a ball, but she still knew there was business to attend to. The Count of Otranto awaited further attention in the examination room, not to mention the little puzzle she'd concerned herself with in the meantime.

Finally as the Orchestra's most beloved songstress began to accompany the melody with her sultry tones, Moretta got to her feet. She set the leather holsters down with the rest of her knives. Running her fingers along the knife launchers, and the gemstones at the back of all the rest of the knives, she tried to calm herself.

"I will *not* let all of this overwhelm me," she coached herself, before kneeling at the hearth again. She wedged the stiletto-like knife into the panel's seam, and worked to wedge it open.

To her surprise, what she found was a selection of knobs, and what looked like a panel of readouts to tell her what she could accomplish with these knobs if she turned them the right way.

She creased her brow as she attempted to decide what these knobs might be for, but the raven which seemed not the least bit intimidated by her hopped over and pecked at one of the knobs.

Moretta moved back to give the bird space, and the clockwork of her mind began to turn steadily. How did this bird know first how to get into the house for warmth, secondly where this panel had been, and thirdly how to act around a human without flinching? Much like so many factors in this new life of hers, it appeared her predecessors had left an indelible mark. How many of the local individual fauna had been trained by those people? What were they *capable* of?

There was a noise from within the closet she'd seen earlier, and even hung up her parasol, umbrella, and cloak. Slowly, she rose, attempting to guess what would be behind the door to greet her when she opened it.

Any number of things could be lurking there, the raven could have let some beast into her house, and it may be prepared to devour her flesh. It could even be some manner of *bestia* that had been part of her predecessors' murder games, programmed to tear anyone in sight limb from limb!

Moretta was distracted from the growing gaping maw of dread opening up behind her eyes by what she saw when she opened the closet door. It was then that the raven had opened *another* gaping maw of dread, *in her floor.*

"Grating gears, where am I living?" Moretta gasped to herself as Renata came running to her side, and climbed up to her shoulder. "I know, it's terrifying," Moretta said as she felt Renata shake. She stroked the cat along her spine to her tail, and stared into the darkness of the passage, which at first had looked something like a closet, but was clearly something different.

The raven began to *caw* proudly, and she turned to see him fluttering his wings, puffing up the feathers on his chest.

"Looks like you deserve a treat, too," Moretta snickered, and lightly tossed one of Renata's treats at the raven.

Renata complained to her that the stranger was getting her treat, so Moretta rewarded the plaintive *meow* with another treat as the raven flew away.

"I'm going to have to investigate this, you know," she told her cat.

Renata gave a longsuffering *meow* and curled up so that her front and back paws framed Moretta's neck.

"Right, well, I'm sure that won't be a problem at all, grateful for your company," Moretta said as she fitted her leather knife-launchers around her forearms. "I think we're on the brink of understanding how our erstwhile Ravens were able to collect so much carrion."

Even though when she'd spoken it had been in a dissonant monotone that *almost* sounded brave, Moretta couldn't completely deny her fear… though that didn't stop her from trying.

"There is *nothing* to fear in that closet." She whispered that mantra to herself as she approached the closet under the stairs. She breathed in and out, summoning her courage as she stepped into the closet.

The closet walls were close around her shoulders, but wide enough that a reasonably average sized man would be able to fit through the passage without any trouble. The passage ahead of her led into the basement, and Moretta gulped in spite of the musty scent which assaulted her nostrils.

Renata sneezed irritably, and flicked her tail in Moretta's face.

"I know, I know, it's not the best idea…" Moretta drew back from the open passage, but a moment later she shrieked.

Her house guest, the raven, flew over her head, and down into the passage, but at first she'd thought it was a bat or someone intent on grabbing her from behind. So he was accustomed to this passage… had he been trained how to navigate it?

Well, one thing she knew for certain was that she *hadn't* been trained, nor could she fly. Moretta turned back to the parlor, and was about to retreat to safety until the lights behind her were switched on.

Slowly, Moretta turned back to the passage to see that it was illuminated just as any ordinary room might be, and she no longer had an excuse to avoid plunging into the depths of the passage.

She took another step down into the passage, and slowly, the further she went down the stairs, which she watched for any sign of weakness, she noticed that the room the raven had exposed was another work room.

There, seated on a perch, was the raven, puffed up proudly and for all the world he appeared to be *smirking* at Moretta.

"I see you there," Moretta snorted as Renata hopped off of her shoulders. She noticed something else as she peered at the raven, and said, "Ah! Your name is *Edgar*, is it?" she asked.

The raven crowed happily, and flapped his wings, nearly brushing against the brass nameplate that had told Moretta who he was.

"How charming!" she cried, and forgot to be afraid as she clapped her hands together. "Edgar! You're my new pet, aren't you?" She trotted through the workshop with renewed vigor; happier than she'd been in… was it months or years?

At the sound of Renata calling for her attention, again, Moretta turned to see her sitting beside a new door, and scratching at it.

"*Another* secret passage?" Moretta asked in dismay, "but I thought I'd found them all!"

Renata flicked her tail impatiently.

"I'm not going to bother with that right now," Moretta told Renata, who flicked her tail again and laid herself down beside the door.

Indeed, she had more to rifle through in this new workshop than she'd thought. There were legitimate medical texts neatly arranged on a shelf, and there was also a rack of surgical tools she may have occasion to use if anyone from the town was willing to visit her.

She was just beginning to think this was an ordinary workroom before she noticed a trough against the opposite wall, with chains bolted to the wall above it. Beside this setup were three barrels, all of which were labeled, "Quicklime."

Moretta swallowed as she realized precisely what she was looking at, and the blood began to drain from her face as nausea overtook her. "Not these things again!" she cried. "Why does it always have to get like this?"

Renata saw Moretta's alarm and jumped up from her place to rub against her leg.

"You're right... I'm not alone... this isn't meant for me..." Moretta trembled as she attempted with all the strength she had to tear her eyes away from what she saw, and stop imagining the ordeals of those who'd found themselves in this room with the madman and his wife... who may have been as mad as he was. She bent and picked Renata up to hold her close, which the cat rewarded with a purr and a rub of her head against her mistress's chin.

It was becoming all the clearer how these monsters had been able to perform atrocities in the name of medicine for so long, but she had no will to further probe the depths of their depravity as yet.

"I asked for this," Moretta reminded herself, for she knew Renata was already aware and needed no reminder. "I thought myself capable of staring into the abyss once more, but it seems I lack the strength..."

Renata gave her a questioning *meow* and Moretta shook her head.

"No, I won't leave until the job is done, but I'm also not going to try and chase down more secrets than I can handle at once."

Edgar crowed, and Moretta spared him enough attention to realize he was pecking at a mechanism meant to feed him, labeled, 'Eddie's Nummies."

"Again, how delightful," she muttered ruefully, and pulled the lever which dispensed a cupful of seeds, nuts and... Moretta held her nose in revulsion, but Edgar seemed more than enticed. "To each their own..." Moretta croaked at the smell of rotting meat. "I'll have to clean this out..." she nearly vomited at the thought. "There will need to be many, many changes around here..."

Yet for the moment, she knew there were other matters to attend to. Grateful to at last be able to justify leaving the underground workshop, Moretta flew to her feet, threw open the door and examined her new parlor, again.

Edgar came flying out of the basement, and with that she decided it was time to close the door on the whole mystery for the time being. "Edgar... closed?" she tried, seeing if the bird had been taught to close the door as well as open it.

Instead, Edgar appeared to have lost all interest in the passage as he'd gotten his food, and was instead flying into what she'd previously assumed was a merely decorative piece of gnarled wood. The way the bird was treating it, however, it was a branch in the stateliest of all trees, and it housed his nest.

"Well, my imperial lord, far be it from me to interfere while you make yourself at home," she said, and closed the window. "Most folk have guard dogs, and I now have a guard raven."

Renata made a disapproving sound, and Moretta sighed. "It's time to close that place up," she said, and knelt at the hearth again to make another attempt at closing the passage, but it still took a few attempts before she'd successfully closed it.

Still, that was not enough. Moretta felt the need to block the passage still more, and cast about for a way to do it. She found a favorable tool in the shape of a small armchair, draped in black lace. Her patron had been kind enough to buy it especially for her, and it was about to come in handy.

She threw all her weight into its journey across the room and into the closet, where it rested neatly in the middle of the tiny room. With that finally accomplished, Moretta ensured that the front door and every window in the house had been securely shut before darting up the stairs, where for some reason she managed to feel safer.

Though she followed more slowly, Renata met Moretta in the bedroom, and stretched out her languid little body before she curled her tail under Moretta's nose, purring softly.

"You're telling me it doesn't matter, aren't you? Well it does. It matters plenty. Where *are* we, princess?" she stroked Renata's back. "I've already had to pick a room I was sure nobody ever made love in, so it looks like a patient's room… that patient

probably ended up in the basement... all of them..."
she held the cat closer, but once she was purring
Moretta felt herself relax a little.

Renata's mouth lulled open and she licked her
own nose, staring pointedly at Moretta.

"Oh, so you think I need a *bath* do you?"
Moretta huffed, and nearly pushed the cat off her lap.
"Well I don't! I am quite well-bathed as of now!"

Renata, unimpressed, climbed up on Moretta's
legs and curled her tail around her paws.

"I'm listening," Moretta said resignedly.

Renata dipped her head low to lick Moretta's
hand, and eyed her pointedly.

"Oh, so it's *not* an insult to insinuate I require a
bath, I see," she huffed again. "That's not how
humans talk, Renata."

Renata lay down, as cats do, and flicked her
tail as if out of impatience with Moretta's nonsense.

With a sigh, Moretta conceded: "I have more
than likely been sweating profusely and into my nice
chiffon and everything. I understand it's quite
shameful, but I don't want to undress just now, it'll
make me feel all vulnerable!"

Renata rolled off of Moretta's legs and batted
her own head with her paws. "You think I'm addled!
You are truly telling me you think I'm addled, aren't
you? Or is that something even more insulting?"

Renata *meowed* in a low roll of sound, and
purred as if she were pleased with herself and
mocking Moretta.

Moretta's fingers jabbed into the cat's belly,
dancing with intentional lack of delicacy over
Renata's fur.

Renata folded over Moretta's hand, nipping at it and batting at her arm with claws purposefully retracted.

"You have won the day, it seems," Moretta said, scooping up Renata in her free hand. "I shall calm my nerves in a bath and you will attack soap bubbles as they come, yes?"

Renata's meow was an octave higher than that which had come before and the cat relaxed into Moretta's arms as the girl carried her to the washroom.

Chapter 7: Dishonest Dealings

Richard trembled all the way to the rendezvous point his masked companion had guided him towards. He had been utterly unaware there was a back entrance to Usher Abbey through a hidden gate... but then again that was something like the point of a hidden entrance.

His thoughts were in such a whirlwind Richard had to consciously scold himself to even attempt to feel competent enough to speak with the Duke. This would be the first conversation with a high-ranking official which he had not begged and scraped for.

What could he possibly offer that had made him worth seeking out? Was it rude to assume the duke even had chosen him specifically? Well, of course, if he'd wanted, Duke Julian could have hired any lawyer in Amontillado, so he concluded there must be something particular to himself that made him the first choice...

"Wait here," the masked man said with some amusement once they were indoors out of the rain, and Richard began frantically trying to dry off all signs that he'd walked through the rain. He couldn't go before the duke looking and smelling like a drowned dog! He was more than happy to wait.

It was much more difficult to compose himself when his masked guide vanished as if he'd never been more than a hallucination. Had he just trespassed in the duke's castle after burning out in his career in the most spectacular fashion possible?

Richard pressed a hand to his forehead, but realized that he was certainly not insane, and yes, he'd made the conscious decision to follow someone... That person had taken him along back streets Richard hadn't even realized were there despite having lived in Amontillado his entire life.

This was a *new* experience, surely, but not one he could honestly discount as a hallucination.

As wonderful as it was to determine that he was not yet a lunatic, Richard realized the unsettled feelings he'd been experienced did in fact have a basis in reality. He was surrounded by sculptures of snakes, and portraits of stately, grumpy-looking people. None of them seemed to approve of him being there, and the fact that the portraits were so tall gave him the impression they were good judges of character.

Anyone who could afford such ostentatious portraits of themselves had to know Richard was embarrassingly poor.

All of them were dressed in the finery of royalty, but he knew they weren't all kings and queens, some of them were simply the dukes and duchesses who had been given jurisdiction over Amontillado in the past. For some reason, the ones he recognized as the leaders of his own community looked much more sinister than their parents.

Was it tradition to dump the least qualified ruler on Amontillado? Richard didn't think that was quite fair. Couldn't the other duchies have the nutty megalomaniacs every third generation or so? Or, better yet... couldn't anyone come to the conclusion that some royals were never meant to rule?

Perhaps it was just him, and royals didn't think the way normal people did, in the least. It could make sense to someone in power to dump their child on a place far away from the capitol without any potential to raise an army.

It couldn't be a coincidence, could it? Someone had to apply logic to the pattern at some point... As Richard pondered these things, he wandered down the portrait hall staring into each painted face, attempting to parse out his kingdom's history.

Perhaps the royal family was secretly much more insane than they appeared to be, and there was no difference between the dukes of Amontillado and the dukes in the other duchies.

"I see you admire my family," he heard a voice echo down the hall, and turned to see the tall, lanky profile of Duke Julian. He'd only ever caught glimpses of the prince while riding through town in his landau, but those glimpses had only left the impression on Richard that the duke was far more mysterious than stately or refined. The impression did not die away now that they were face to face.

"What citizen would not admire his betters?" Richard asked, and bowed.

Duke Julian gave a nobleman's chuckle which made Richard slightly uneasy. There was no logical reason to be unsettled, he was sure, but instinctively, that laugh bothered him. Perhaps it was because when he heard that sound, it was clearly something that would have been at home on the lips of every portrait in the hall he'd judged equally unsettling.

"Come along, my good man," Duke Julian gestured for Richard to follow him, and Richard was glad to be out of the hallway, out from under all those eyes. The only trouble was, the study they entered had a window open onto the town, and an arctic draft was sweeping through it.

By the time he was shown to a seat, he was already frozen, nearly into a block of ice. He held himself absolutely still, terrified more of doing something rash he wouldn't ever recover from than he'd been of the man shooting up the Bacchanal. He knew he ought to look at the duke, but he was paralyzed by his own terror that the duke would see something unworthy in his eyes.

"You must be wondering what could possibly have caught my notice about someone like you," Duke Julian drawled.

Richard looked up at him, and furrowed his brow, his arms still stiffly fused to the arms of the chair he sat upon, and his heart beating painstakingly slowly. It ought to be racing, but instead, he felt as if he were freezing from the inside. His high collar, though it hadn't been nearly starched enough, seemed to likewise restrict his breath.

He had to speak, had to show that he was not an imbecile — and yet the duke spoke first.

"The fact is, I've decided you are the one who needs my business most out of all the men down there in that festering pit. In fact, you are the most bound to show me loyalty as our business proceeds."

"I have always endeavored to be unflinchingly loyal, your grace," Richard forced out, exerting a great deal of effort to prevent his teeth from chattering.

"*Yes...*" Duke Julian smiled, and Richard noticed that he was being mocked, if subtly.

He had already referred to the duke as one of his betters, there was no room for going back on that now. As a mere citizen, he had no right to demand respect from the son of a king. "I have always been loyal to my chosen profession, for example," he said, keeping his voice even only due to intense concentration.

"Despite the depths it has dropped you to," Duke Julian said with another of those unsettling laughs of his.

"I admit... I have faced more hardship than most who pursue my profession..." he knew he was beginning to shake, and eyed a tea service on the side table directly next to the duke's arm. If the duke would be just a little generous and offer him tea, Richard may stop shaking...

"Of course, you have! Look at you! You're the son of a factory man who didn't even have the decency to make something more entertaining than buttons!"

Richard couldn't help flinching. "He financed my studies, and in return I am no longer a burden on the family," he responded evenly.

"But you're no help to them, either, are you? Now, see, you're here so that you and I can change that! Are you willing to hear what I've got planned?"

"I do not have the will to tear myself away," Richard replied. "As you say, I need the business."

It was then the duke called for his servant to pour the tea for them.

Richard accepted his cup only to find that when he took the first sip, it was already cold. He ought not to have been surprised, it fit in with the rest of his luck.

Though the duke's tea must be equally cold, to Richard's dismay, the fellow not only appeared unbothered by frigid tea, he seemed to enjoy it. Was this a trait peculiar to the individual, or a family trait?

"As concerns that nasty business in the Bacchanal Hall, I heard you were in attendance, were you not?"

"I was…" Richard wished the duke hadn't brought it up, especially not in such a cavalier manner. It was already difficult enough to ignore his steadily growing panic, he didn't need it to get more difficult still!

"What was it like?" Duke Julian asked with a glint in his eyes.

"Oh, the party?" Richard paused to shuffle through the confusion which had ensued the moment the attack began. Already his memory was a jumble, but he needed an answer to give the duke. "Well… honestly it was horrific… there were people dying everywhere, screaming… running… I barely got out, myself… How many survivors were there? Are we any closer to catching the killer?"

Duke Julian waved his hand. "The dead have been dealt with, and the living souls have been compensated. All save for in one case, which is why I called you here."

"Oh…" Richard stared as the duke received another cupful of tea. "But where have all the bodies gone? I spoke with the new Raven and watched the other citizens run past her without paying her any heed… so did you send the bodies to the morgue, after all?"

Duke Julian smirked at him, and smoothed his silken vest. "I have graciously housed the bodies on my own estate until such a time as the families can finance their funerals. However, I did not call you here to speak about that, and I am afraid my time is more valuable than yours. Thus, I wish to discuss the matter of Count Udolpho of Otranto. He died in our city, and is without heirs. Thus his estate has fallen into my care, or at least all those holdings which are within town limits. That includes his town home."

Richard's eyes widened as he all but salivated over the idea of an estate up for grabs. "What would my role in dealing with this estate difficulty be?" he asked.

"I believe the local aristocracy has grown too powerful," Duke Julian took another sip of his tea. "I think it is time to set up a new local hierarchy."

Despite the chill which had pervaded Richard's heart, he could feel warmth well up from his core as those words sank in. Nothing said opportunity more clearly than restructuring.

"I see I've piqued your interest," Duke Julian's smirk was back in full force. "We'd best begin our preparations, immediately."

"Do you have any papers I could —" Richard was cut off as another servant entered the room with a stack of legal documents, and set them on the table before Richard with a resounding *thud*. "Well, I'll get to work, straightaway, then… What sort of stipend can I expect for my time?"

Again there came a laugh which Richard utterly despised, but could not protest. His mind was racing but he still could not decide exactly what the duke thought was so funny. "We will decide that on a basis of how much you actually accomplish. In other words, we will discuss that when I decide you've already begun working."

"With all due respect, your grace, I believe you chose me for a reason, over all the other options. Thus I think you do value my help highly, and I would be remiss if I entered a contract without learning what the terms are."

Duke Julian was no longer smirking. Instead, he was giving Richard a calculated look, and actually attempting to appraise him. "We will give you a starting allowance of 1,000 *chrysi*, and then we'll negotiate further after you've done some real work."

Richard was already reeling from the suggestion of 1,000 gold coins, or at least a note which entitled him to them, but the prospect of earning still more than that was what truly staggered him. "Th-thank you, your grace..." he stammered, and felt himself begin to come apart at the seams. All that composure he'd been forcing on himself was quickly eroding, and he had to get out of sight before he dissolved into an utter simpleton.

"Don't thank me yet," the duke said, tilting his head at Richard as his eyes flashed over a smile that was not quite *right*.

Still, Richard was not one to stab at a rocking horse once it rolled up on his beach, so he rose and bowed to his new patron. "I will not disappoint you, your grace," he pressed a hand over his heart. "This is my most important endeavor, so I will devote the entirety of my vitality to your cause."

For a silent moment, the Duke smirked at Richard, swirling his tea in his cup, before saying in a low, thoughtful tone, "I shall hold you to that, boy. See that you do not disappoint me."

Chapter 8: Evidence to the Contrary

Moretta left her home once the inclement weather eased slightly, so that the clouds merely brooded overhead, rather than pouring forth a deluge upon the helpless inhabitants of Amontillado.

She bore a missive that she would send directly to her aunt, for it was surely only her who would heed her words. She had spent the morning embalming the count and preparing him for burial, but she had a missive for his next-of-kin, as well… if only she could find them!

Her map of Amontillado did at least guide her to the office of the postmaster, and she handed over her envelopes to the postmaster's clerk, but he would not speak to her.

"I beg your pardon!" she called after him as he turned his back on her and disappeared into the back room. "I'm looking for the estate of Count Otranto!"

There was no reply until she heard someone ask, "Raven?" There was only one person in the town who had become acquainted with her was Richard Phaal, and for this reason she knew who it was before she turned to see his bewildered face.

"It is good to see you again, Master Phaal," she said, and dipped a curtsey.

He bowed, and tipped a hat she didn't remember him having. "My dear young lady, I believe I've been caught off-guard by seeing you alone about the town. Might I have the honor of escorting you? I feel remiss leaving you to swim upstream in a sea of strangers."

Moretta knew she was blushing, but she pressed her fan over her heart. "I would be equally honored to accept your invitation, my good man... might I ask that you escort me to the estate of Count Otranto? I believe it is of the utmost importance and I require immediate access to his next of kin."

Richard blinked, and she saw the confusion play across his face. "Surely, my lady, I cannot determine for what reason you may wish to visit such a place. Do you not already live in a dead man's house? Why seek another?"

"Do you know that he has died," Moretta sighed. "Do you imagine that his family is equally aware?"

"He hasn't got any family, at least not in the duchy of Amontillado. You'd be better off sending a letter to wherever he hailed from."

Moretta sighed. "Perhaps then I ought to send his body their way, as well."

"I should think Duke Julian would be willing to send his mortal remains to them," Richard said, and a moment later he puffed himself up slightly. "I could help you get in contact with him."

Something about him had undoubtedly changed, but the question was whether Moretta considered it an improvement. He did not seem to lack confidence as he once had, but perhaps he had grown too at ease with himself. He seemed to have overestimated his own prominence in promising her the ear of the duke. "I would prefer to circumvent such ostentatious means," she said quietly, and watched his surprise cross his features.

"Is that so? He has taken personal responsibility for the bodies of the victims which were taken from this life by the madman at the

Bacchanal. I do not doubt he would take this body off your hands, as well."

"It is my responsibility to care for all those under my roof, be they dead or alive, for I am not an ungracious hostess. I beseech you, Richard, for the kindness of your time in escorting me to the home of the deceased. This map of mine only tells me where the noblemen's homes are, not to whom they each belong."

Richard sighed, and bowed to her request. "I have several appointments laid out for me today, but I can spare the time to escort you across time. I could never bring myself to deny a lady."

True to his word, Richard did escort Moretta across town, and all the while he conversed in little pleasantries as he introduced her to the local haunts he enjoyed, and the ones which he aspired to one day patronize.

Among the latter number was a triple-story boutique, whose fanciful curlicue sign declared it was known as, "Bon Bonnie's Boudoir Boutique." This establishment had been painted a pink so garish it nearly triggered Moretta's gag reflex, though once she controlled that, it had a certain charm to it. Only the truly bold would dare to paint an establishment of any kind that shade, so she had to admire its proprietors for that.

The windows were tinted bottle green, and she even caught sight of an advertisement in the window which boasted of the boutique's very own creamery and saloon. Their signature flavors both of ice cream and spirits revolved around peppermint, but that was nothing compared to the boasts they posted about their bonbons

"It appears to be a catch-all for the ladies of the town," Moretta observed as she debated seriously entering the establishment. "Surely you don't want to go in there," Moretta huffed, scandalized by the very thought of a man entering such an establishment.

"They do have a men's section," he qualified with a blush. "But... I really want to go because—" he stopped abruptly, and Moretta traced the focus of his gaze to the second story of Bonnie's.

Through the pastel pink of the windows, she saw that he had focused on several women who were certainly oblivious to them both.

"Do you know them?" she asked, wondering how often he stared at women and whether he was indiscriminate as to which of them he ogled.

"Lenore..." Richard muttered as if he were speaking the password to enter some arcane society's deepest, darkest sanctum.

"I see..." she could see pure adoration, bordering on *veneration* on his face. This was the look of a man who had spent years fermenting an admiration for a woman, and a small part of her broke. She had no right to him, she reminded herself.

She couldn't tell which of the women was Saint Lenore, but she knew she did not wish to linger. "Shall I continue on my own?" she asked. Perhaps if she left, he could enter the shrine of his favorite saint, and she would be able to mend her poor wounded heart. It was better to remember not to lose her mind, she couldn't afford to.

"No, miss, I… I promised you that I would escort you all the way to your destination, and I would be forever shamed if I had abandoned you in favor of my own passions."

To keep from flinching, Moretta reminded herself that he was nothing more than a handsome acquaintance. This shining example of beauty he had glimpsed through Bonnie's window had certainly wormed her way into his heart long ago, and she was not in the business of dislodging other women from their rightful places out of jealousy.

Still she was silent as Richard led her along, which was thankfully simple as he appeared to be lost in his thoughts.

"This is it," Richard said at last, and brought Moretta's attention back to their actual location. "Otranto Manor… so what's the deal, did you have an appointment with the count?"

"You could say I've already had a meeting with the count," Moretta's lips curled with a hint of irony. "He's something of an unexpected house guest, in fact."

Richard stared at her without comprehending, but she waited for him to come around to what she was attempting to communicate gently. "Are you… *absolutely* sure… I mean, I think the duke has everything under control, it's possible he's just holding it for someone." His blush belied some unspoken truth which made Moretta dread uncovering deeper truths behind his words.

"That's right." She produced the invitation she'd salvaged from the count's pocket and showed it to Richard. "He was not killed in the same manner as the others. You said they were shot? He was hit with a poisoned dart. He was assassinated. The rest of the attack was only a cover-up."

She watched as Richard's face colored, and wondered what the cause of his apparent embarrassment might be. Still, she waited for him to deal with his reaction rather than prodding him and perhaps further obscuring the issue.

"I can't believe… he doesn't seem to have any relatives, so…" Richard drew Moretta's attention to a notice which had been pinned to the iron gate of the manor. "Everyone's been talking about it…"

Moretta stared at the notice, looking from the information on Count Otranto to Otranto manor seeking some difference that would tell her she was not seeing what she thought she was.

Except that there was no denying it. She was looking at the very manor the duke had acquired as the spoils of not an accidental or random manslaughter, but a targeted assassination with scattershot sprayed about the room in order to cover up the attack's true intent.

"You say everyone's been talking about this?" she asked. "What do they think happened?"

"Most everyone believes the count was part of the random attacks perpetrated during the Bacchanal."

"Of course, they do," Moretta sighed. "I wish I weren't correct in my assertions as often as I am."

"What do you mean? What did you assert?"

"It's… it's becoming clear this was no random attack. Don't you wonder why no perpetrator has been found? I believe Duke Julian is doing this out of greed. He murdered Count Otranto in order to buy up his land at a marked-down price, or even seized it because it's within his purview… Richard, we're dealing with a serious criminal here. How long do you think he's been abusing his power?"

She watched the blush she'd seen begin to fade on Richard's cheeks return in full force. "It could be a misunderstanding," he suggested weakly.

"What sort of misunderstanding?" she pressed. "I understand, you've lived under his command perhaps your whole life, but… you can't believe this is normal. Real leaders don't do this to their people, they don't cannibalize them and they don't terrorize them. This is filth, Richard, and I'm going to put a stop to it!"

Richard stared at her as if she'd just suggested overthrowing the king and calling herself Empress of the Mad. "Raven, you don't really know what you're suggesting!" he gasped, utterly scandalized.

"Of course, I do," she folded her arms at that remark, and the fact that she'd just gotten called by a nickname which was stained with blood. "Richard Ambrose Phaal, you have to understand one thing and you have to grasp it well: not everyone in power is a just ruler. Some of these people need to be reminded that they're human, too."

"You don't know the Duke, he's not a criminal," Richard asserted, folding his arms to mirror her stance. "I've spoken to him, he's incredibly generous and magnanimous!"

"Oh, that's impressive!" Moretta snapped. "How cute, the charlatan can put on a show! I suppose if you met a man who wanted to sell you a translation of an ancient book he found in a hill you'd never ask to see it before you believed him, now would you?"

"Look, I'm not an idiot," Richard gritted his teeth, and Moretta could see she wasn't getting anywhere with him. "I know for a fact that Duke Julian is kind, and you're the one who's making assertions without evidence!"

"In every case, the party which benefits from the death in question is the primary suspect." Moretta forced her voice to remain as steady and soft as possible, so as to prevent the argument from turning into a friendship-shattering boulder. "That is why when I see the duke buying up the count's manor days after his death, which I know was no accident, I have to conclude that the duke is the one who benefits, and is thus the guilty party."

"You can't know that for certain, not when your investigation has just begun!"

"Why are you really defending him?" Moretta knew the words were counterproductive to her maintaining a friendship with Richard, but her sharp tongue had cut before she could force it to stay sheathed. "What do you get out of this?" she asked in a softer voice, reining it in once more.

There was that telltale blush again, his heart pounding with guilt that would soon be unearthed if Moretta had anything to say about it. "I…" Richard sighed, and she knew he was giving up on hiding the truth from her, at last. "Yesterday, he invited me to the Abbey, and he told me that he would need me to help him with smoothing over the count's affairs… it's the first big case I've ever gotten… I *need* this,

Raven, I need it so badly you can't possibly understand!"

"Of course, I understand," she said softly. "Richard," she offered him a hand on his shoulder, and he didn't pull back. "Listen, I understand, too. I understand that you feel you're disadvantaged and I can see why you would feel that way. But I don't think you need someone like the duke to raise you out of these circumstances. I think you're capable of doing it for yourself."

"I haven't been, so far," Richard rebutted, but did not pull back from her steadying hand.

"I know you have ambitions, and you feel this is the best way, but trust me. Getting involved in the duke's nefarious dealings is going to ruin you. He will use you until he no longer needs you, and then you will be painted as the only criminal in this business when it comes out that something was done shamefully."

The frantic denial on Richard's face told her that he knew she was right, but she was equally aware that he could not face that reality. She couldn't blame him for that weakness. It would take time before he was willing to accept that.

"I don't think we ought to remain here much longer," Richard said. "Someone who works for Duke Julian might think we're here to vandalize or break in."

"Someone like you, perhaps?" she asked gently, but without being the least bit vague on the fact that she was actually leveling this argument.

Richard gave her a disapproving look, but he had no rebuttal. He turned his back on her and began to walk away.

She watched him go, unwilling to call him back and thus prolong the argument and widen the frigid gorge between them. She did not even say anything in farewell to him. Perhaps it was for the best that they no longer spoke to one another. She was probably better off alone.

Chapter 9: Moneyed or Moral

If he had been honest with himself, Richard would know that his new friend had been correct. And yet, this offer was the best thing that could have happened to him, so he could not relinquish his hopes for a better life.

He returned to his apartment in a new suit, and he would have felt completely at ease with himself if not for the fact that the barber he'd hired to fix his hair had botched his new style. He now had two curls of coal-black hair on either side of his brow, and he felt either like a sleazy android-salesman or a schoolboy.

At least out in the world he was able to wear his hat to cover it up, but once he was in his apartment it was somewhat inappropriate. Thus, when he heard someone knock on the door, he jumped in as much surprise as if he were guilty of a crime... and perhaps now, he was...

"Come in..." he said as he went to the hat rack for his new hair shield. It was quite smart with its bobbing pheasant feather, but still at the sight of it, Braxton still saw him the moment before his hat went on.

"Oh, I'm sorry," he said, setting down a box of shining, polished brass devices. "I thought Richard Phaal still lived here, I didn't realize he'd been supplanted by a choir boy."

Richard snorted and ushered Braxton is, though with his blush still burning his cheeks he kept his hat on. "Very funny, Brax, what do you have there?"

"I need to show someone else these inventions before I come utterly unscrewed in the cranium," Braxton explained as he lifted one of his inventions out of the box, itself bearing all the seeming of being naught but a wooden box with something peculiar carved onto its lid.

"Are you sure that's an invention?" Richard asked. "It looks like an art project."

"Bear with me a moment," Braxton said, and held the box up. "This is a sensor."

"What does it sense?" Richard raised a brow and tilted his head.

"That's just it…" Braxton held up a finger and set the box down on Richard's table, then opened the lid.

There was a small brass device inside, the display face of which showed something along the lines of a compass. Beside it were three pocket watches… or at least Richard assumed they were pocket watches until Braxton opened one of them and revealed that it was a similar radar device.

"So… it's a tracking device?" Richard asked. "And… anyone who takes one of these little devices with them will find their way back to the main device?"

"Precisely!" Braxton cried excitedly. "This could do wonders for explorers! Imagine a network of these showing everyone the way home!"

"So you'd better slap a patent on it," Richard nodded, and smiled with how impressed he genuinely was. "If you can sell it to private companies it could open up a whole new series of opportunities."

Braxton grinned and packed that box away, tucking it neatly in with the others. "Next is something for home use," he said, and lifted out another device. "What do you think of that?"

Richard took it to hold up for a better view. He turned it over in his hands, noting that once it had been an ordinary clock Braxton had harvested it for parts. What he found at the end of his examination was that opening a panel in the side of the clock was a complete refitting of the mechanisms.

He opened the entire device to find that there was a space in the device for a phonograph cylinder. It was from there he realized that there was a small cone like there would be on a phonograph or gramophone.

"What... how does this work?" he asked as he turned the device around again to show that there was netting where the clock face normally went.

"This is to amplify music more than current technology allows," Braxton explained. "If I can manufacture versions of this that are much larger... Just think of the possibilities... They could be mounted outside concert halls and opera houses so that the populace can hear the music... they can be set up on street corners to give emergency alerts..."

Richard's eyes widened still more. "Wow... you're right..." he felt almost as if he were holding a holy relic. He set it back in the box carefully, closing all the panels.

"So you think both of these will work?" Braxton asked, wringing his hands together nervously.

"What's this?" Richard asked, at a loss to identify the small rectangular leather object with brass fittings, about the size of his finger, and opened the lid. There was a metallic sort of claw that made Richard ask, "Is this a weapon?"

"No, no," Braxton waved his hands, "this is for containing data!"

Richard quirked his brow and turned the little leather object over in his hands. "How?"

"It'll hook into the interface of any computing engine and take the data it contains."

"So... rather than in a massive device that takes up an entire room you can keep the data in the palm of your hand?" he asked.

"Even if the person *with* said monstrous device doesn't know it..." Braxton's eyes were aglow with pride.

"Don't... don't let anyone but the royal family get ahold of this... it could revolutionize espionage..."

"I'm sure it will," Braxton plucked his invention out of Richard's hand. "It'll need fine-tuning, of course."

"Right, don't start selling quasi-completed gadgets…" Richard smiled, but in his heart he fretted that his neighbor and friend was about to rise and leave him as the last vagabond in town. His eyes itched for the sight of the documentation he'd abandoned for this meeting.

"What are you up to?" Braxton asked, carefully securing all his inventions for his trip back up the stairs.

"Oh, I've got my first client in a long while…" Richard paused, wondering if he ought to maintain the duke's confidentiality. He couldn't remember any orders not to reveal that he was working for the duke…

"Do you? How stupendous for you!" Braxton said with genuine enthusiasm. "So who is it?"

"I… I don't think I can say… but I'll let you know it's someone quite prestigious, and I think this will be the most momentous case of my career. It could launch me to greatness for life… or plunge me into infamy."

"We could go down to the pub and drink to stave off ill fortune for us both," Braxton suggested. "Perhaps we'll catch the fancy of a lady or two, out there in the wild."

Richard tilted his head, remembering his earlier fascination with the idea of encountering Lenore at her favorite boutique. "I could go for a drink at Bonnie's. That's where the women will be."

Braxton tilted his head and considered that plan. "Those are the women what we'd have to bribe to spend time with us, aren't they? High society wouldn't have time for us."

"Perhaps they wouldn't have before, but we're moving up in the world," Richard noted. "Look at us, we've got ambition and we've got style. What girl wouldn't want to hop aboard our train to prominence?"

"A girl who lives near prominence station and lets her daddy drive her there?" Braxton guessed.

Richard waved his hand. "Maybe, but I think we're capable of even netting a girl like that. You bring one of your fancy gadgets and I'll... well, don't you think this hat is fetching?"

"Maybe if you wash that pomade out of your hair you'll still have a shot when that hat comes off!" Braxton snickered.

Richard frowned and his hand went protectively to the brim of his hat which hid the embarrassing hair style. "You have a point there... think you've got an invention that could help me?"

Braxton gave a laugh that was almost harsh. "No, friend, the day I invent something to fix hair like that is the day I become a barber! I'm afraid you're on your own!"

In the midst of Braxton's laughter, Richard snorted and ushered his neighbor back to the door. "Let me get ready and look over my papers, all right? We'll meet at sundown."

Richard allowed himself to spend some time preparing, after all it was of the utmost importance that he made a good impression.

Still, his eyes kept drifting uneasily toward the stack of papers he'd received from the duke. Surely if he really looked into them he would find that Raven had been wrong, but if that were the case, why was he afraid to look?

He took a deep breath and finally broke into the first page and began to read. The preliminary notation all revolved about the prospect of legally binding Richard to supporting Duke Julian and ensuring that he was well aware of the consequences should he betray him.

Should that concern him? Richard knew he'd been selected because he was more likely than most to stay loyal, so it made sense that the duke would be concerned in writing as well as in person. This was nothing out of the ordinary, he decided, and anyway he *needed* this opportunity.

He scanned further down the literature, and shifted to the next page. This was concerned with Richard's duties, so he eagerly read into it for his instructions. He was meant to oversee the transfer of all Count Otranto's assets to the accounts of the duke's household.

Raven's words echoed in his mind, and sweat speckled his brow as denial became more difficult to maintain.

Perhaps it was within the duke's rights to absorb the count's estate, and Raven's wariness had been mistaken. In order to avoid facing the truth, or at least what Raven had vehemently attempted to convince him was the truth, he peered out his window. Below him was the town which passed him by every day, with very few citizens every paying him the slightest hint of attention.

If he were foolish enough to turn down the duke's offer, they always would. Worse, if it were true what Raven said, perhaps he would find *himself* assassinated rather than given the chance to reveal what he knew.

With these considerations in mind, Richard could not see an alternative to signing the contract. If he were lucky, he could drink away his guilt.

Before he was ready to leave his brooding thoughts, Richard heard another knock at his door. Perhaps it was for the best that he didn't descend into his ruminations so deeply he couldn't be extricated. Life was to be lived, and he was unwilling to miss his opportunity.

It was an odd feeling, realizing that for once he wasn't ashamed to be seen in public with Braxton. It was one thing to be seen with a poor man who could not better himself, but a man who had created worthy gadgetry that could benefit society was a worthy companion.

He would be proud to be called this fellow's companion, so he strode with confidence out of the clock tower with his pheasant feather bobbing in his hat.

"Are you sure we've got enough to afford Bonnie's?" Braxton asked when they were halfway there, cutting into Richard's thoughts.

"If you don't, I'll buy something for you. I was paid in advance."

"Well, I did get some grant money, and it hasn't run out yet..." Braxton considered.

"See?" Richard asked, distractedly. "Naught to worry about."

When they actually arrived at Bonnie's, Richard could hear the music wafting down from the upper levels as if it were the sound of angels plucking their harps. Except of course that this was the sound of an erratic and whimsical string quartet accompanied by a harpsichord; angels almost certainly didn't sound like that.

"Are you ready to go in?" Braxton asked, just before they were stopped by a caped man entering with a woman on his arm.

"Richard? Is that you?" In the gaslight burning a halo around Bonnie's, Richard recognized his cousin, Hans. He was leaning on a walking stick, and wearing a pair of rosy spectacles. "I didn't think Bonnie's was your scene!"

"I'm trying something new," Richard explained. "I'm moving up in the world now, and my social circle needs to reflect that."

Hans was beaming with pride, but the pride faded out of his eyes as they landed on

Braxton. "You're still bringing him along?" he asked.

"Well, I'd say the best friendships are those that start close to home," Braxton said before Richard could salvage himself from his instant shame. Why was Braxton so much better at this friendship thing than he was?

"Not to mention you shouldn't underestimate my friend here," Richard set a hand on Braxton's shoulder as he envied the power of gesticulation he was sure Hans's walking stick gave him. "He showed me some of the inventions he's created that are awaiting patent approval, and I must say I was quite impressed! I believe the man you see before you will achieve fame, fortune, and a legacy one day, and he shall do it overnight!"

He almost felt like a good friend after that speech, and didn't dare check Braxton's face to see how well he'd succeeded.

"That so?" Hans appraised Braxton, then Richard. "Well, I must say your hat does make you look much more distinguished than you were before... I suppose we can forgive the lodgings you currently occupy..."

The brunette woman at Hans's shoulder cleared her throat, which gave Hans a start. She had an impressive hat, silken and somewhat swooshy... was that an appropriate word to use in appraising women's clothing? It was the only one that came to Richard's mind, and he was fairly sure that meant something was wrong with him.

"Ah! This is my dear acquaintance, Charlotte Wilson! Of late, her father has given me permission to escort her to her evening activities."

Both Richard and Braxton bowed to the woman bowed to pay honor to the lady. In the filtered light, it was difficult to tell what color her dress was, but the cut of it was unmistakably fine, festooned with ruffles and bows in a fashionable pinstripe. Likewise, her face was slightly obscured by the nighttime and the mist, but it was definitely visible as round and friendly-looking.

"Charlotte, this is my cousin, Richard Phaal, he is a solicitor… who has apparently found work for himself."

There it was, the first reminder of the "opportunity" he wished he could forget. He found himself cringing, but he took a deep breath to compose himself.

"Indeed, and the work is quite good, you may be assured of that!" He just wished he could be. That would be nice…

"And who is his friend?" Charlotte whispered to Hans.

"Ah…" Hans paused as he furrowed his brow at Braxton, while he groped around in his mind for the answer.

"Braxton Coy, at your service," the inventor said as he bowed. "I am responsible for providing the local mines with gunpowder and bombs in order to open up deeper veins of ore. I work on side projects on occasion, as well."

"I was unaware of the mining thing," Richard admitted.

"How do you think I stave off starvation?" Braxton asked. "Now, let's not stand outside in the fog and let it soak our skins, we ought to go inside and warm up. I hear," he pointed to one of the boastful signs in Bonnie's window, "that they have impressive absinthe cocktails."

Richard had to hand it to Braxton, he didn't harbor the least bit of insecurity about his position in society. He led the rest of them into the boutique bar without flinching, holding his head up as stately as a king.

Remembering the way he'd forced himself to stand at the Bacchanal, Richard took his cue from Braxton. If an inventor could be this confident, why couldn't the duke's solicitor also be proud of who he was?

He set his impressive hat on a hat rack, though he was concerned that with it had gone much of his magnetism… if he'd had any.

Stripped of his hat and his coat, Richard nearly felt naked. Everyone could see his threadbare shirtsleeves, even though he'd rented a silken vest which ought to impress with its forest green crispness and the silver buttons.

He stuffed his hands into his pockets and prayed nobody would scrutinize him too closely. Perhaps he was just being self-conscious, and he was much more conscious of himself than anyone else was likely to do.

Was the fact that his hands were in his pockets bringing more attention to him?

He fumbled with his hands, feeling they hung awkwardly at his sides, and were even starting to sweat. Was it just him or were they too big? It was simply unsightly! No gentleman would have hands like these!

"Are you feeling unwell?" Charlotte asked him, which brought Hans and Braxton's eyes around to scrutinize Richard.

"I think you need a drink or two," Hans suggested with a wink. "That'll get some courage in you!"

Richard forced himself to laugh, albeit awkwardly. "You're probably right," he admitted, and followed Braxton past the wooden and silken changing screens which had covered up the dresses and other wares normally sold on the bottom floor.

The first time he entered the party at Bonnie's, he was startled to find that the dancing was of a variety he'd not seen before. Legs were kicked into the air, and skirt ruffles were fluttering like the wings of so many disturbed doves.

He'd never seen so many ankles in his life! At least all the women were wearing stockings… that would keep them relatively decent, he told himself, so he didn't have to be overly abashed by the sight of them.

Hans pushed him forward toward the bar, and Richard watched as Braxton approached the bar with a blend of a swagger and a shuffle. It was almost enough to make Richard think the fellow had already had something to drink before they went out for the night.

There were too many people for Richard to actually discern whether he recognized any of them, but for the time being he was more concerned with not being outmanned. He needed to be seen drinking a heroic degree of absinthe and befriended that infamous green fairy he kept hearing about.

The woman behind the counter wore half a mask, but he could still see the beauty mark at the edge of her lips, which were painted, somewhat appropriately, in pink and green stripes to match her dress. "What can I get for you?" she asked in a smooth voice that somehow managed to put Richard at ease.

"I think I'll take one of the peppermint drinks," he said, like a complete novice.

He watched her smirk and knew he hadn't said the right thing. It was no wonder he never impressed anyone—he seemed intrinsically incapable of it.

"Which one of them?" she asked sweetly, just before Hans thumped Richard's shoulder and said, "He's not acquainted with the green fairy yet, Miss. I believe he's asking for the Menthe Twist, which is what I'll be ordering as well, incidentally."

"Right away, sir," the woman turned away, so that the pink and green ostrich feathers in her hat bobbed with her movement.

"Have you decided what you'd like, my darling?" Hans asked Charlotte as Richard found the Menthe Twist on the menu and counted out the money to pay off the barmaid.

"I'd like a Jaded Shrew," Charlotte said, primly seating herself on one of the bar stools.

In the meantime Hans counted out the money for that drink as well as his own, and paid the barmaid when she turned about with the two Menthe Twists in hand.

She was kept busy as she instantly turned back to the array of mixtures to prepare the Jaded Shrew, and in the lull Richard turned to survey the dance floor again.

"Thinking of going out there?" Hans asked Richard. "You're going to need some serious quality steps to keep up with the rest of us, you know."

"I might," Richard said, hoping against hope that he would see Lenore among the dancers. "I don't think I'm quite drunk enough, yet, though."

"I hear that!" Braxton chuckled from Richard's other side. "Miss, if it's not too much trouble, I'd like a Black Mango."

"A *what*?" Richard re-examined the menu. "How do you even *make* a black mango? Do you slather it in black licorice?"

Braxton widened his eyes to convey the gravity of that truth, and nodded slowly.

"Someone always asks that question," the barmaid snickered. "That's why we called it that, it's a good way to catch a customer's eye." She set said drink before Braxton, and Richard noticed that her hand lingered against Braxton's fingers for just a moment longer than necessary.

"At least it's you that picked it, not me," Richard finally summoned the courage to drink his own brew. Along with Hans, he performed an abbreviated absinthe ritual, as they could be reasonably assured their barmaid had already performed the other half.

The moment the Menthe Twist touched his lips he felt the acrid burn of peppermint combined with absinthe… it was possibly one of the reasons peppermint was advertised on the window.

Once the burn was over, his head seemed to clear and let in such clarity he couldn't believe he was drinking highly concentrated alcohol. It seemed counterintuitive, but perhaps that was why someone might give the drink such a mystical nickname.

All his insecurities appeared to roll off his shoulders as if he were shrugging off a cumbersome cloak. Nothing around him changed in his eyes, it was only him that seemed to change and grow slightly taller.

No need for someone like him to be intimidated!

"So have you heard the latest gossip?" the barmaid asked, distracting Richard from his preparation to conquer the dance floor.

"What's that?" Charlotte asked excitedly, and Richard felt his ears prick up.

"They say Count Otranto is dead," the barmaid said, and instantly a fist seemed to close around Richard's heart.

"How dreadful!" Charlotte cried.

"More than that! Before the bidding war could even get off the ground, Duke Julian snapped it up! He's such a hawk about these things!"

"But what is he going to do with *another* manor?" Braxton asked.

"They say he's going to pass it on to one of his friends," the barmaid shrugged, and Richard took another drink in hopes of clearing away the worries Raven had implanted in his mind.

It didn't quite work, but it did give him a way to disguise his own insecurities, which was honestly the best he could ask for. Why did everyone have to make him doubt his choices? He needed this... he may even get to move into decent lodgings... if only people would stop casting aspersions and doubts on his dealings with the duke.

"Typical," Braxton sighed.

"As long as it's someone who deserves it," Hans said, and Richard gave his cousin a hopeful look. "Perhaps this will improve matters in town."

"How?" Charlotte asked. "A friend of Julian's is just someone who'll run things the same way he does, right?"

"That's possible," Hans conceded with a disappointed sigh.

"That isn't necessarily a bad thing," Richard said, thinking perhaps nobody would guess he was a potential candidate after he came into the discussion so late. "What if this person was entrusted with a higher station in order to make things better for everyone else? After all, he could know what it's like to live in the lower levels of society even after ascending... that could be a perspective Duke Julian values, couldn't it?"

His drinking companions eyed him thoughtfully, and he took another drink. Had they guessed that he was hoping to take up residence in the count's vacated manor house?

"You may have a point," Braxton said at last. "When it comes down to the facts we don't know them all. So it's best to stay optimistic, no matter which town we happen to live in... even if it's this one."

"This town isn't so bad," Richard said defensively, "it's still full of possibilities, no need to denigrate our home."

"Oh, good heavens, do I know you?"

Richard's heart beat so powerfully that it made his chest ache, and he slowly turned to see that it was indeed *his* Lenore! She was standing, as she so often did, with four of her friends flanking her.

Slowly, he got to his feet, and said, "We've met..." he smiled at her, and for the first time he was able to look her in the eyes without fear or flinching. "I am Richard Phaal, solicitor. It has been my privilege to cross paths with you on many occasions... though most recently it was at the Bacchanal which..."

Lenore gasped, and he hadn't the heart to continue describing the events. There was no need to aggravate her delicate constitution.

"You were the fellow who saved her life, weren't you?" asked one of Lenore's friends.

"But you didn't save Agnes!" Lenore cried, pointing an accusing finger at Richard that made him step back in horror. "You had the chance to save her but you *didn't*! How could you fail her?"

"I am but one man," Richard said, finding a strength he didn't realize he was capable of. "Lenore—"

"You haven't the right to call me that!" Lenore shrieked, and even though the music was still going, many of the dancers stopped mid-step to stare.

Nothing was more enticing than town gossip, and Richard found himself in the center of it, even when he'd just begun to escape the depths of scorn!

"Forgive me!" he cried, and fumbled again, something between bowing and shaking his head as if to absolve himself. "By Jove, Miss Roget, I did all I could! Had we stopped to find your friend we may have died!"

"You can't fault him for rescuing you in a way you didn't like when you were rescued, at all," Braxton said, though Richard didn't feel entirely entitled to the support.

He wasn't one to complain when he had so few allies, but he glanced at the women who surrounded Lenore. "These girls were also there... they got out... now, how did you ladies escape?" he asked.

Silence ensued for a long moment, but finally one of them said in a soft voice that was barely audible over the music, "the shooter just... lost interest... It was as if he'd ticked off his list of people to shoot and then... disappeared... We were hiding behind a table and..." she shook her head, and began to cry.

Three of her friends turned to comfort her, but Lenore's eyes were still firmly riveted to Richard.

He took a deep breath to strengthen himself to withstand the scrutiny, but he knew his heart would pound its way out of his chest if he looked back into her eyes for too long.

"I suppose your little toad has a point..." Lenore said at length, and while Richard was wondering exactly what about Braxton made him worthy of that particular slur she continued. "I should be grateful to my knight in shining armor for whiskering me off my feet and rescuing me from that heroing experience."

Having listened to Lenore's passionate declaration, Richard was proud of himself for having kept a straight face rather than laughing at the silliness of her malapropisms. He did have to wonder, though, how much of a gallant knight he could consider himself, seeing as how he'd abandoned these four ladies to however long it had been... just waiting for the killer to stop killing... His heart broke for them.

"We came here to *forget* that," one of Lenore's friends scolded from the huddle they'd made of themselves.

"I'm deeply sorry," he said, and pressed a hand to his heart. "I deeply regret what happened to you, and I equally regret mentioning it in front of you..." It was odd to find himself capable of focusing on someone other than Lenore when she was standing directly in front of him. Maybe it was the absinthe.

The four women in the huddle looked directly at him, and he knew he had no right to expect he would pass their inspection.

"Apology accepted," said the woman who'd been crying.

"My deepest gratitude," he said. "For still the burden of guilt at not being capable of rescuing you all weighs heavily on my heart."

"None of them got hurt," Lenore pointed out.

"But they were... in their hearts," Richard stepped forward, and bowed deeply to all the women, including Lenore for he knew better than to slight her. "Is there anything I could do to offer you some relief from your pain?" he asked them.

"Oh!" three of them exclaimed, hiding their mouths behind their fans.

Richard became painfully aware of how many people were watching them now. Dancing had almost ceased entirely, and the only people still swaying to the music were doing it to look as if they weren't eavesdropping.

People could say what they would about absinthe, but gossip was far more addictive a drug.

The one girl who had remained silent said, "I think… if you'd like to… we might all like a dance with you."

Richard's first instinct was to decline — he was right in front of the lady whose heart he wished to win, after all… and yet… he realized that was *precisely* the reason to accept the invitation.

"I would be honored, and though it is the least I could do, I will offer more if you can think of what you'd like." Did that sound wrong? He'd really meant it innocently, but the way they tittered behind their fans told him something may have been lost in the ether between him and his audience.

Still, he'd made a promise, and he was loath to lose his reputation as a man of his word. He escorted the first lady of the quartet onto the dance floor, and a new song began as the dancing recommenced.

The way she smiled into his eyes gave him the impression there were untapped thoughts hiding behind her gaze which might make him blush. He hoped he would not receive confirmation of that theory.

"Lenore told us what you did to save her while we were hiding," she whispered. "You know really, I recognized you, but I've never noticed you could be so dashing…"

So it was true that heroes had better luck with women. It was just too bad she wasn't Lenore… He simply could not encourage her admiration further.

"We all have our destinies," he said gently. "I suppose all I did was seize mine."

She was still beaming at him, and he realized he may have said something terribly romantic by accident. He gave her a twirl just to take her eyes off him for a moment, but they trained directly back onto him as she turned back into his arms.

They hopped together along with the melody, and he gave her a polite smile. The dance finally ended, and though he was relieved. It was nothing against the lady, who was light on her feet and sweet as a spiced pear, but he was glad to be extricated by the awkward situation.

He was out of one of those situations, sure, but the next woman in the group took his hand and her turn began.

"Lenore's watching us," she whispered in a giddy little giggle.

"She is?" he was about to look, but he stopped in order to prevent her from realizing he knew. What was she actually watching? Was she watching because she didn't trust his friends with him?

"She was just telling me—"

"My dear young lady!" he shook his head and clicked his tongue. "I do not wish to hear what she said, if she said it in confidence!"

It was a lie. He wanted to know so badly his ears were practically on fire.

"But..." the woman pouted and bounced up and down as if it were that difficult to hold in what she wanted to say.

"What is your name?" Richard asked instead. "I would love to spend this time getting to know you."

Even though the lighting in the room was pink, he noticed the deeper saturation of the same tint on her cheeks. "My name is Rosaline," she said softly. "I'm so pleased to meet you..."

Richard could understand why Lenore had chosen this girl as part of her retinue. She seemed like a genuine sweetheart. "Surely the pleasure is all mine," he returned. He spoke out of politeness, and yet there was truth in what he said.

She tittered, and he gave her a spin before they kicked up their heels to the music. When their dance ended, Richard didn't even have the time to breathe before someone else caught hold of him and led him back onto the dance floor.

"Greetings, miss," he said as he wondered whether any of them knew it was the man's duty to escort a woman onto the dance floor.

"I have to tell you something," the woman whispered, "I know it wasn't an accident, what happened to Amelia!" her eyes were wide and watery, and she gave Richard such a desperate look he could do nothing but glance around in concern that someone might hear what she said and do her harm.

"You must speak more quietly, miss!" he urged her. "What you say could be the death of you if you do not temper your words with caution!"

"But you can help, can't you? I know what you did for Lenore and... and you're a solicitor, couldn't you... couldn't you do something legally? If I know it was an assassination?"

Richard flinched at that word, remembering with painful clarity how Raven had laid out the very same argument only that morning. It could be no coincidence if not only the mortician who'd examined one victim but the witness of another death on the same night had come to the same conclusion.

"Who was your friend? I mean, I remember you called her Amelia, but what was her family name?"

"She was Amelia Otranto," the girl whispered, as if saying the name would summon her friend's ghost.

A shiver rattled Richard's spine and he cringed. Father and daughter assassinated on the same night, after which Duke Julian seized control of their property?

That was such a damning batch of evidence he would have to be a fool if he were blind to it. But what could he do?

If he confronted the duke, he could be thrown in prison for insubordination. Not to mention, the duke considered him an asset, and this door to a glittering new life that had opened up for him would snap shut forever!

"What's the matter?" the girl fretted.

Richard stumbled, having forgotten that they were still mid-dance, and bumbled into one of the other couples. "My deepest apologies," he told them in a voice he was sure sounded just as hollow to the objects of his apology as it did to him.

"Well?" the girl asked expectantly as Richard attempted to collect his thoughts from the jumbled mess they'd become in his mind.

He felt like a simpleton who'd dropped something valuable on the ground and was attempting to gather it up off the ground. No amount of scrambling would put it all together, again, but he kept trying.

"I don't know…" he said, wondering if that made him sound as stupid as he felt.

"Why not? I thought you were a hero!"

Richard stopped with a sigh.
"Because… I feel as if I'm not the right person to come to with this…"

But part of him knew it was possible for him to do something… if he were someone else, perhaps he would already know what to do… but what if he didn't? What if he did the wrong thing? His heart was beating like a humming bird's wings, but still he thought his fingers were going numb.

What could he do?

"I…" the girl pressed a hand to her heart, and ran back to her friends.

Richard swallowed, but he didn't have time to panic. The fourth girl left the huddle and took her turn with him.

"My name is Genevieve," she said.

"Richard, pleased to meet you," he returned cordially in spite of his internal calamity. He was putting up a good show, but he wasn't much for conversation. He knew she was speaking, but he could only hear something along the lines of a blathering monotone.

Before he knew it, their dance had ended, and he was bowing to the woman who was his dance partner as mechanically as if he'd had a wind up key in his back.

He was eager to get back to the bar for another drink of green fairy, but instead he found none other than Lenore standing in his path.

"You've danced with all of us except for me," she said, and he wondered how he could ever have found occasion to be unhappy despite the opportunity to dance with her.

What sort of chivalric knight would lose the delight of his lady love? Well, he wasn't a knight, he was a solicitor... so he ought to remember that.

"I need a drink first, my lady, for my strength is flagging," he said. "Would you care to join me at the bar? I can offer you whatever you would fancy."

Lenore tilted her head, and he wondered what she was thinking.

"I haven't made this offer to anyone else," Richard told her, "I mean this invitation for you alone."

It was then Lenore smiled. "My favorite drink is a Cherry Fairy," she said, and primly sat herself at the bar.

Richard obediently sat beside her and ordered himself another Menthe Twist along with Lenore's Cherry Fairy.

"My friends really seemed to enjoy their dances with you," Lenore said quietly.

"I try to make spending time with me worthwhile," Richard said in an equally hushed voice. "Otherwise nobody would have a reason to do it."

Lenore chuckled, and Richard realized he was actually having a real, human conversation with her. This wasn't a dream, despite the fact that it had only happened due to his drinking absinthe. "It must be hard for you, isn't it?" she asked him.

"Yes, a little," he admitted.

"People don't notice you the way they notice me. Even I didn't notice you before you rescued me…. What's your name?"

Richard blinked in dismay. Had he not introduced himself to her, yet? He was fairly certain he had, but what was he to say now? Could he possibly point out that she ought to already know his name?

"My name is Richard, my lady," he said, "and I am glad to finally make your formal acquaintance. I have wished for the honor for years… I wish it had happened sooner. Perhaps if I had been with you at that party sooner, we could have made our escape with more of your friends at once."

She watched him steadily, but he could not discern what she hid behind her eyes.

He turned away from her and back to his drink, his heart once again thudding painfully in his chest. Had he said the wrong thing? He cycled back through what he'd said to her, as if it were a cylinder he reloaded into a phonograph.

"You may be right," Lenore told him softly. "My gaggle of friends and I have spent a great deal of time as spinsters now, and we began to grow too at ease with being ladies without men to help us."

"There's nothing wrong with that as long as you have one another," he said, "and you seem to do well on your own."

"We don't, anymore." Lenore reached out and placed a hand on his wrist, which did no favors to his overworked heart. "I'm willing to think we might need you."

Richard swallowed, but his throat was dry. "I… well, actually… I would love to help you…" he said, and the pounding in his ears began to have an effect somewhat *lower*, which was all the more humiliating.

"Then…" Lenore whispered in his ear, "let's dance…"

Perhaps he'd had too much absinthe, though he'd heard that drink would actually clear one's head rather than clouding it.

The dance that Lenore led him into made him feel like a puppet had taken his place, and he was watching it as a stage performance. Had it not been for the fact that he could feel her near him, and was capable of feeling the heat off her breath and the hands at his wrist and back, he might have given his mind over to that impression.

Still, he knew better. In fact as time went on, he was convinced the absinthe was making his mind still clearer, and he was better able to grapple with the fact that once again, he had found himself fortunate.

By the end of the night, during which Lenore clung to him, he was guiding her and her friends home, with Braxton's help.

The Lord only knew where Hans and Charlotte had disappeared to, but Richard hoped that now that he had become respectable, his cousin would not taint the family name. He'd just gone to the trouble of fixing it!

"Meet me tomorrow for lunch, back at Bonnie's," Lenore whispered to him, and when he returned home, his mind had been made up.

Chapter 10: Grave Occasions

Moretta locked the door behind the pall bearers who took the coffin of Count Otranto away. Apparently his family had a plot waiting for him somewhere to the east, and he would molder in his native soil.

"Farewell," she whispered to him, and hoped the flecks of light she saw surrounding the coffin were a sign that his spirit was leaving her house. It was crowded enough, already.

It would seem that the mystery of who had assassinated the count was out of her hands, as she had turned over all the evidence, but Moretta was no less troubled.

As she had devoted her early morning to preparing the house for visitors, Moretta was able to brew herself a pot of tea. It almost felt like home, alone on this hill.

Renata hopped onto the newly-polished counter and rolled onto her back, so even though Moretta preferred to keep cat fur out of her food, she gave her precious kitty a gentle, generous petting.

"I love you too, Rennie," she whispered, and on second thought scooped her into her arms. "Come on, let's get away from the food.

She knew the whistling of her teapot would tell her when it was ready, so she had no qualms leaving it unattended in the kitchen.

Upon entering the sitting room, freshly dusted and with incense chasing away its former mustiness, Moretta shrieked.

All was not as she had left it: she had specifically *not* left this pallid woman sitting patiently on her couch with a bullet wound through her chest.

Renata did not jump out of Moretta's arms as she usually did. Instead she kept purring as if to remind Moretta's heart to beat steadily in spite of it all.

"H-hello...?" Moretta forced herself to ask in the most cordial tone she was capable of.

The woman pointed one finger at Moretta, then at the couch facing her. Moretta paused, realizing that she had just been asked to sit and speak with a ghost. Was that a good idea? This was still a human...

Renata made a little sound to get Moretta's attention, and batted at the cameo necklace she wore as if it were a bell on a string.

"You're right," Moretta sighed, and clutching Renata to her, she slowly seated herself in the seat which had been indicated to her. Still giving the ghost woman a wary look, she stroked the fur along Renata's spine. "What brings you here, my lady?" she asked, noting the refinement of the ghost woman's garb and not wishing to cause offense.

The woman's smile twitched as if with irony, and she gestured to the hole in her chest.

"Ah... so this is a counseling meeting," Moretta stroked Renata's fur a little faster, her uneasiness beginning to well up in her heart. She had to keep her focus. "Ordinarily, I would be having this talk with your family… and I'm afraid—" that was much too true, even still.

She could hear her teapot begin to whistle, but she still jumped as if she didn't know what had made that sound.

When she turned back to her guest, she saw her gesturing for Moretta to attend to her tea. Clearing her throat and swallowing awkwardly, Moretta set Renata down on the couch and gave her head another affectionate stroke. "Renata, darling, will you please attend to our guest while I fetch the tea? I wouldn't want her to feel abandoned."

Renata gave her a *meow* that seemed to confirm her agreement, and Moretta slowly extricated herself from the parlor.

Once she was back in the kitchen, she panted as she released her tension. She took a while to adjust to the fact that once again a ghost was petitioning her for help.

She was still taking her medicine, she reminded herself with a glance at the bottles beside the kitchen sink. She hadn't lost her mind, so this was real.

Moretta had always told herself that ghosts were just as they had been in life, so why should this stately, even somewhat friendly lady frighten her?

A thought occurred to her, and rather than filling one porcelain teacup painted with delicate pink rosettes and lined with gold, she strained tea into both.

She brought it all back to the ghost along with cream and sugar on a tray, and set it on the table between the couches. "I wouldn't want you to feel at a disadvantage," she said, and held up one of the teacups. "Dear, would you prefer cream or sugar?"

The ghost seemed to glow a little more brightly, and pointed to the cream, then the sugar, twice.

"Oh, certainly," Moretta said, finding it much easier to continue as if this woman still breathed. The only difficulty was imagining how the specter would drink it… Still, she poured some cream into it, and pinched two cubes of sugar into the cup before edging it toward the ghost.

Rather than try to drink it, the ghost merely sat there giving Moretta a smile, and gestured for her to tend to her own tea.

"Why thank you," Moretta said, and piled three cubes into her own cup, along with more cream than she usually drank. Her hands were shaking as she lifted the tea to her lips.

As if she had noticed this, Renata rubbed her head against Moretta's side, and then curled up there, still purring and keeping her steady.

"I often wonder what I would do without my dear pussy cat," Moretta noted by way of conversation, and having said so, she sipped her tea.

The warmth spread through her, and even managed to stop her heart from shivering.

She noted that when she looked back at her guest, she looked just as calmed and happy as she felt. Even the cup of tea in front of her was just a little bit emptier.

"It occurs to me that we may have some difficulty in communicating, my dear," Moretta said. "It seems that you cannot speak, and what you wish to communicate to me must be conveyed with the utmost clarity. How might we bridge this difficulty?"

With delicate, graceful movements, the ghostly woman pantomimed writing.

"Ah... will you be able to move a pen?" Moretta asked.

The woman shook her head with a smile, then pointed at Moretta before gesturing back at herself and then once again pantomiming writing.

"I am to write for you?" Moretta asked. "How can I do such a thing for you if I do not know what you wish to say?"

Renata *meowed* for Moretta's attention, and pushed her head against Moretta's arm, which made it move. Thankfully this was not the one occupied with holding the tea.

"Ah..." Moretta stroked the cat's fur once more, and gave her guest a quizzical look. "Has my cat guessed rightly?"

This question received a nod of confirmation, and so she sighed. "It seems the plan is settled. Will you accompany me upstairs to my writing desk?"

The woman nodded, and the two of them rose from their seats.

Renata jumped up on the table and pointed at Moretta's cup with one paw, as if telling her to bring it along.

"Ah… I may need this," Moretta acknowledged, and took the whole tray along with her as she led Renata and the ghost up the stairs to the room in which she had taken up residence.

Renata darted in front of her and stood on her hind legs so she could open the door for the over-laden Moretta.

"Why, thank you dear," Moretta said, and set the tea set down on one of her end tables before turning the gaslights on. "Now—" she clasped her hands together, as she had always been an awkward hostess, and gasped at seeing the ghost so close behind her. She paused to recollect her composure. "I believe we ought to begin with your name. I would like to know how I ought to address you, madam."

She seated herself at the writing desk, hand shaking, but with her off hand she reached over and got a sip of her tea. Once she'd had her sip, she was able to hold her hand still again.

Slowly, perhaps out of a desire to prevent Moretta from panicking, the ghost's hand closed around Moretta's.

"Right… go ahead…" Moretta said, using her own willpower to dip the quill into the inkwell

The chill of the ghost actually exerting power over her hand made Moretta squeak, but Renata hopped onto her lap and began to purr steadily again.

"Right, right…" Moretta murmured, then took another drink of tea before she set her free hand on Renata's fur. "I can do this…"

Slowly, still shivering with deathly cold, Moretta's hand was made to spell out,

"I am Amelia Otranto."

Moretta swallowed. "I sent your father home today… I'm so sorry I didn't realize you also needed help…"

Amelia's hand lightly touched Moretta's back, and though Moretta squeaked at the cold, she could feel the intent. At least Amelia meant to calm her, and tell her it wasn't her fault.

Moretta swallowed another sip of her tea, and poured some more. "I'm ready to go again," she said. "Tell us what happened to you…. Please."

Amelia took her hand away from Moretta's back, a welcome mercy. Still, her frigid hand was moving again, and scratched out a longer message.

"I attended a party at Bacchanal hall with my friends, Lenore Roget, Yvette Montgomery, Rosaline Degas, Vivienne Delacourt, and Genevieve Sucre. We were having an excellent evening, and all was well...." Her hand halted, and drew back from Moretta's.

"I know..." Moretta released a frantic hiss of breath, and clutched her right hand to her chest, trying to warm it.

Amelia knelt beside her, and gave her hand a concerned look.

"I'll be fine," Moretta got a squirrel belly fur coverlet and wrapped herself in it before downing another cupful of tea all at once.

Renata had jumped up onto the desk when Moretta got up from the chair, and sat on the up-tilted end of the desk, flicking her tail.

"I know you're waiting for us to finish, pretty kitty, but I don't want my fingers to freeze off, and Amelia here is working through her trauma."

Renata stretched out, so that her back and her tail both curled, and lay there at the top of the desk preparing for a cat nap.

Amelia reached up and stroked the cat's fur, a contented smile on her face. She met Moretta's eyes once again, showing that she was ready again.

"I think I'll get my woolen gloves first," Moretta said. "I would rather not freeze my fingertips off, I'm sure you understand."

Amelia nodded graciously, so Moretta got up and armed herself for the next round of writing.

"Now," she said, taking a bolstering drink of tea, "we may begin again."

Chapter 11: A Newly-Minted Man

The fact that Richard awoke mid-morning rather than at the crack of dawn startled him, and frightened him somewhat as well. Before he checked the time, he was terrified that he had missed the one and only arranged meeting with Lenore in his life.

His panic slowed down and he moved to pressing his shirt and vest and then his trousers as he did his absolute level best to contain himself. How was he supposed to talk to her without alcohol in his veins? He had to be in a suitable state of mind, but how would he get into it?

She would smell his fear, he knew it, and then it would be over!

His eyes darted over to the stack of papers from the duke, and decided he ought to take them back to confirm his dedication to the project. It was the only way to maintain his status, and his shaky rise.

With another glance at the clock, he decided if he caught a cab he could make it all the way to Usher Abbey and then to Bonnie's.

Not only did he wish to ensure with the utmost certainty that the duke directly received the paperwork, he was adamant that it should happen without delay. Thus he could not take it to the postmaster general's office.

Though he was well assured of his aim, he stuttered through the instructions he gave the cabbie, and blushed at his own feelings of inadequacy. "I-I just would really like to g-get to Usher Abbey, please," he finally managed to spew out, and smiled awkwardly at the cabbie.

"Climb in," the cabbie said, somewhat exasperated after having to listen to Richard's botched attempts at saying the same.

It was a nicer cab than he'd ever flagged down. Once he was inside, he admired the red velvet interior, and stroked it lightly as if it were the fur of a dog he was fond of.

It had been all he could do not to drool over the polish on the exterior and the *bestia* horse which had been harnessed to it.

He could only imagine what it would be like if he could own something like this, along with a stable full of his own *bestia* horses... one for every occasion. These could go along with the several carriages he would require for travelling in the country and the town.

It really was astounding, he thought to himself as he bounced along the cobblestones, how only a day previous it had been just short of ludicrous to expect owning just *one* carriage!

The very fact that he had cause to visit the duke, the highest-ranked member of the aristocracy he'd ever met, still had the power to dizzy him.

As they went up a hill, and turned down a side street, he caught sight of the Raven's house atop the hill across town. Guilt stabbed its impertinent self back into his heart, and he quickly closed the curtains on that side of the carriage.

He knew that the Raven would be furious with the choice he was making, but it was necessary. He could not rise above poverty without sacrificing himself to a slight risk. She would understand that, wouldn't she? And who had elected her his conscience, anyhow? She didn't know as much as she kept insinuating she did.

No matter what she said, he knew that he could trust the duke. It was even possible he could inform the duke of the suspicions which had been cast on Count Otranto's death, so that perhaps the two of them could prepare their counter arguments.

But if Raven were correct, then it would be inadvisable to tell the duke that he was under suspicion. A guilty man would take that as a signal that he ought to cover his tracks immediately… so it was a good thing that he wasn't.

So why didn't Richard still feel comfortable with the idea of informing him?

An abrupt stop told him that the time for ruminations had ended.

"I'll try to make it quick," he promised the cabbie as he climbed out of the cab, clutching the papers to his chest.

He got a drowsy nod in return, and took that as a hint to hurry before his cabbie fell asleep and he had to either wake him up when he would be grumpy or walk all the way back down to the main streets to hail another.

Rushing up the stairs, Richard did all he could to gather the shreds of his composure and make something of them. He had to be on his best behavior, he reminded himself. If he weren't, he may lose this shining opportunity.

One of Duke Julian's servants peeked at him through a panel in the door. "What is your business with the duke?" he asked.

Richard cleared his throat, suddenly feeling quite short, and regressing to a time when he'd been at school and the nun minding him had caught him trying to hide that he'd wet himself. He held up the papers. "I have this for the duke," he said meekly.

The fellow behind the door rolled his eyes. "The duke is indisposed. Give the papers to me."

Richard expected the door to open, but instead, another panel in the door opened, and he saw the fellow's hand waiting on the other side of it. "I would feel more comfortable if I gave this directly to Duke Julian," he said, shifting his weight from foot to foot.

"As I've said, the duke is indisposed! I am in charge of all his business until he is prepared to reassume control of his business again. Give me the papers."

"Is the duke ill?" Richard asked.

"No, he is attending to sensitive business that requires his immediate attention, and that is why he cannot bother with you, simpleton! Give me the papers!"

Richard flinched as surely as if he'd felt the nun's harsh switch of discipline against his fingers. "Well…" he wavered, but finally relented. "Just make sure he sees these as soon as possible, please. This is also quite important business."

The man behind the door snatched the papers out of Richard's hands. After a brief pause during which the fellow on the other side of the door glanced over the papers, he made a thoughtful noise to himself and asked, "You are Richard Ambrose Phaal, who resides in the clock tower?"

Richard blushed to admit it, but nodded.

"I was meant to give you this if you showed your face here," the man said so ominously Richard took a step back in alarm.

Instead of the barrel of a gun, the fellow reached out of the slot in the door with a pouch of coins in hand. "Do what this what you will," he said. "The duke wishes to reward your loyalty."

Though his palms were sweaty, Richard was able to grip the sack of coins rather than drop it. "Thank the duke on my behalf!" he cried, imagining how well he could treat Lenore on this new budget.

Rather than confirm that he would, the fellow slammed both slots in the door shut, and Richard waited a moment before returning to the cab.

"Now I'd like you to take me to Bonnie's," he said, and gave the cabbie an extra two silver *argenti*.

Not a hint of sloth or fatigue remained in the fellow's aspect any longer, and it was a relief when Richard climbed into the back of the cab again.

Lenore was just arriving on the street corner outside Bonnie's, so Richard realized he had the unique opportunity to shine in her eyes. He pulled the bell chord which told his driver to stop, and climbed out, just in time for her to see him.

"Oh, hullo, Richard!" Lenore exclaimed. "How lucky am I to be seen with a man like you?"

Richard puffed up his chest. "I venture to say you're rather lucky, indeed."

Since he'd paid the driver in advance, the fellow drove off abruptly, and left Richard alone with his lady love.

"So," he started, "Lenore, I think it's time I—"

She cut him off, looking instead at a poster which had been pasted to the lamp post. "Look, Richard! Duke Julian's left us a lovely notice!"

Richard blinked, and wondered if this missive had been what had consumed the duke's time to such a degree that he had not been able to greet him at the door to his castle.

There it was, this missive from the duke, which read, "Be it known among all the people, that since the evenings and nights of the coming spring have been predicted by our finest almanac compilers to be wondrous breezy and sweet, it is advised that as many household windows ought to be left ajar. Please avail yourselves of the delights of spring, this is your duke's wish for you in the coming months."

The seal at the bottom of the parchment made it official, but Richard could still not believe his eyes. He had so many questions he couldn't comprehend why the duke didn't seem to... and how had writing this silly thing been more important than meeting with him? He was more than a ragamuffin, and he had thought the duke had acknowledged that.

"What is he even thinking?" Richard grumbled under his breath, staring skeptically at the paper as if he were intent on winning a staring contest with some malevolent entity.

"Most probably the duke is thinking of how the spring will renew our spirits in spite of our losses!" Lenore exclaimed, but he still saw tears straining for freedom on the edges of her lashes.

Richard knew it may be impertinent, but still he reached out and took her hand. "Miss Roget... I hope spring brings your heart gladness... in spite of everything."

Her hand tightened on his, and though she wore lacy gloves and he wore thicker cotton ones, he could feel her nails dig into his palm. "If I'm right, you may be able to help me there," she said.

"I hope that's true..." it was symbolic, but he still pressed a kiss to her lace-gloved fingertips.

"So I have to ask," she whispered, "what do you have against open windows?"

"I don't think it's safe," he shrugged. "We live in a busy town, filled with all sorts of people. If the weather were so stiflingly hot nobody could breathe unless the windows were open, then keeping them open might make sense. Except, that's incredibly rare here, and besides, spring is the rainy season."

"I suppose you have a point there," Lenore admitted, and her lips twitched.

Richard could sense that her thoughts were drifting toward the madman who had murdered her friend, and he kissed her fingers again. "I think you ought to keep your windows closed, Miss Roget, but I don't want you to live in fear. Keep them closed out of practicality. My guess is the weather will be just as damp as it usually is, and you wouldn't want any of your silks and satins getting wet with rain water, would you?"

Lenore gasped as if he'd bitten her hand. "No!" she cried in alarm.

"Hush, sweet lady," Richard whispered, and slowly hooked his arm around her corseted waist. "There's nothing to fear... You and I ought to enjoy ourselves. It is a new day, remember? We must be strong and rebuild our lives from the ashes... that is the way to survive."

"Not all of us," she whispered softly, and he caught her tear on his gloved knuckle.

"After we spend our time out on the town, we can go to the chapel and offer up our prayers for your friend... Amelia."

She met his eyes, and slowly, she began to smile. "I'd like that," she whispered, and he took that opportunity to lead her into Bonnie's for some much-needed respite.

He'd never been in the shop during the day, and he found there was a tremendous difference between the ways it looked during the night as opposed to the way it looked during the day.

"Now that you have money, I think you should court me," Lenore said, startling Richard into looking at her rather than the strings of crystals and pearls hanging from the ceiling. He found that she was not looking at him, and instead she was gazing at a dress that was on display, a much-ruffled silken confection in pastel pink and yellow.

"Well, if… I suppose I could speak to your father about it… where is he now?"

"He's…" she sighed. "He has some business he's conducting at the capital… he's been there for so long, I… I don't know if it's going so well."

He squeezed his arm around her waist and gave her what he hoped was a reassuring smile.

She leaned her head on his shoulder. "I've got you though, so I'm sure it could be worse."

Richard blushed, but his knees started to knock together as they proceeded up the stairs. This was his lifelong dream, so why was he so nervous and panicky when it finally happened?

Surely by this time it wasn't going to go wrong. He already had her leaning on him, and she saw him as her strength, so… so of course she wouldn't toss him away when she got the opportunity. Why was he even thinking of that? He was jinxing himself!

"Is something the matter, my darling squire?" Lenore purred into his ear.

He didn't even get to be a knight? Well, he was a probationary gentleman, so perhaps he had to prove himself before he was a knight. He'd just have to keep his hands clean in the meantime. "Nothing's the matter, nothing whatever," he tried to be reassuring for her, but really it was also for his own sake.

"I think you need some frozen courage," Lenore diagnosed with a pat to his forearm while he tried to filter through what she had just told him. "Come along, dearest." She took over leading him, to his great shame, to the bar.

It was strange to be back so soon, but he saw that the menu had changed, entirely. Rather than alcoholic beverages, he saw several flavors of ice cream.

"*Oh...*" he chuckled softly as he realized what Lenore had been implying to him. "I think I've got a good idea of what you'd like, then," he said, winking at her.

"Straw-cherry swirl, please," Lenore chirped, and Richard mechanically handed the woman behind the counter an argent coin.

"Now you get to choose yours," Lenore said, rubbing Richard's arm while the other maiden prepared her share of ice cream.

Richard scanned the menu, but still hadn't decided what he would prefer by the time the maid had turned about with Lenore's ice cream. It was a small crystalline bowl with a delicate silver spoon planted like the shovel at the top of a mound of soil displaced for treasure hunting.

Why did he keep getting distracted from a moment like this? What had he awaited longer than this moment? He should be *in* the moment, not drifting down these broken, pot-holed paths...

"I um... chocolate..." Richard stuttered.

"Will that be in a bowl or with a cone?" the maid asked patiently.

"Um... bowl." He would probably drop a cone if he were given one, and he couldn't afford to make a bigger fool of himself.

"And will you want any toppings?" she asked in a sunny voice.

"I... think that'll be all right," he said, and gave her a half-smile.

"You had a lot of fun last night, didn't you?" the woman asked, winking, and Richard realized she was the same one who had been masked the night before. It must have been part of the nighttime atmosphere closing up the daytime version of the shop. Like the screens downstairs, the lady's friendly face had been masked for the sake of atmosphere.

"Yes, but I was also well-rested."

"So what's the matter now that you're with me?" Lenore asked with an edge to her voice.

"Perhaps it has finally caught up to him," said the barmaid gently, and set Richard's bowl of ice cream down in front of him. "Eat up, fellow, you'll need some sugar strength."

Richard snorted, and did in fact take some of his ice cream as he sheepishly set down some more *argenti*. "There's an extra for making me laugh," he said.

Lenore's hand clamped along Richard's wrist, startling him so much he nearly covered his nose in ice cream. "What will we do next?" she asked, her eyes and her grin equally wide.

"I could... take you to another floor and... buy you something... Would you like that?"

She gave a thrilled little squeal, and Richard gave an internal sigh he didn't dare release aloud.

The rest of the day did little but exhaust him, but he always bore in mind how lucky he was. Even when he dropped Lenore back off at her home, his pockets much lighter, he told himself this was the first day of the rest of his life.

Chapter 12: In the Pink Palace

As distasteful as the idea of venturing into town was to Moretta, she needed to eat. Especially after her harrowing experience in "ghost writing," she felt the need to pamper herself in order to recover.

But where would a girl go for a thing like that? The only place that kept echoing through her mind was that absurdly feminine shop, Bon Bonnie's or whatever it was.

Perhaps she shouldn't go to a place like that, it could be the most pretentious place she'd ever found in her life.

Well, she may as well try something new... There would even be some people there who may not run away if they didn't notice her. She seriously needed to be around someone other than her cat, who was tucked into her velvet-lined hood, and her ghost friend.

As pleasant as Amelia's company had become, the land of the living had to have *someone* in it who was willing to carry a conversation with Moretta. She was well aware of the fact that these people felt uneasy around her due to her predecessors, but perhaps she could make a better impression if they gave her a chance.

Despite knowing better, Moretta forced herself to be optimistic on that point. Somehow she managed to slip into the shop without any suspicious eyes landing on her, and she was even impressed with the stately way in which the shop was adorned.

She had seen actual royal halls, and knew how well this place mimicked them. She had to smirk at the coat of arms they displayed at the end of the hall beside the stairs. Pink and quartered, thus contained four sections, one with needle and thread, the next with a bowl of ice cream, the third with a green fairy, and the fourth with a bonbon. Its motto written on a green scroll beneath it read, "*Glamour of the Ages*," in fanciful cursive.

It may be boastful, but that was the point of a business. She heard the voices of a couple descending the stairs, and she froze. It sounded like…

She saw Richard with a woman on his arm, and despite her better judgment she jumped behind a mannequin. They passed her without noticing, and she watched them go merrily down the street.

She had no right to Richard, she reminded herself, yet again. She was being ridiculous. It didn't matter how amiable he'd been, or how dashing he was. He had lived a whole life in this town, and she was merely passing through.

"Can I help you?" a friendly voice asked, and Moretta jumped, then turned to see a genial woman in a pink and green pinstripe gown she wouldn't mind buying if not for all the pink.

"I think... I might need more clothes..." she said awkwardly, somewhat embarrassed to even be asking."

"Of course, dearie," the woman said. "I can have you all measured in a matter of minutes." She held up a tape measure she'd retrieved from one of the lace-lined, heart-shaped pockets in her whimsical pink apron.

"Then we can go right along with that," Moretta nodded, and offered a small smile. At least here was someone talking to her. If she were lucky, the seamstress — or the woman who seemed to be a seamstress — would never found out who she was.

"With your coloring, black is really a good choice, but have you considered purple? Oh! You would be ravishing in red!"

Moretta blushed. "Ah... I've always found those a bit too... ostentatious for me..."

"Certainly they would compliment you tremendously! But a deep eggplant can be subdued as well as elegant, and you already seem to have a flair for the dramatic."

Moretta's heart seized in her chest at the idea of being what someone may call 'dramatic' in front of an audience. Surely she would be shamed eternally! "Not really..." she admitted in a small voice. "I'm a... well, I've been in mourning for some time, but now I'm out of clothes that aren't for mourning."

"Ah... I am sorry for your loss... Come, let us brighten your palette somewhat."

"Just not too much, please."

For some reason, she had feared it would be much worse than it was in actuality.

The staff at Bonnie's was sunny and cordial, and she did not even regret stepping through their door when the seamstress applied a gauche yellow color swatch to her shoulder and suggested just giving it a chance.

"I really couldn't..." Moretta blushed and flinched away from the yellow. "It could not suit me, I would melt away in a dress of this shade... I would die of my nerves."

For this admission she received the seamstress's indulgent smile and a pat on her back. "I understand," the woman said gently. "I think we should give you an emerald gown in addition to the eggplant... and maybe the longer we work with you, the more willing you will be to attempt a bolder shade."

Moretta considered it, but she chose the sample drawings from the catalogue that she would like for each gown, and the trimming styles as well, and placed the two orders with her down payment in *chrysi*.

It was once these arrangements had been made that Raven brought herself to travel up the stairs. As dusk was approaching, she saw the staff setting up the change over from the daytime bar to the nighttime.

Some of them had already donned their masks, and Moretta shied away from these as much as possible.

"Can I help you?" one of them asked through a half mask with brilliant rubies set into the center of her forehead and dotting the centers of both her cheeks.

As lovely as the mask was, Moretta couldn't countenance looking into that face. She quickly tore her eyes away from it. "Oh, no, I was just... I'll go to the next floor up; I can see you're busy."

"We still have leftover ice cream," the masked woman said, and though her voice was friendly, Moretta could not bear to look back at her as was polite to do. "We give it away free since it's more expensive to store than to give away."

Moretta considered. "Sure, I'll take some of it."

Before leaving the second floor for the second, she was carrying a bowl she'd promised to return filled with various scoops of ice cream, and she had forgotten what all of them were.

Mostly they were variations on chocolate, with one pomegranate mixed in, and that was enough for her.

As she took tiny spoonfuls to make it all last, Moretta ascended to the third level.

One wall was devoted to a selection of bonbons so staggering it made Moretta's mouth water until she scooped more ice cream into it.

The opposite wall nearly made her drop her bowl, however, as it featured a collection of something like a hundred masks of all sorts.

She stood shivering, knees knocking subtly together, but she reminded herself that she had in fact spent her morning preparing a corpse for transportation and her afternoon writing the tale of another's death over tea.

What were a few masks in comparison?

Hundreds of hollow eyes stared at her, daring her to question their potency. She could hear them laughing at her until she tore her eyes from their faces.

"Can I help you find the perfect mask?" a masked woman asked from behind the bonbon counter. "They're perfect for any occasion! I can find one that will project your personality for everyone to see!"

Moretta swallowed, but her throat was still dry. "I... really I couldn't..."

"You're not afraid of the price, are you? I assure you, many of our masks are available for any budget!"

"No, no, it's... not that..." Though Moretta did wonder if, were a mask available to her, she may be capable of erasing the stigma she'd inherited from those mad folk. If only masks weren't so menacing...

There was silence, except for the malicious laughter Moretta knew she was imagining. She had to get out of there!

"I'll come back another time!" she cried, knowing full well the woman could guess what the matter was with her now.

She gobbled down the rest of her ice cream just to be polite, and with frostbite in her skull, she hurried out of the shop.

On the street corner, she found solace while leaning against a lamp post. Perhaps she ought to begin acclimating herself to masks for the sake of her survival in a town that seemed to like them so much. Otherwise she may have a panic attack at an inopportune moment.

But for now… it was much less unsettling to return to her haunted house. She trudged back through town, somewhat stronger than before.

Chapter 13: From the Horse's Mouth

Richard woke to note affixed to a flying mechanical *bestia* dove at his window, complete with the royal crest painted on its wing just before where the synthetic feathers stuck out. This mechanical dove was pecking at his window, and he knew precisely who had sent it.

"Take me to dinner tonight!" the note read, and it warmed Richard's heart to see.

Apparently he had made a successful impression on Lenore on their first outing, and he would have occasion to partake in a more formal ritual a mere day later.

He thought the best thing to do would be to arrange for a reservation at one of the fancier restaurants, though already he was growing anxious over how much money he had left from the duke.

It had been so easy to toss it about at first, but now that he had done it for some time, he wondered exactly how long he could keep going at this pace.

He was almost too afraid to think it through, he was already too accustomed to paying for what he wanted in the moment without a care. Why should he stop living the good life so soon after it had started?

In the meantime, his day ought to consist of preparing for this dinner with Lenore… perhaps if one day they married, his advantageous marriage would earn him a permanent place among the *crème de la crème*. He could certainly dream.

All the finest restaurants in town all but bore his nose prints from how often he'd dreamed of dining there, but he found each time he inquired with them that no tables would be available that evening.

Panic settled in like a flock of screeching magpies. Restaurant after restaurant was booked solid, and his mind was racing out of control with how he would reconcile this fact with his imperative to keep his thoughts in order to find a solution.

His salvation arose in the form of a sign hanging over the street, swinging there in the mist and illuminated by its very own gaslight lantern. It read, *The Lavender Garden*.

Why hadn't he considered this place?

He quickly pulled the door open, which caused the lilting tones of a chime hanging beside the door to sound its dulcet signal that he had entered. Naturally, Richard had never been in this place, so he took stock of it quickly to make sure it wasn't some perfumery.

It was certainly a restaurant devoted to fine dining, and he sighed with relief, but reminded himself that it had not been fully confirmed that he could eat here.

The walls were painted a soft pastel purple, in keeping with the theme, and lavender shades tinted each source of light to match. Paintings, mostly of lavender, and even some dried lavender adorned the walls in neat regular rows, and each delicate glass vase which had been set out on the tables contained spears of lavender.

Naturally, the sweet, calming scent of it permeated the air, and Richard couldn't help the fact that it calmed him, and kept him tranquil even as the maitre d' approached him.

This fellow wore a white suit with a purple silken ascot and cummerbund, and even two sprigs of lavender in the purple top hat he wore. Neither was more impressive than the sheer confidence of the way he carried himself, and bowed to Richard. "How may I serve you, good sir?" he asked.

"I require a reservation for this evening, should that be possible," Richard said in a rush, intimidated by the way the man's confidence outshone his own despite the influence of the lavender scent.

The maitre d' smiled, his finely-manicured beard and moustache perfectly framing his friendly grin. "We would love to host you for the evening. Shall you be accompanied by a fine young lady, good sir?"

"Yes," Richard said, his confidence returning to bolster him in holding up his head. "Mark me down as a reservation for Phaal and Roget, party of two."

"Right away, sir," the man's pen — topped with a synthetic lavender flower — flickered across his records book until he looked back up with that smile of his. "At what time will you arrive with the lady?"

"I believe we shall arrive at six o'clock, provided that no external forces intervene to postpone our arrival," he replied.

"See that they do not," the fellow said, and Richard tipped his hat at him, departing from the restaurant, his heart burning with joy. Forget how much he might have to pay, at least he'd found a place to pay it to!

Though his first thought was to travel to Lenore's home and leave a card with her to inform her of when he would arrive to escort her, he was prevented.

A mechanized black horse strode up to him, rider-less and still autonomous due to its programming. He could barely even hear the mechanism at work inside it! As he stared at it, he saw it go utterly rigid, then shake stiffly as its mouth dropped open and something began to print out of it where the horse's tongue ought to have been.

He tilted his head, seeing his name as the first words the horse printed, so he knew that it was certainly meant for him.

Only one person would go to these lengths to get into contact with him, so Richard froze in place, hoping to appear on his best behavior. The horse's eyes may be equipped with cameras, after all!

That would explain the faint sheen on them, for one thing, and for another, it would make a great deal of sense for whoever had programmed the horse to also drive it from a remote location and prevent it from getting damaged in traffic, or worse, stolen.

Once the entire message had been printed out, Richard heard a faint ringing noise, and that signaled to him that he was meant to pull out the message.

He was a little on edge as he reached into the mouth, and hoped it would not snap shut on his fingers. Thankfully, he was able to examine the letter with all of his fingers intact.

It was from the duke, as he had expected, and it ordered him to mount the horse and ride back to the castle on urgent business.

Richard instantly blushed t the realization that he was not on his own time, but another thought occurred to him as he held still again under the horse's and thus the duke's scrutiny. If he did good enough work for the duke, he could get more money for dinner with Lenore, and imagine if Lenore happened to see him riding a mechanized horse as if it belonged to him!

He eagerly climbed into the saddle, and tried to right himself, so he would look as if he were used to perching on horseback. There was a pair of riding goggles in a little compartment hidden by the synthetic mane, so he slipped those on. He may not be a nobleman, but he certainly wished to be one, someday, so he may as well put on the appearance of it until it was truth.

Thankfully, that façade did not require him to actually navigate the streets on this horse, so he gained all the appearance of sophistication without being truly sophisticated.

Rather than the hoped-for encounter with Lenore, Richard passed the post master general's office, he saw none other than the Raven emerging, with her arms full of packages and her black cat perched on her shoulder.

"Raven!" he called to her, and startled her to such a degree she fumbled all her packages, and dropped them to the sidewalk and the puddles there. "Oh!" he exclaimed in his guilt, and attempted to pull the horse to a halt, but it kept plowing forward. "I'm sorry!" he called. "I can't dismount!"

The Raven stared at him as he went, her mouth slightly hanging open as her cat made loud noises in her ear and rubbed her head against her cheek. She mechanically raised one hand and waved weakly at him.

Richard's lips twitched as he faltered between a grimace and a smile. He didn't dare dismount the horse and anger the duke, not when it was of such dire importance that he appease him, instead.

Still, he felt guilty about abandoning his new friend with nothing but soggy paper protecting whatever delivery she'd just received and possibly irreversible damage. He blushed at the utter shame of knowing he'd

done something so ungentlemanly to a lady,
but still he proceeded as the duke had
mandated, receiving the castle just as a steady
hum of rain began to pour down on the city.

Chapter 14: Gathering Mists

Moretta smoothed out all the precious documents that she'd been sent before hanging them from a chord and clothes pins beside the roaring fire.

Once again, she reminded herself that it hadn't been Richard's fault that she'd dropped them, instead it had been due to her own weakness.

"I'm such a twit," she whispered to herself, fretting over the ink that could run out of place and obscure the messages she'd been sent. Photographs were included, and these had thankfully been insulated enough to preserve the images on them, at least for the most part.

Small portions were somewhat obscured, but she hoped that when she began her examination in earnest, she hoped she would be able to make as much sense as possible out of them.

Renata rubbed against her leg, purring steadily, as if to reassure Moretta that she would not lose all the information which had been sent to her through the network.

She went for her tea once again in order to steady her nerves, but yelped at the sight of Amelia Otranto's ghost hovering much too close.

Amelia gave her a sheepishly apologetic smile, and pointed to the papers to indicate that she had only gotten so close out of an interest in what they said.

"I informed your family that you are dead, but your body is missing, and I included the message you wrote to them," Moretta said between deep breaths she hoped would steady her. "They are inquiring with Duke Julian as to why your body has yet to be recovered, but they are being careful to circumvent any implication that I had a hand in it. I cannot lose my cover, or I'll be paralyzed."

Amelia set one chilling hand on Moretta's shoulder, and although Moretta shivered, she knew it was only a comforting gesture.

"Let's see what this first letter says," she pointed at it. "It says… Oh, *sweet Lord…*" Her words caught in her aching throat, and she sighed, skipping over the frantic introduction.

Amelia turned away, having already read ahead of Moretta's halting eyes. Her outline shifted as she stretched out on Moretta's couch and began to weep, covering her eyes as for the first time Moretta heard her make a sound. It was a banshee's wail, and it carried with it the despair of ages.

The wailing began to shake the house, and Renata ran to Moretta, who caught her cat up in her arms.

"I know, I know, I know!" Moretta stroked Renata's fur frantically as the cat's claws dug into her forearm with the tension. "Hush, girl, relax, please don't scratch me, anymore, ouch!" she cried.

Realizing her mistake, Renata retracted her claws and instead began to lick Moretta's forearm through her lacy sleeve.

"I'll make this right!" Moretta cried over Amelia's wailing sobs. "I will get you the justice you deserve!"

Slowly, Amelia looked up at Moretta. She slowly shook her head, and pointed at the bullet hole in her chest.

"I know, I cannot bring you back to life," Moretta sighed, "I cannot work miracles… but what I can do is… *wait*…"

Amelia raised both her brows and tilted her head at Moretta as if she'd begun to babble nonsense.

Moretta took a few halting steps toward Amelia, fixating on her wound. "That wound was larger before…" Moretta noted. "I'm no expert, but I don't think wounds get smaller *post mortem*… so what's this I see?"

Amelia was dumbfounded, so Moretta fetched a mirror to show her.

"I'm telling you, something's different," Moretta insisted. "I think… I think we need to reevaluate your situation."

The living and the dead both stared at the wound. While neither of them knew what the answer to this fresh enigma was, they both determined to investigate.

Firstly, Moretta took out an anatomy book which discussed the newest understanding on the stages of decomposition.

As she flipped through it, Amelia watched eagerly over her shoulder.

"You see...?" Moretta pointed. "It's been a few days, already, you shouldn't be healing..." she glanced back at the wound to find it even smaller than before, but there was something else. "Your clothes have changed, as well!" she cried in surprise.

Amelia glanced at herself and found that indeed, she no longer wore a ball gown, but a simple smock, the sort which could be found in any sanatorium. She gave Moretta a terrified look, and Moretta nodded rapidly.

"I know, I know! Someone had to change your garments! Those aren't the sort of thing for a burial, someone is trying to do things to you!"

The outline of the ghost went erratically flaring as if she were on fire, but Moretta waved her arms.

"Someone could be trying to heal you!" Moretta cried excitedly, trying to inject some positivity into the situation.

Amelia appeared to consider it, and her aura stabilized as she did.

"See... now the real question is... who has your body and what would they want with it? It can't be your relatives. They want you back so badly they can't possibly have you..."

Amelia shuddered, and gazed out the window of Moretta's parlor. Moretta followed her gaze to the opposite end of the town. There she saw the duke's castle.

Chapter 15: The First Obfuscation

Richard sincerely hoped that one day he would grow accustomed to Usher Abbey, but that day had yet to arrive. It still yawned out in front of him with its ominous stretch of shadowed halls.

The archways overhead were pointed as a cathedral, but somehow they looked pointed enough to harm him if he were unfortunate enough to somehow touch one of those spindle-like edges which pointed inwards along the arches.

This and the fact that he was about to meet with the duke again contributed to his discomfort, and all he could do was hope he would successfully hide that somehow.

His uneasiness did not abate on command, however, especially not when he heard approaching footsteps. Instead he stood rigidly and waited for the duke to come across him, with frequent glances at the clock to calculate how long he had before he would be late for his appointment with Lenore… well, the one he hadn't been able to tell her they had…

"I see you are not as happy to see me as I expected," the duke said from the end of the hall, and his approach put Richard further on alert. "After all, I am now your employer; am I not? Have I proven a poor one?"

"It is my privilege to appear before you, your grace," Richard said, bowing. "However, I am sure you understand that I have recently begun to court a woman, and I have plans with her, tonight."

"Ah…" the duke smirked. "Is that so? I don't remember giving you the day off, though, you are at my disposal."

A chill stiffened Richard's spine. "F-Forgive me, your grace…" he stuttered.

"You are forgiven," the duke said as he swept past Richard into his library office.

Richard swallowed once the duke's eyes were no longer on him and followed him into the office, seating himself slowly.

"I believe we can conduct this business simply, and quickly enough to let you get back to your little game of courtship."

"That is quite gracious of you," Richard said, and glanced anxiously at the clock. It was a quarter past one, so normally it would have been no great difficulty to get prepared.

However, he could not guess how long this business meeting would last. He would need all the time he could to let Lenore know that they were meant to meet at the Lavender Gallery specifically and at six. What if they both took too long to get prepared?

"I can see your mind is occupied with something outside this room," the duke said in an increasingly suspicious tone. "I do warn you that the longer you are distracted by other things, the longer it will take us to cover all the portions of our agenda for this meeting."

Richard swallowed, folding his hands in his lap. "Please, familiarize me with the agenda, you have my full attention." He just hoped the duke didn't notice how little truth there was in that statement. Now he was worried about being kept in the castle longer as a form of punishment.

"I have received a letter from the Otranto family demanding the body of their daughter, Amelia in the wake of their somehow recovering the body of the count without my ever being able to find him. I ask that you make them stop."

Richard blinked at him. "You mean... tell them to stop asking for the body?" he asked. "Do... do you have it?"

If indeed the duke *had* the body of the deceased, what was he *doing* with it?

"Of course, I do, but you are my lawyer, figure out how to keep them from demanding it of me."

Richard stared at the duke until he produced the letter and slid it across the table, and then Richard stared at that. At least he had the opportunity to divert his attention and make himself look as if he hadn't been completely stupefied.

"Do you have any initial thoughts?" the duke pried, nearly startling Richard to such a degree that he dropped the letter.

"I have to ask... because I don't know what to tell them yet... for what purpose are you withholding their relative's body from them? She is surely destined for a place of honor among her ancestors, why deny her that?

Why deny her friends the chance to take part in her funeral?"

"My reasons are my own," the duke said, steepling his hands on the desk before him and leaning forward. His shoulders squared in subtle menace, but Richard recognized it.

"But how am I to argue if I do not know the truth? What if we both say different things?"

"Do you honestly think I plan to talk to these people?" the duke asked.

"Well, I... yes, in fact, I was under that impression. Have none of them sent a representative to speak with you? Did nobody call you?"

"I would not call these people," the duke said. "They are outside my town, I do not owe them anything."

"I...." Richard remembered Lenore's friend and the pain in her eyes as she talked about what losing her friend had been like. He remembered how she had implored him for help... why must he instead cater to the duke's callous whims?

"You will do precisely as I said, won't you?" the duke asked, leaning forward again with a vicious fire burning behind his amber eyes. "You signed the documents which told me you would obey me and do precisely as I said, or have you already forgotten the opportunity I gave you?"

The back of Richard's neck was glazed with sweat, so though it was hot, it was also cold. "You see... the inquiries cannot simply be set aside, and a grain of truth is like the yeast in dough... it will make the rest of what we tell them more acceptable..."

He watched as the duke leaned back in his chair, his fingers still forming a steeple as he looked up at the ceiling. "Yes, what you say is true," he said at last. "Suffice it to say... we are keeping her out of a need to study the scientific realities of her death."

"Oh..." Richard sighed, and expected the weight to lift off his chest, but it did not disperse entirely. "So then, we will release the study to them along with her remains when the time arrives?" he asked, eager for this justification to prove true.

"Yes..." the duke said slowly, giving Richard an appraising look. He may be wrong, but Richard thought perhaps this meant the duke had just lied to his face and was waiting to see if the lie had taken hold.

"Well, in that case, I shall draft a letter to them and submit it to you for your approval," Richard nearly rose from his seat, but he reminded himself that his social better had yet to rise, so he had to hold still until the duke chose to move.

"Do it now," the duke said, pulling out his own stationary and a fountain pen.

"At this very moment? I don't think I've done enough thinking to know how to do the best possible job," Richard said.

"Stay here until you've done it the best you possibly can," the duke said, tapping the stationary expectantly.

Richard swallowed silently; but finally he reached out with one shaking hand for the pen he'd been offered. "I will do the job which is expected of me," he said obediently.

If he played his cards right, he could make it out of this office in less than an hour and net more money out of it, as well.

His first draft did not meet with the duke's approval, as he held it up and with a contemptuous huff said, "Your writing is plebian! Why don't you use any better words? Do not rush through it this time!" the duke produced another page of stationary for him to write on, and Richard's heart sped up.

This could take another half an hour, at the least! Richard steadied the paper with a few weights, and forced himself to subdue all his flighty nerves.

The second time he leaned back again and offered up his best work to the duke, it met with approval, instead.

"For your good work," the duke said, still looking the words over, "here." He lifted a coin purse out of a drawer in his desk and tossed it at Richard.

With barely responsive reflexes, Richard successfully caught the purse, and asked, "Might I ask you for permission to leave?"

"Yes, go," the duke said, reading over the letter again with a dismissive wave of his hand, crossing one leg over the other and leaning back in his chair.

Richard took his lack of interest as the chance for him to escape before he could be told to do something else he might possibly find distasteful.

Chapter 16: Vanity's Incitement

Amelia could not maintain her manifestation much longer after she and Moretta had begun reading for information on ghost sightings.

Moretta considered it somewhat understandable due to the fact that she had been so greatly upset by the revelation they'd both uncovered.

It should have been a relief to learn she wasn't dead, but knowing that something about her body's circumstances had changed. Unfortunately, she had also learned that someone had undressed her, which was most unsettling for the both of them.

Moretta herself would have abstained from further probing the secrets of death and states between life and death, but for the fact that Amelia had been her house guest. Of sorts, anyway.

All she knew for sure was that she had to get out of her house, because there was only so much one could learn from books. Perhaps if she went out to the place where the incident, itself, had occurred, she would have a chance to pick up some clues.

Renata stood scratching at the door as Moretta put on her overcoat and laced up her boots as she set aside her silken house slippers.

"I don't think you ought to go with me," Moretta told her gently. "The owner of the place might not allow animals in."

Renata made an irritable face that would have been a pout if she were human.

"I know, I know, we're a team, but I think I ought to do this one thing on my own, and you should stay here, where you're safe."

Renata flicked her tail impatiently, but Moretta still picked up her umbrella and leaned it on her shoulder.

After a moment's stare-off, Moretta said, "Well… maybe if you hide very, *very* well. But then the onus will be on you, understand?"

Renata fluffed up a little, and hopped onto Moretta's shoulder, curling into the ringlets which hung at the back of her head while Moretta pulled the hood up for her to hide in.

Moretta locked the door to her house behind herself, and glanced up at the sky. A parliament's worth of ravens were converging on her house, but at least she wasn't alone. "The map says we need to be in that sector of the town," Moretta said, pointing to the eastern quarter nearest the hill. "See that large rectangular building with three stories and a peaked roof? It's where they used to have parties. I don't think there will be too many people scrambling to host another one there for some time."

Renata *meowed* as if that had been completely obvious.

"Well, sorry my human intellect is dwarfed by your feline genius," Moretta snickered before starting on her way to the crime scene.

She wondered, the further she got into town, whether she would encounter Richard, again. The fact that he had admitted to his poverty the first time they met and was now riding fancy horse-modeled automatons made her wonder just how well he had been following the duke's orders.

He could probably no longer be trusted, concerning matters of actual import. Not when he was a pawn so firmly painted in the duke's personal colors.

It was really a shame, he'd been her one friend… or at least the only one who could speak to her and answer her questions. Perhaps if she were able to cure and free Amelia from whatever was ailing her, the two of them could be friends…

That was foolish, she admonished herself. She had duties in Amontillado, no matter what she would prefer to do. She was equally certain Amelia would prefer to return to her family.

At least no matter what, she had Renata.

Those who had seen her walk into town from the house on the hill shied out of her path, despite the smile Moretta offered them. Perhaps she ought to hold a garden party?

Oh, that wouldn't work. The only thing she could call a garden was the patch of grass overlooking the cemetery, and a precious few would actually find that enjoyable. They wouldn't want to go into her house, so she would have to return to that plan when she had more information attendant to the possibilities.

She paused on a street corner to flip the map over a few times and reorient herself. So if she turned down Pepperfrost Lane to the third intersection, she would know to turn right down Umberholdt Street…

In the midst of her planning, someone knocked into her from behind, and bustled on past as a flurry of laughter assaulted Moretta's ears. It was a somewhat less pressing issue than the fact that Moretta had collided with a lamp post.

Her nose had gone numb, but her hand flew to it only to collect a warm stream of blood. The laughter became all the more grating then, as she realized her assailant found *that* amusing, as well.

She turned to see the woman that had been on Richard's arm the day before standing in the center of a group of well-appointed young women. They stood in a well-practiced tableau, as if they had choreographed it to their best advantage.

All she could do was stare at them, utterly baffled by their behavior. What could she say?

"Some *Raven!*" the woman tittered. "Nothing like the last ones! Who was in charge of bringing her here? They made a serious error in their appointment!"

Moretta briefly wondered if she ought to ask whether the woman would have preferred her as a brutal serial torturer and murderer, but she refused to lose her grip on her decorum.

"And she doesn't even have anything to say!" one of the other girls mocked loudly, and pantomimed tracing a trail of blood down from her nose with an exaggerated frown.

Moretta held her handkerchief up to her nose, letting the blood soak into it and hoping the handkerchief would not become uselessly saturated with it.

"Nothing to say for yourself?" another one of the girls asked. "Why don't you tell us what happened to Amelia?"

Blinking in dismay at their shocking lack of decorum, Moretta took a step closer. To her surprise, the others all shrank back from her. Amusing.

"Do you mean Amelia Otranto?" Moretta asked. "I don't know what happened to her, but I'm here looking for evidence."

The entire group stared at her in dismay until the blonde at the center turned and waved her handkerchief at someone on a street near them.

"Oh, Richard!" she called. "Please come help us! We found a pesky Raven here to pick on our bones!"

Moretta quickly turned her head around to protest her defamation, seeing Richard rush along the street to meet them.

"Ah! I'm glad you girls have finally met! Raven, this is Lenore Roget, the most beautiful woman in all Amontillado!"

Moretta stared blankly at him, and Lenore's friends folded their arms irritably at him. "That was perhaps not the best manner in which to earn your approval."

Richard blushed sheepishly. "And Lenore... Raven is quite clever."

There really wasn't any point correcting him about her name, Moretta told herself, all she was to these people was her job. Her loathsome, tainted job that may just save someone's life... *How dare she?*

"You know what? I've got business in town," Moretta said, sidestepping the lot of them. "I won't impose my presence on you, any longer." She successfully maintained her composure, and her voice kept its even keel, save for an edge she could barely hear.

Oh well, she deserved a bit of an edge after what these callous cretins had done!

"Raven, wait..." Richard grasped Moretta's arm as she passed him, and slowly moved her handkerchief away from her face. "Good lord! What's happened to your face?"

"Get away from her, Richard!" Lenore's shrill voice demanded. "She's a witch!"

"Don't be ridiculous!" Richard snapped, clicking his tongue. "She is no such thing!" He turned his eyes back to Moretta, and she saw concern in them. "Here, take mine," he said, and offered her his much larger, pristine handkerchief. "Will you tell me what happened to you?"

"It is beneath my dignity to say," Moretta said, holding herself up though in spite of herself she began to cry.

"Oh…" Richard dabbed at the last remaining drops of her blood, then folded it over so that he could dab at her cheeks and her lashes with another, clean portion of it. "Should I escort you home?" he asked.

"Excuse me?" Lenore demanded. "You have an *obligation* to me!"

Moretta raised one brow. "Is that how courting works?" she whispered.

"It's the way she wants our courtship to go, and I've waited for her my whole life," Richard responded, equally hushed.

"Why are you whispering?" Lenore demanded, stalking toward them. "Richard! Such closeness to another woman is a fault I cannot countenance!"

"I must be a gentleman," Richard said, still patient, somehow. "I suspect that you could have been more charitable to my friend here, as well."

"Are you suggesting that I lack moral fiber?" Lenore demanded.

"Well, you know, Lenny… we did…"

"*Silence*, Yvette!"

"What did you do?" Richard asked in a low rumble. "I must hear it from you, Lenore, or our evening is at an end!"

That threat successfully mollified Lenore, and she said, "My friends and I slipped on the sidewalk and we tripped into her."

Moretta gave her a disdainful look. She couldn't even justify what she'd done. Her heart was full of rage, but she contained it with all the force of her willpower.

"Is that what happened, Raven?" Richard asked quietly, and the husky concern in his voice made Moretta sigh softly.

"I didn't see it until it was over," she said. "All I ask is that they apologize."

Richard put a hand on Moretta's shoulder, and turned to the group of women. "She has been especially gracious to all of you," he said firmly.

"We're sorry—*I'm* sorry," said not Lenore, but the woman who had been called out as Yvette.

"I accept your apology, Yvette," Moretta said gently, and subsequently, three others apologized, leaving only Lenore staring at Moretta and Richard as if they had been the ones who did something to her.

"I have our evening all planned out now, and I went to extra pains to ensure I had extra money to make it as special as it could be," Richard said. "Are you honestly going to throw all of that away over pettiness?"

Moretta could have interjected if she had a sharper tongue, but instead she focused in Richard's profile, from the strong set of his jaw to the sharp glint in his eyes. This was a side of him she had yet to see, and to her dismay, she found herself beginning to fall for him, again.

That was sheer insanity, and she scolded her heart, adamant that it had to stop. She really ought to know better at this juncture, she'd thought over this same situation before!

"I am so sorry," Lenore said at last, and pressed her hand to her heart. "I simply cannot believe this would happen, it was not my intention."

Moretta recalled how Lenore had laughed at her expense, and wondered whether it would be suitable to point this out to Richard. He was courting this woman, after all, and it may be in his best interests to protect his heart from a harpy like this.

"I accept your apology," Moretta said evenly, meeting Lenore's eyes, which were the sort of reddish brown that made them resemble spiced cider. "I accept it, on the condition, of course, that you explain why you laughed when you saw that I was in pain."

Lenore's mouth dropped open, and Moretta knew she was about to protest her innocence, but the guilt was plain on her companions' faces.

"I can't believe your behavior," Richard said coldly.

"I only laughed because I didn't realize you were hurt!" Lenore's words rushed from her lips and her blush was stark, though she held Moretta's gaze as if defying her to protest to the contrary.

Moretta held her head up with a stern frown. "Very well, Lenore," she said. "I have business to conduct, and I am tired of your presence impeding me. Thank you for coming to my defense, Mr. Phaal. I can wash this handkerchief for you, I would deeply regret asking you to carry it about with you in that state."

"I do not find it the least bit inconvenient," Richard said. "It is a badge of honor to pay respect to a lady in distress. As a matter of fact... Miss Roget, it appears that this evening, you and I owe our friend Raven here a deeper apology than a few words can provide."

Moretta stared at him, feeling his hand close around her elbow and imagining her knees melting out from under her.

"What are you saying?" Lenore demanded, taking a step closer to them. "You owed *me* an outing tonight!"

"And in the future, if you want that outing, you'll have to behave in a manner which warrants the troubles I went to in order to arrange that for you," Richard said. "From what I see, the looks on your friends' faces have spelled out how you lack integrity in this instance, and I expect better of the lady I am courting. Lord willing, our paths will cross tomorrow, but for now, good afternoon." He tugged on Moretta's elbow, pulling her away despite Lenore's shouts and pleas for him to return.

"I can't believe you would jeopardize your courtship like that," Moretta whispered to him, finding it difficult to keep her footing on the cobblestones as they walked.

"If I set no standards now, there will be none in the future," Richard said, plowing ahead down the street with a resolute set to his features. "You don't actually have to have dinner with me..." he brought Moretta into a small boutique and pulled her just out of sight from the street view. "I only said that to get my message across, you are under no obligation to me. Please, accept my sincerest invitation, which you are equally free to accept or decline... I thought it only fitting that after that display you be compensated."

Moretta took a deep breath, and in order to think more clearly, she focused on the boutique's wares. Once she did she realized that the sweet smells which perfumed the air originated from the fact that they stood in a soap shop.

Some of the soaps had been molded to mimic the shapes of artisan breads, and others resembled fine cheeses and vivid fruits she was tempted to bite into. Others had been formed as rainbow cones or abstract shapes, swirling with vibrant creativity.

Finding that she had successfully facilitated a return to reasonable thought, she smiled at Richard. "Nothing would lift my spirits more… I wasn't lying, I did have some business in town, though… Would it bother you if I conducted that business before reconvening with you?"

"My dear young lady, should it be your wish, I will accompany you on this errand. I would not wish for you to meet with further misfortune due to my own negligence."

Moretta tilted her head as she considered it. She had previously decided that he was untrustworthy, but if he had been unwittingly manipulated by the duke, he may turn on him the same way he had turned on Lenore. There was no shame in reevaluating her circumstances.

"Do you wish to aid me in conducting an investigation? I am trying to find Bacchanal Hall. According to my map, we are close to it."

"That place has been shut down pending further investigation," Richard said, though she could see curiosity in his eyes. "Why would you want to investigate such a place? Do you think you could find something that the duke's investigators have not?"

"That depends… and mainly it depends on what they're looking for."

"How would your investigation be different? And exactly… how are you qualified as an investigator?"

"I have reason to believe that evidence is missing in the case of Amelia Otranto," she said, and watched Richard's features twitch at the name.

Ah, so he had heard her name! What else did he know?

"You could be right about that," he said reluctantly, and hung his head.

"A grave injustice has been done, and I believe we may be capable of rectifying it, but only if we can learn something new about the circumstances of the crime."

He met her gaze and held it steadily. "Again, I agree, however... we should not conduct such an investigation in daylight. Come to dinner with me, and when the twilight passes, we shall search for our answers."

The fact that Richard had stopped them in a soap shop proved an advantageous one. Since Moretta knew where their dinner destination was, she purchased a little kitten-shaped bar of lavender soap, and went into the washroom to clean her face and both handkerchiefs free of all her blood.

Once she was alone in the washroom, Renata hopped onto the counter and met her eyes with a serious, almost scolding expression.

"Yes, I know, I wasn't going to trust him before," Moretta sighed quietly. "But he's my only friend here."

Renata *meowed* reprovingly at her.

"Except for you," Moretta acknowledged, "but he's different..."

Renata flicked her tail, giving Moretta a cold blink of her eyes and another flick of her tail, which splashed some of the lavender-tinged water up at Moretta.

"Get back in my hood," Moretta said with a roll of her eyes. She dried off her new bar of soap and held it up for her cat's inspection. "Isn't it a lovely likeness? And you love lavender, don't you?"

Renata tilted her head as if she found the answer to that somewhat ambiguous.

"Well, it's really for me, anyway," Moretta said, tucking the soap into her pocket.

Renata jumped up onto Moretta's shoulder, and made herself comfortable hiding in her hair.

"Who were you talking to in there?" Richard asked when Moretta emerged, apparently all alone.

"I've… I've smuggled a friend along with me," Moretta confessed, "my cat."

From within Moretta's hood, could be heard Renata's *meow* of protest at having been revealed.

"Ah, I see… do you take her everywhere with you?" Richard asked.

"Only when she approves of the destination," Moretta shrugged, and felt Renata catch her balance along her shoulders.

Richard smiled. "There's something quite charming about that, actually. Well, are you prepared to go?"

Moretta handed him his handkerchief. "It's still rather damp, but I think it's going to return to normal, soon."

"Thank you for going to the trouble," he said, and bowed as he accepted the handkerchief back from her. "I am glad it served its purpose well." He tucked the handkerchief away and offered her his elbow.

Forcing her hand not to tremble, she laced her arm through his, and allowed him to lead her out of the shop.

Chapter 17: Lavender and Spite

Some traitorous fragment of Richard's mind was concerned that he had made the wrong choice as soon as he had gotten sufficient time to think through the choices he had made.

Surely Lenore would consider this his betrayal of her, and he would never get a second chance with her! Still… he could not deny that Moretta had suffered maltreatment at her hands.

If Lenore were willing to mistreat a stranger, she could very well transfer that animosity into her other relationships. She had to be made aware that Richard would not tolerate it.

"You wish you were going with your beloved, don't you?" the Raven asked in a quiet voice. He met her tranquil silver gaze and blushed at the quiet assurance there.

"I wish she had proven herself worthy of all the trouble I went to," Richard said. "But after I saw what she did to you… I knew that if I sided with her, she would never stop mistreating people. She needs to suffer consequences."

"You know that you are not her father, do you not?" Moretta asked quietly.

"I do, but her father isn't here. Perhaps she is learning the lesson a bit late, but the important thing is that she learns it."

"I can honor that perspective," Moretta nodded, and her fringe and ringlets both bobbed along with the movement.

"I know it's not ideal, but if I really want a life with someone, if I truly expect her to be the mother of my children, I have to expect that she will be something more than a lovely face. I cannot doom my children to a cruel mother."

"I respect that position still more, your thinking is quite forthright," Moretta finally smiled, and he almost could have imagined that his friend had been unharmed.

Unfortunately he could see pinkness pooling under the ivory of her skin, with a dash of purple mixed in, and knew that he would be dining across from the evidence of her wounds. Poor thing...

"Is it bad?" she asked, her fingertips fluttering up to where the worst of the bruising was, and flinching when she touched it.

"I'm afraid so..." he sighed. "I am truly sorry you had such an unfortunate encounter... I know I was not personally involved, but the woman I am courting was, and citizens of my own hometown, and I feel most aggrieved that they represent me to some extent."

"Do not trouble yourself. I do not consider you the least bit culpable. The extent of your concern does you credit, however... Let us talk of happier things..."

He watched as she chewed on her lip, as if in search of a pleasant topic to discuss. Her eyes were darting around the streets until they fixated on something and she finally smiled.

"This place looks gorgeous," she gestured ahead to where he could see the Lavender Gallery illuminated down the street with a soft aura of peaceful lavender. "I'm lucky my face hit that pole or I'd never have seen it!" she gave a delicate giggle, which made her appear more adorable than he remembered.

"Then perhaps by some measure it was as fortuitous as you say," he led her along with more eagerness, less concerned with the negative consequences. "I hope you like art! The name is quite indicative. I saw some lovely paintings on the walls when I entered to make my reservation."

Her subtle smile grew and she trotted along with him, though still within the confines of ladylike behavior. "I haven't seen good art in days!" she cheered in as soft a voice as an exclamation could permit.

At last they stopped in front of the restaurant, and Richard opened the door for Raven, doffing his hat and bowing to pay her honor as they entered.

They were quickly ushered to the table reserved for them, and Richard saw her eyes widen more than he'd ever thought she could. "So beautiful…" she whispered, and as he gazed at the wonder on her face, he noticed a pair of luminous green eyes watching him from amongst her ringlets.

He could see the cat's tail flicking as it bounced her mistress's ringlets o n the opposite side of her head than where the eyes were. Why was he so nervous about being stared down by a cat?

"I will cover any expense you incur for the evening," he told her, bringing her eyes back onto him, though it was her cat's which maintained more of his attention.

"I could at least contribute half," she said, and began to flip through the menu.

"Perish the thought, not when I am giving you a gift."

She looked back up at him, and he was forced to look away as her gaze was nearly blinding. "Thank you," she said softly. "I do not feel as if I'm worthy of such a gift when you are courting another woman, however I will take you up on the offer. Nothing so pleasant has happened to me in… a good long while, actually…" she bowed her head for some reason, and Richard wondered whether it would be appropriate to probe for more information.

All the while he wondered this, he noted the cat's eyes narrowed on him with suspicion. He decided he didn't dare broach the subject. As she had suggested, they ought to focus on pleasant things.

"I think the lavender lamb would be quite pleasant," he said.

"I think you're right about that," she taped the watercolor illustration of the recipe in question. "I was also considering the lemon drop partridge. Apparently, the chef is able to stuff it with an entire spiced lemon!"

"That *is* interesting…" Richard tilted his head. "How about we get both and split them?"

"Oh! How adventurous!" she clapped. "Let's do that! It'll be such fun!"

Richard couldn't help but grin at her. "And what would the lady like to drink?"

"Their signature red wine looks delightful, I've never tried it with lavender before, and I'm sure it'll enrich the entire dining experience."

"I'll purchase a bottle, whatever we don't finish you can take home."

"How supremely generous of you!" she grinned, and he heard an exasperated feline noise just below her voice.

"It's the least I could do," he said, and glanced over to check on their server. He was speaking to a fellow dressed in a cape and an *il dottore* mask, which made Richard wonder if it were the same man who had recruited him into the duke's service.

If he were, should Richard offer him his gratitude? For some reason, his spine was tense with foreboding. His heart would not relax, either, for it seemed impossible to know for certain whether this fellow were trustworthy.

"What's the matter?" Raven whispered to him across the table.

"It's… it's nothing, I just saw that the server is busy."

"That's no trouble, we can talk in the meantime… we haven't really gotten to speak in depth, and that's a sorry foundation for a friendship." He noted the light blush dusting her cheeks, and decided to comply.

At least it would take his mind off the mysterious man at the door, and he would blend in more, just in case the fellow had come to spy on him.

"What would you like to know?"

"You could tell me about your family, to start with. Are your parents still living?"

"Indeed they are, and my father still runs his old factory, even if it is only buttons. He's not as active as he once was, owing to his age, but Mother keeps him in good spirits. I visit them when I can, but most of my time is devoted to… well, it *used* to be all about looking for work. Now I have more leisure time, I can visit my family more often."

"How lovely! And have you any siblings?"

"Well… there is my sister, Hyacinth, but I hardly call her family. He watched her frown and held up a hand. "Yes, we are estranged, but it is much better for my health that way."

Her brows rose. "That is a dreadful circumstance, I would be quite at the end of my sanity if my relationship with my sister were like that!"

"I had time to grow accustomed, rather like a boiling crab. However, I had the great fortune to hop out of the fryer before my demise could come about. Unfortunately, Hyacinth is a constant presence at my parents' house, and it is partially owing to her I do not see them as often as I would like."

"Has she not married, then?"

"Who would take her? No, she is a spinster, and quite the damnable harridan about it, as well."

"Such a shame, it seems you acquired all the fruits of virtue from your family tree."

"And her vintage is pressed from wrathful grapes," he nodded, and glanced over to see their server approaching them.

They ordered quickly, and the efficient man did not keep them waiting, merely zipped away behind the double doors with porcelain lavender sprigs decorating each one.

"So tell me about your family," he told Raven. "What of your parents?"

He watched as all the color which had painted her cheeks moments before was blotted out, and she bowed her head to obscure her eyes behind her ebony fringe. "They are no longer with us, may God rest their souls."

"Ah... Forgive me, it is utterly rude to discuss such distressing things," Richard blushed, and reached across the table to put a hand over hers.

With a hiss, her cat's paw lashed out from hiding and scratched at his hand, though not too deeply.

"Renata is quite protective," she said apologetically, then guided Renata back into hiding. "It is my turn to apologize. You did not say anything I did not ask you first, and my cat reacted poorly."

"I deserved it for chasing away your smile," Richard said before he had the chance to think of how it would sound, and blushed to the point it was painful once his mind caught up with his tongue. "Ah! I am sorry if that sounded too forward!"

Already he could see her eyes widening, and knew her blush must hurt as much as his did, but she only watched him silently a moment before saying, "I thought it was sweet."

They broke off speaking as a woman poured their wine for them out of a graceful, regal purple bottle. Each of them swirled the wine in their glasses.

"Are you ready for your first taste?" Raven asked, lifting her glass.

"I think I just might be," Richard said, lifting his as well.

"On the count of three," she said, and began to count down slowly, with a sly, catlike smile on her lips. It was really no wonder her cat was her best friend, since they had so much in common... he just hoped she didn't start clawing at him.

"Go!" she whispered, having reached the count of three, and Richard nearly missed taking the first drink with her.

The wine was warm as it flowed down his throat, rather than burning its way through him. The light floral aftertaste blossomed then, and he sighed, leaning back to enjoy it.

"I know... it's fantastic..." Raven sighed as well. "I'm so glad we chose this..."

"So..." Richard sat back up straight and gave her a lopsided smile. "What is your sister's name?"

"Rina," Raven said quickly. "Or... sometimes she asks to be called Katie... Really those are both nicknames but she gets rather particular."

"How very interesting," Richard said sincerely, cocking his head thoughtfully. "So why would she do a thing like that?"

"It depends on her mood, at times she will not even acknowledge that she had ever been called by the name she wanted you to call her by the hour before."

"Is she..." Richard lowered his voice, his brow knit with concern, but even then he could not bring himself to ask the question.

"Yes... something dreadful happened years back, and that is one of the ways in which her pain was made manifest."

"Might I inquire...?"

"You may, but I cannot actually reveal very much to you… I may break down in tears if I do… but suffice it to say, our parents' death had a great deal to do with it."

"Ah…" Richard blushed. "Sorry for bringing it up again…"

"Don't even worry about it. So what made you want to become a solicitor?"

"I read a lot of heroic legends when I was a child. I wanted so desperately to be a hero I tried to decide how I could do that… But you know, there's not much demand for knights and roaming heroes anymore."

"In the right circles, that sort of persona goes a long way," she said with a faint smirk. "So you perceive working as a solicitor a form of heroism?"

"It worked for Cicero," Richard noted.

"Ah, that is a fair observation. So are you planning to uncover a Cataline-esque conspiracy and topple the rebellion?"

"Oh, had I only the chance!" Richard snickered as their food arrived.

"Here's to you one day getting that chance," she said with a wink, and held her glass up for a toast, which he gladly accepted.

"And as for you?" he asked once he'd had his second sip. "What drew you to the Raven—I mean, necromancy—that job you do?"

"I became a coroner because I'm interested in dignity for the dead. I believe we ought to be more aware of the role death plays in life, and the impact a good funeral can have on the family of the deceased. Practicing medicine on the living is somewhat more incidental, but I prefer to prevent deaths when possible, as well."

"But… how do you deal with being around dead people? Doesn't it frighten you?"

"It's not like they're going to sit up and attack me," she snickered, though she paused, and shook her head. "Well, one did once, but that was different."

"Really? Tell me about that!"

She glanced anxiously around the restaurant. "Perhaps when we are no longer in polite company, I will tell you the whole story, but I would not wish to spoil anyone's meals… now let's divide up our own."

Richard was the one who did the most work of dividing it up, and by the end of it, they each had half a pheasant and half a side of lamb. "What do you think?" he asked when she had her first bite of lamb in her mouth.

"Heavenly…" she sighed, and closed her eyes as she enjoyed it. "I want to eat here every week…"

"That sounds like a good plan," Richard agreed once he'd gotten his first taste of the pheasant.

"We're staying for dessert, right?" she asked. "I'll pitch in the money for it if I have to."

"You'll get no fight out of me," he said, and swirled his wine in his glass before taking another drink.

The door to the restaurant jangled open and it was so abruptly loud that both Richard and Raven whirled around to see who had opened the door so indelicately.

There stood Lenore on the arm of *another man*! Richard stared with mouth agape as he realized it hadn't even taken her two hours to find someone else to parade in front of him. Her smug smirk indicated to him that he had done it precisely because she wanted to taunt him.

"Don't give in." Raven's hand was on his forearm. "She's putting this on as a ruse to toy with your emotions, do not allow it!"

Even knowing that she was hissing the truth at him did not completely save Richard from the effects of the wound Lenore had inflicted on him.

"What did I do to deserve this?" he whispered to Raven.

"Simple: you didn't lie down on her bed of knives," she returned, and her nails dug into his sleeve. "Stay calm. Don't give her power over you."

Lenore flounced over to them, dragging the fellow who appeared somewhat stiff and uncomfortable along with her. "Look, Algie, it's *him*! He broke my heart!"

Richard got to his feet. "Did she tell you what she did to my friend's face?" he gestured as politely as he could at Raven's face, and the fellow looked, as well.

"That isn't something I would expect from you, Lenny dear," Algernon said. "I don't understand why you dragged me out here when clearly—"

"Oh!" Lenore smacked Algernon's chest. "Come on, Algie! I want some lentil stew!"

Algernon sighed, and gave Richard a look that said somehow Lenore had called in a favor and she had manipulated him into this.

"I've still got a chance!" Richard hissed to Raven, who raised one skeptical brow.

"I think so, but I'm wondering how much you'd benefit from actually *getting* that chance. Do you want to be *him*?" she jerked her head in the direction of Algernon.

"No, I want to be myself, the man she wants to make feel jealous with the help of some poor sod."

"I don't think she's such a catch if she's resorting to that kind of tactic."

Richard had to admit that was another point against Lenore, but he couldn't let himself believe she was heartless. Not when she was so... *idealized*... in his own mind. Did that actually reflect who she was as a person?

Living in denial could hardly change who she was, and how long would he spend pining after a woman who did not truly exist?

He tried to look at Lenore with critical eyes, but had not the willpower to do it. He looked back at Raven, instead. "I have to believe, at least for a little while longer, that I have not dreamed so long in vain."

"If that's the case, just try not to look at her. She's probably going to be aggressively attacking your senses."

"She can do that from all the way over there?"

"Of course, she can, she's a woman. We can all do things like that. That's why you should only trust us when we're your friends."

He smirked, finally finding it possible to tear his eyes away from Lenore and focus on his new friend. "Is that so? This wouldn't be one of those manipulative tactics, would it?"

"If I wanted to manipulate you, I could cause you to go have a fight with lard-for-brains over there, or cause you to court me, instead. All I'm doing is giving you honest advice because as your friend and confidant I insist that you protect your heart, is that understood?"

"Quite clearly, actually... I'm rather flattered, thank you..." It was somewhat difficult to comprehend someone doing a thing like that for him without an ulterior motive, but his life *had* begun anew, so why not?

"Don't thank me too much, I'm still a woman," Raven said with a smirk. "Now just don't look at her. We're having fun without her, and right now *she's* the one who's jealous of *you*. Keep it that way and you'll maintain the upper hand."

"I will?" Richard glanced over at Lenore, who was tittering just a little too loudly with her escort Algernon. "I don't even feel like I have it now!"

"Hush," Raven said softly, "don't let her know that... Have some more wine, and then some lamb, it's divine."

He knew she was right, but it was still difficult for him to eat when he was so frantic over Lenore. Even so, he looked at Raven instead, and saw that she was eating contentedly. He remembered what it had been like before Lenore had arrived, and how righteous he had felt in the choice he had made.

If this were a sign of desperation on Lenore's part, why shouldn't he be glad? The more desperate she got, the more likely she would be to beg for him to approve of her. Assuming she didn't actually fall for Algernon...

"You're still worried, aren't you?"

"I cannot resist thinking that I've forever lost my chance with Lenore..."

"I'm surprised you still want anything to do with her, after seeing how petulant and toxic she is, but do you know what I think?" Raven asked. "I think Lenore and Algernon look *quite* similar. Do you know much about her relatives? I think he may be her cousin."

"What do you mean? Why would you think that?"

"You have never seen him before, and she was able to get him here swiftly... I think he is her relative masquerading as a possible lover. He is not a threat, he is a mask."

"You could be right…" Richard realized. "Does that mean she loves me?"

"It means she thinks you're useful. Have you been buying her things?"

Richard blushed. "Yes…"

"Has she seemed more excited to spend time with you after you offered to buy her things?"

"Yes…" never in his life could he remember feeling more like an imbecile.

"Then what you have trying to make you jealous is a stuck-up twit who wants nothing more than to manipulate the life's blood out of you for money and other perks. As your friend I insist that you stop wishing she cared for you, because I am unconvinced she can care for anyone but herself."

"Don't you think that assessment may be a little harsh?"

"Only if she actually has hobbies other than walking around with her friends and laughing at the expense of others, but otherwise… I think it is a fair if blunt assessment. As for you, do you want to sacrifice a happy evening for a woman who doesn't even have anything in common with you?"

"We're not that different…"

"So what do you have in common? Has she expressed ambition? Does she want to make something of herself? You have said you want to be a hero, does she wish to be a heroine?"

He'd never thought of that before. "Can't just any woman be a heroine? All women are members of the fairer sex, you are innately — "

"Manipulative, prone to hysterics, slothful… these are traits both men and women can possess. We are all fallen creatures, and I suggest you stop idealizing people before you discover the truth in what I say only for it to be too late. What kind of a lawyer can't understand that people commit crimes?"

"Surely women don't do things like that."

"I'm a coroner, Richard dear. I've seen men and women both, killed by men certainly, but do you know who primarily kills with poison? Women. Because unlike men who tend to kill in a fit of anger, a woman will calculate purposefully how much poison to murder you with, over a long period of time. Scheduling how long it will take you to die while smiling at you and even caring for you while your symptoms worsen. Every famous poisoning case was perpetrated by a woman, at least in this country."

He stared at her in wonder. "I've never heard a thing like that!"

"Of course, you haven't! It's because we're so good at polishing our image."

He stared at how calmly she ate her pheasant, picked its bones clean and then drank more of her wine. As he was so stunned, he ate his own mechanically, trying to determine what to ask as a follow-up question.

At last he asked, "How much have you learned from working with… well, corpses?"

She swirled her wine in her glass and considered. "Mostly impolite things. But I don't take myself too seriously anymore. Our bodies are all built the same way, even if we do have personal variations. I suppose there's something philosophical in that."

"I'm sure there is…" Richard nodded, but his eyes drifted over to Lenore despite himself. "She's watching us…" he whispered.

"Of course, she is, because she doesn't know how to have fun."

He smirked at her. "And you do?"

"Watch," she cut a slice of lemon, and slipped it into her sleeve. Then in a flash of an instant, she whipped around and sent the slice of lemon flying at Lenore's head, then returned to sitting still and quiet as if she hadn't moved.

Lenore, on the other hand, exploded in indignant screeches that brought a server over to her.

"Oh my…" Richard stared at her. "How did you…?"

"I learned from my mother. She was a mistress of knife-throwing, and she taught me a great deal of it…" She paused as the server assured Lenore that he had no concept of how the lemon could have gotten caught in her hat, but offered her a plate of hors d'oeuvres, which finally mollified her.

"Now she'll be looking around for lemons falling from the sky for awhile," Raven whispered. "Though maybe we ought to cover the cost of the hors d'oeuvres in our bill, I can cover that cost since it's my fault."

"That's very generous of you, considering how much of a troublemaker you are," Richard noted with a smirk. He also noticed that Lenore had gotten her hors d'oeuvres but was now pouting sulkily in his direction.

"She's looking at you again, isn't she?"

"Unfortunately, yes…"

"Tell me how your business is going. You appear to be doing rather well for yourself… for instance: do you own that *bestia* horse I saw you riding before?"

"Oh, no…" Richard blushed to admit it. "However, I am hoping to afford one soon. That one was just sent to collect me."

"Oh, well, aren't you special, then?" she snorted. "Someone went to a great expense to 'collect' you."

"The duke does not like to be kept waiting, it seems. The thing printed out the message that I was supposed to go and then it took me right there. I have to admit, now I really want one of those. I used to only want it as part of the carriage setup, but now I'd like to have one for its own sake."

"What sort, a quick-stepping thoroughbred? From what I hear, they have the most horse-power."

"I think I ought to aim a bit lower, if I get a thoroughbred it'll eat up twice its cost in oil and repairs — plus, have you heard how sensitive those knee hinges are?"

"Very true, if I were to get one, I might lean toward a Frisian. They make a bold statement while being a sturdier model. I think they're more reliable while still being attractive. Besides, for someone as small as I am, I would appreciate rising above the crowd."

"So you wouldn't go for the customized pony models?" Richard winked to accompany his smirk. "I could see you with a pink one, maybe with a cotton candy mane?"

"Oh, could you?" she purred, leaning back and reaching into her ringlets for Renata, who Richard could hear purring.

Richard snickered, and could *feel* the heat of Lenore's glare on him. "Perhaps you're right, a Frisian model would be just your color, black as coal."

"At any rate, our hair would match!" the two of them snickered, though they were able to keep the volume of their laughter to a minimum.

"We ought to order dessert, we'll need our strength for what comes next," Richard said at last.

"Did you have your eye on anything in particular, by some chance? I don't care too much beyond the fact that it needs to be chocolate."

"You really *are* a woman, aren't you? That's no trouble; I'll just focus on the savory."

"There's this petite little rosehip chocolate pound cake," she suggested, pointing it out.

"Hmm.... It comes with gentleman's relish on toast as the savory accompaniment, would you mind that?"

"That's the one with the *patum peperium*, isn't it? Just hope they don't use too much of that, you can only take too much pepper paste."

Once they'd ordered that, it didn't take long before Lenore was towering over them with her hands on her hips. "Why were you mocking me this whole time? You should be gravelling at my feet right now! Apologize for how you've treated me!"

Richard gave Raven an awkward, panicked glance as he weighed whether it was appropriate to tell Lenore she had used the wrong word, but Lenore snapped her fingers and drew his attention back to her before he could make up his mind.

"Why do you keep ignoring me for her? Don't look at her, *I'm* asking you a question!"

"The fact is, my friend and I were having a good time before you came along," Raven said when Richard found himself incapable of replying.

"Do you honestly expect me to believe you consider him nothing but a friend?" Lenore inquired, leaning forward and giving Raven a look of sharp scrutiny.

"I do expect you to believe that, because I am an honest woman," Raven said quietly. "I understand if you cannot grasp the concept."

Algernon was at Lenore's side and grabbing her by her shoulders before Lenore could spit out a coherent response. "It's time for us to go," he told her sternly. "I'll have to tell my aunt what you're doing, and then we'll see when you next leave home!" he scolded. With a quick respectful nod Richard and Raven's way, Algernon wheeled Lenore out of the restaurant, leaving a generous pile of gold on the maître d's desk.

Though first Richard and Raven ate their dessert over a hushed discussion of just how punished Lenore would be, they kept it quick.

"Next time I come," Raven whispered to him when they left, returning to Amontillado's streets, "I hope she isn't there to ruin it."

Chapter 18: A Mirthless Bacchanal

The glow of their enjoyable evening together faded as all the town clocks struck ten. There was a misty silence which permeated the streets and made Moretta supremely uneasy.

At least now she felt justified in pressing close to Richard for comfort, after all, now they were friends. When she had first arrived, she had thought that perhaps Richard considered being seen with her an embarrassment, but perhaps she had been wrong to start with.

"Are you cold?" Richard asked.

"Oh, no, my cape is quite warm, and I've got Renata generating constant heat against my neck, but thank you for the concern."

"I'm still responsible for you, so I have to ensure you're as comfortable as possible," he reminded her.

"Such a gentleman," she blushed. "Will we be at the Bacchanal Hall soon?"

"Quite soon, n fact it's just around this... corner..." he halted in his tracks as they stared at the once grand hall, with its windows busted out and boarded up.

Wind whistled through the upper windows, sounding like a wailing horde of ghosts. The building itself was a great skeleton devoid of the liveliness that had reportedly once filled it.

"It's... it's like looking at a dead friend's cadaver..." he murmured.

"I suppose it would be," Moretta sighed, looking up at the ruin. She had actually seen her dead friends, and she hoped Richard would not share the experience one day. "The one good thing about this is how open it will be to investigation," she pointed out, and gestured to one of the windows, which hadn't been completely covered over with the boards.

"How will we get in without..." Richard stopped when she revealed one of the knives which were hidden away in her belt. "Don't worry about that, I've handled this sort of thing, before."

"As a... coroner?" Richard asked in dismay. "Do you... you don't break into *coffins*, do you?"

Moretta snorted, and she heard Renata make a similar noise near her ear. "No, but I have learned to do things like this in case of emergency. I'm double as an ordinary doctor, you know."

"And a rescue worker?" he asked, one brow rising.

"They told me I was one of the only people who would do a thing like this in town, so before I came I was prepared for just about anything." She could tell him that much, she reassured herself, it wasn't a lie. She just couldn't tell him any more than that.

"You shouldn't have such a heavy burden just to yourself," Richard said softly as Moretta began to pry at the nails which barred them entry to the hall.

"I'm not bothered by it, but your concern is endearing," she said, and tried not to grunt with her effort. Such noises were unladylike, but regrettably unavoidable.

"Let me do that," Richard said, lightly touching the wrist of the hand which wielded her knife. "A lady should not have to do a thing like that."

"How kind of you, Richard dear, however, I'm the one who has been taught how to do this without harming myself, and I cannot in good conscience ask you to take over for me. After all, I'm going to be finished soon."

She pried off all four boards, and then kicked at the vestiges of glass which still clung to the window sill.

"Careful with your skirt," Richard cautiously gathered the lacy expanse of her skirts behind her as she prepared to walk through the window.

She knew she was blushing, but was grateful for the darkness veiling that fact from Richard. She thanked him breathlessly and climbed her way through the window.

Once inside the tile-floored atrium, she pulled out her small lantern to light their investigation. First she had to unfold it, and wound up the mechanism's key in order to generate enough energy to produce the light which shone from it.

"That's… quite handy," Richard said as he hopped into the room and then stood close at her side. "Just be careful," he whispered to her. "There could be evidence, but there could also be a criminal returning to the scene…"

"I am aware, unfortunately," she sighed, "but remember… I am armed. Aren't you?"

The look she could see illuminated on his face by her lantern told her he was not, even before he sheepishly shook his head.

"You may wish to invest in a weapon. A man of obvious wealth is a target for the unscrupulous among us."

"You're just full of advice, aren't you?"

"If it annoys you, I'll stop, I just want you to be safe," she shrugged, and turned to examine the ticket office. "This is undisturbed," she noted, "so it seems whoever got in here didn't break in, at least not from here. He either showed a legitimate ticket to the man at the desk, or he got in some other way."

"And do you think that indicates anything in particular about him?"

"Mainly that he was good at disguising himself if he came to the window here, but it could also mean the manager has a lax entry policy. It could also be that he is an upstanding member of society nobody would suspect."

"Surely not! Why would someone who was so well-off want to attack people?" he asked.

She gave him a sad smile. "Because something was deeply wrong with him, or he was hired as an assassin… though in that case something is wrong with him, as well. Speaking of whom, did you get a good look at him?"

"He was masked..."

"But did you note anything about his build? Was he tall or short? Slim or stout?"

"I... I really couldn't say..." he said as vacantly as he would have if he were a dullard, but Moretta held back her disapproval. He was probably kicking himself internally without her input.

"Well, we can still find some evidence further in," she said, hoping to dismiss his shame. She led the way deeper into the shadows, before she opened the door further into the Hall.

"Are you sure we can get in here without tripping some sort of alarm?" he asked.

"That would imply someone still has an interest in a derelict building, and if so, I would like very much to know who those people are."

The tiles on the floor in this new hallway were somewhat lopsided and loose in places, which necessitated extra care as they walked forward.

"I don't know for sure that I would..." Richard said as he picked his way along the shattered floor behind Moretta.

"It's better to know your enemy than let him strike from silence," Moretta told him.

"Better to have no enemies than be killed by one."

"Do you think everyone at this party *knew* there was someone planning to kill them? That was their enemy, and they were completely unaware of him… or them."

"You can't predict everything."

"But you can protect yourself in case of an emergency. You can be armed, you can be trained. That is the sort of thing my parents taught me, and that's why I wear knives wherever I go."

"Wouldn't a revolver be more effective?"

"Well, I wasn't going to mention that I had one in case it made you nervous," she smirked, and forced the door ahead of her open even though something was in her way.

Richard joined her in the effort, and she could feel his scrutiny on her. "Is that really something ladylike to do?"

"Do you see what I'm doing here? Do I look like an ordinary lady? Anyhow, if it's ladylike to be attacked and faint helplessly, then I must be something else."

"That's certainly a fair point…" Richard put his shoulder into pushing the door open, and it finally screeched open.

What they found there was the grand staircase with its two wings, one reaching up to the two ballrooms it housed, overshadowed by a massive crystalline chandelier.

"It must have been beautiful once," Moretta noted, and glanced back to check Richard's face.

He appeared deeply troubled, and she couldn't blame him for it. She would be disturbed as well. He pointed at a long velvet curtain which was stretched and torn from the second floor down to the one they stood on. "That's how I got down here," he told her quietly, "I can't believe how this whole area was so full…"

"It looks like that whole thing was quite difficult to execute… congratulations on your success. How are you feeling now? Is it too much yet?"

"Even if it were, I wouldn't abandon you here, and I know you won't leave on your own so I have to stay."

"I'm sorry I let you know where I was going, then," she sighed. "If it gets to be too much for you—"

"Don't worry about that, I won't let it overpower me." He ushered her up the stairs with a firm hand on the small of her back.

The further they got up the stairs, the more Moretta prepared for a possible ambush.

"Have you ever done something like this?" Richard whispered to her. "What kind of doctor are you?"

"I confess, I have had unorthodox training, but I'm meant to help people in any way necessary," she said, hoping if she could just wrench the ballroom door open, they could both get in without discussing the matter further.

Instead of letting the matter rest, Richard asked, "Who do you work for?"

"I work for none but the Crown," she replied, and for once found herself revealing part of her true identity in stark honesty.

"The Crown?" he repeated, but at this she hushed him.

"We are about to begin investigating digging into portions of the building people will clearly see our light from. If at any time, someone is planning to come after us, it will be after seeing us up here."

"I'm ready," he lied, but there was a greater degree of bravery than cowardice in his voice when he lied.

Moretta turned the handle of the door, and it was this which finally opened without protest. "Either they only wanted to close up the outside, or it's the one part still being used," she whispered to Richard.

"But used for what?" he asked.

"That's what we're here to discover," she whispered back, and tiptoed into the ballroom.

The crime scene was still hauntingly similar to the way it must have looked during the attack, itself. Tables were overturned, and blood stains were splattered across the floor in a macabre testament to the death and mayhem which had reigned over the Bacchanal.

"Why didn't anyone clean this up?" Richard croaked from just behind her, and Moretta turned to appraise him. He had pressed a hand over his mouth and was staring with horror which she was sure would give way to tears at any moment.

"I know," Moretta said quietly, "But I'm going to go further in... I think I see something."

In fact, she held her lantern out so she could see a trail of blood which led from one of the windows all the way across the ballroom.

"That's where I saw Lenore's friend go down," Richard said hollowly.

"Amelia," Moretta said softly. "She's my friend now, so I have to learn what happened to her." She started at the initial blood splatter, and followed the trail, watching how it had certainly been smeared under the weight of Amelia being dragged along.

They hadn't even bothered to pick her up? No respect... how disgraceful!

"How do you know Amelia?" Richard whispered as he followed her.

"She's been haunting me... we were supposed to discuss this at dinner, weren't we? Well, it was more pleasant since we didn't..."

"Ah... I was made to write a letter to her family which said that her body is being used for science..."

Moretta's brows shot up and she whirled on him. "What did you just say? Used for science?"

"Yes... I asked the duke why he hadn't just turned her body over to them, but he wanted to make absolutely certain it was *me* writing that letter…"

"He wants your fingerprints on this mess… and you do realize — you *must* realize — that what he's done is illegal! Nobody can take someone's body for the sake of science without either their own pre-mortem written consent, or that of their family! I've been getting letters from them, as well, and they're all desperate to bury her! The duke should be made to face consequences for doing this!"

Richard held up his hands defensively. "I know this looks bad, but — "

"You're a legal expert! You ought to know precisely how wrong this is!"

"I… I do," he admitted, "but I can't fix that if I'm dismissed from the duke's service. I won't know what he's doing next, and he will completely discredit me if he considers me a threat."

Moretta scrutinized him. Based off of what she knew about him, she considered his perspective a trustworthy one. He was the most honest person she remembered meeting in some considerable while, so if he said he was doing his best against the duke, he most likely was.

The trouble remained, however, in the fact that he had not only benefitted from the arrangement but had taken no opposing action. Perhaps he only needed a nudge?

She considered this as she followed the trail of blood through the room, past the overturned tables, where there were more splotches of blood. Rather than let herself be distracted by these, she followed the trail left by Amelia all the way to the furthermost corner of the room.

"Why wasn't Amelia taken out the door?" Richard asked.

"Oh, she was taken out through *a* door, just not one you would expect," Moretta said, stopping where the trail met the wall.

"Oh... Oh, good lord!" Richard cried. "A secret passageway?"

Moretta hushed him, again, and waved a hand somewhat frantically. "If anyone's here, they may be on the other side of this door," she whispered to him. "You have to be quiet... can you handle a firearm?"

"I... well, I... *could*... I have before..."

"Right, then," she gave him her gun, which she had to pull from its secret pocket in her skirt. "It's loaded, take it off safety mode and point it at the ceiling."

She watched as he swallowed, but failed to calm himself entirely. This was the face of a man who had never willingly engaged in combat; that was for certain.

"Everyone needs a bit of excitement in their lives..." she muttered, "even solicitors."

He returned that sentiment with more of a grimace with a smile. "Are you sure it's necessary to do this?"

"Do you want to know what's happening in this town or do you not?

Remember we're both tangled up in this mess, and whoever did this must pay. It is our duty to bring them to justice."

She watched as he slowly agreed with what she said, culminating in another swallow and a deliberate nod.

With that taken care of, she slipped a knife out of its holster and searched with its point for the hem she knew had to be there. At length, the tip of her knife sank into the seam she'd been seeking, and she dug it deeper.

She slid it to about the same height as the average locking mechanism and handle would be, and jiggled it as she would have if she were picking a lock that she could see.

"What are you doing?" Richard asked, but she hushed him again, tilting her body so he could see what she was doing for himself.

If it hadn't been for the fact that she moved aside, the door may have hit her when it came swinging open. At first she thought it was her doing, but the moment Richard screamed and shot her gun off, she knew otherwise.

From within the shadows were rushing men wearing red masks and long black capes, arms out-stretched to make a grab for them. These were all Zanni masks, characterized by their exaggeratedly long and crescent-curved noses, and these also had puffy synthetic moustaches, so Moretta did not take them for more than foot soldiers. Why should they be aught else when they wore the masks of stock servants?

Servants or not, they were extending the rather hostile arms of a master who wished her ill. They would have to go.

"They've seen our faces!" she shouted, and thrust a dagger angled up into one of the men's throats.

While he gasped and bled out, Renata jumped off Moretta's shoulder and lunged for another one of the men in the red masks. Even as she did, a harsh side-sweep from a man's arm knocked the air out of Moretta and sent her crumbling to the floor.

"Raven!" Richard cried, and though she couldn't see him, blocked as he was by her assailant, she knew it was he who shot that man in the back of his head.

In the wake of the gunshot and the shouting, all was silence, save for the man slumping down to his side as his life bled out of him.

"Three of them..." Moretta croaked as her breath returned to her.

Renata was rubbing her head against Moretta's hand, and so she began to pet her by mechanical instinct. The cat really knew how to calm her mistress... a bit of purring from her dear pet and she didn't feel so horrid, any longer...

"Are you all right?" Richard asked, edging the fallen masked man out of the way with one foot so he could kneel in front of her.

"Yes, yes, don't you worry, I'll be just fine in a moment…"

"Have you been able to deduct anything?" he asked, holding a hand out as an offer to help her to her feet.

"Yes…" she took a deep breath, and accepted the assistance of his outstretched hand. "I'll take my gun back, thank you. I think someone probably heard that, so we should conduct our investigation and then hurry home."

"Who *are* these men?"

"Enemies… they heard what we were talking about, and these were the men you were worried we would encounter."

"It's a good thing I was here, isn't it?"

"Indeed, you were a great help," she said, and gave him a half smile she hoped would bolster him and chase away some of his fear as she tucked away each of her weapons with care.

Renata resumed her place on Moretta's shoulders, and purred just a little frantically once she was there.

Moretta reached back and stroked her cat's fur, hoping to ease the frantic purring as she pressed on and entered the little room she had uncovered.

Against one wall was a desk upon which had been laid out a series of papers which Moretta instantly swept up into her arms without looking at them, and then folded.

"What are those?" Richard asked. "Are you going to let me see?"

"No, you work for the duke, and I don't want him to extricate what's on these papers from you." She didn't watch his face this time, reluctant to see the effect her words had on him. "I think they've been here for a long time…" Moretta said, indicating the wall where hazy sienna photographs were hung along the wall.

"Were they here when parties were going on?" Richard asked.

"Possibly… I think whoever perpetrated this attack was involved in their conspiracy."

"But what did they want? Does this absolve the duke?"

"By no means does it completely absolve him, these could be his agents," Moretta pointed out, even though she knew he wouldn't like to hear it.

"So… they were hiding back here… waiting for the right chance to strike at us…" She heard the shiver in his voice without having to look at him.

"And organizations have heads," she pointed out to him. "Someone had to give them orders."

"But we can't prove who their leader is… unless the answer is in those papers of yours… You should let me see them!"

She edged away from him. "Later. You can visit my home tomorrow, or the day after, and we can go over these papers when we are at our leisure to do so. At this moment, we are in a rush."

He frowned but had no response, so she turned back to her investigation.

"Is that a…" she knelt and her hand went to a ring on the floor. She gave it a quick tug and found that yes, it was a trap door.

"Don't go down there!" Richard yanked her back with one hand on her shoulder. "You don't know how many of them are down there!"

"Maybe I don't, but we can't leave this without investigating!"

"Yes, we can! We've already killed three of them, there's no telling how many of them live down there!"

Moretta had to admit he had a point. "It's getting late… we should adjourn, and return to our homes."

Richard insisted on escorting her home, and it was fine with Moretta. She was reluctant to be left on her own, especially since she was still suffering the after effects of the sudden attack. She even asked if he would stay the night with her due to how uneasy she felt, and after a brief hesitation, he agreed.

"You don't have to sleep on the couch this time," she said, guiding him up the stairs. "I've discovered I have guest rooms."

"I'm glad I can make you feel safer," he yawned as she opened the guest room door for him.

"And I'm glad I didn't have to send you home in the dark."

When she closed the door behind him, and she was met with Renata's skeptical gaze, Moretta sighed. It was time to put on the gramophone and hope that she could get some sleep.

Chapter 19: Red Masks

When Richard woke in the unfamiliar surroundings of the guest room, he'd forgotten where he was. His first assumption was that the men in the red masks had kidnapped him and put him somewhere to await interrogation, but he was much too comfortable.

At last he remembered that he had fallen asleep in the Raven's house after a night of investigation, and a blush spread over his cheeks. What would people think?

He'd fallen asleep twice in a woman's house, and she wasn't remotely related to him! Lenore must already suspect that he was courting Raven, instead, so why shouldn't she assume the worst if she discovered where he had laid his weary head?

Richard scrambled to his feet and hastily arranged the bedclothes before straightening his own clothes.

His nerves were instantly calmed when he smelled someone making breakfast downstairs, and knew that his hostess had thought of everything.

When he made his way downstairs to greet her, he found her in the kitchen, manning several different preparation stations so that she could simultaneously prepare tea, eggs, bacon and pancakes.

"You are *amazing…*" Richard leaned on the kitchen table. "I don't remember ever being so happy to smell breakfast!"

"Harrowing experiences tend to put the simple pleasures of life in focus," she said softly, giving him a small smile.

"Does it really? I suppose it does… I'm amazed it seems you've done this before…"

"Many times," she assured him, returning her attention to her multiple tasks. "You could call it my true calling."

"But you're a lady…"

"You keep saying that, but I'm not like most ladies."

"I know, but that makes you more deserving than most of the protection owed you."

"Does it seem that way to you? I would assume the opposite."

"I suppose you do enough for yourself… but that just makes you special."

"Well," she smiled, and turned around to offer him a plate full of what she'd made, "If I ever want to go on another adventure, I'll take you along with me."

"I think I'll get my own gun just in case, it's not fair that only one of us has one."

"Good idea, I certainly suggest a revolver."

Richard watched her as she poured the tea for both of them. She was a peculiar sort, not merely because she was one of the few women willing to bother with the dead. She had also shown a great deal of bravery the night before, which indicated she was a different breed of woman entirely from the ones he had met. She was even braver than him, in that instance.

Was it possible that now he had become somewhat braver for having been exposed to the previous night's danger?

He ate some of the bacon which had been given to him as he continued to mull over those considerations. He stopped when he noticed the tea he had just sipped was tinged with lavender.

A smile blossomed on his lips and he met the Raven's eyes. "That was sneaky," he snickered at her.

"I thought you might appreciate that. I'm not one to hurry a house guest out, but I imagine you don't want to be seen at my home, is that correct?"

Richard blushed. "It's not owing to who you are, I mean it is, but—" When he found his tongue useless, she nodded her understanding.

"We are both unmarried, and some may misconstrue our time together as indecent."

"Some may consider our time together indecent no matter what we did or didn't do," he pointed out, and his blush burned more harshly than before. "You're right, and thank you for accommodating me..." he shoveled his food down his throat and glanced at her apologetically. "I wish the circumstances were different."

"Well," she stirred cream into her tea, "unless you plan on proposing, I don't think it will."

"That's a good point!" he laughed at what he assumed was a joke and rose from his place at the table. "Good day to you, madam. I hope you will grace me with your presence again soon."

"The sentiment is mutual," she curtseyed as informally as such a gesture could possibly be.

He left in a hurry, and just in case someone might notice him, he left out the back door, which at first Raven was reluctant to show him. It was out through a secret passage, and he started to wonder if Amontillado were full of more secret passages than he'd ever guessed.

"It goes out through the graveyard," she warned him, "I would go with you, but it seems you're much too ashamed to be seen with me," she wrinkled her nose playfully at him.

"Oh, well, I'll have to pay the price for that one," he sighed, and tipped his hat at her.

Still, he was glad to get out of the creepy old house, and especially the secret room she'd shown him. No matter how she tried to downplay the fact that there were chains on one wall, he couldn't shake the fact that he'd seen them even as he began to walk into the graveyard.

The graveyard ought to be far more disturbing than a room he couldn't confirm had any dark secrets. He *knew* terrible things had happened in this graveyard.

People had been heard screaming and groaning as they tried to escape the Ravens, tried to stumble to freedom in the dark calling for help that seldom came.

Even in the early morning mist, Richard clutched his coat more tightly about himself, and expected phantasms to arise from the blurry shapes before his eyes.

The infernal practices of the last Ravens had persisted unabated for years, and it had only been going away to University which had saved Richard from the daily influx of tragedy.

Now he shivered at the thought that the dead may rise up against him for living in the shadow of this house and not lifting a finger to help them. It wouldn't matter to them how young he'd been, and that legally nobody had recourse to stop what the Ravens were doing with inadequate proof.

He stumbled over a low tombstone, and whimpered with fear rather than pain despite the mild twist he could feel in his ankle and his smarting toes.

No revenant or ghoul had risen from this grave yet, but he didn't wait around to see if one did. The threat of his imagination was stronger than the knowledge that nothing was actually there with him.

He tripped through the graveyard, squinting in the mist at each shadow, scrutinizing it for signs that it was haunted by an infernal specter. Fear propelled him further through the cemetery, and his heart raced further on ahead.

It occurred to him that he didn't particularly know how to get out of the grave yard, and he couldn't possibly know in this mist whether or not he was going further in! Panic rose to a heightened fever pitch, and he thought he could hear the cries of the languishing victims of the Ravens.

Clawing sensations on his back and shoulders made him cry out in terror, and he began to race for the gate.

His run for safety ended abruptly as he tripped over a grave stone and toppled face first into the grass, with the air bashed out of his diaphragm.

Wheezing and desperate, Richard imagined he was surrounded by accusers, he could hear far-off screams echoing in his memories and growing louder. They were calling his name, shouting in voices both male and female, closing in on him as a red light grew in his eyes…

"Richard!" a particularly familiar female voice said as at last he felt a hand on his shoulder.

He screamed at the sheer terror of it, but instead of attacking him, the person who had touched his shoulder pushed him off the tombstone.

The red light was still hovering over his eyes, but what he saw despite the haze was the Raven's face, eyes wide with concern.

"I realized the gate was locked from the outside, so I was going to unlock it for you…" she told him. "I'm sorry you… I should have accompanied you, and I would have if you hadn't… I'm so sorry."

He wheezed up at her, and squeezed her arm. "Thank you… saved me…" he croaked.

"Nothing was out here," she said gently. "Though I suppose you could have gotten lost and fallen into the lake… come on, you were almost out of the graveyard."

"I was?" he asked sheepishly. "That's embarrassing…" he allowed her to assist him to his feet, and while he recovered she led him to the gate.

"Next time we can walk through here together… in fact, I really should walk through here on my own and get to know the place. Are you going to be all right walking through town?"

"Much better than walking with the dead," he nodded emphatically, and stumbled gratefully through the graveyard gate.

On the other side of it the air felt lighter, and easier to breathe. He turned to see Raven still standing in the graveyard, porcelain pale and clad all in black. Her hair was not pinned up as it usually was, but her ringlets were still in place. She looked like someone out of a ghost story, and he couldn't keep looking at her when he saw her that way.

He ran down the hill, grateful for the cloak of mist which defended him from the prying eyes of gossips he knew were hunting for him. They always were in this town.

When he arrived home, it was with the intention of changing his clothes more than anything, but he found a note on his door.

He plucked it off with trembling fingers, his mind instantly inventing a reason for this note to be there. Had the duke discovered it was him who had helped the Raven break into Bacchanal Hall?

No, he realized when he broke the seal on the note and opened it to reveal that the duke was quite angry that *someone* had broken into the crime scene and left fresh bodies for him to dispose of. His services were demanded immediately.

Richard swallowed. As long as he could convince the duke this was the work of vandals... he should be fine.

He ducked into his apartment in order to make himself presentable before he hurried across town in a cab to the castle.

Unlike the other times he had visited the castle, someone was there to swing the door open instantly and drag him through the imposing ancient halls rather than leaving him waiting.

What made him cry out in alarm when he saw this fellow was how similar the scarlet mask he wore was to the ones he'd helped kill the night before.

There was the duke, pacing his office, in a state of disarray. His clothing was out of sorts, and he looked as if he were in the latter stages of a descent into madness. He would not have been so surprised except for the fact that he had expected that to take much longer than simply overnight.

"What are you *doing*?" the duke demanded of him, jabbing his finger in Richard's direction as if it were a loaded flintlock. "How are you helping me? What use are you?"

Richard stood stunned in the doorway, trying to assess where that question had come from. "I... I don't understand..." he admitted.

"I have a solicitor and still there are bodies piling up on my doorstep!"

"I can really only help you after the fact..." Richard stammered, grabbing hold of one of the edges of the book shelf beside him. It eased some of the tension but could not fully erase it.

"Then help me now!" Duke Julian shouted, and drew aside a sheet to show Richard the three bodies of the men he and Raven had encountered the night before, still masked.

"Who are they?" he asked numbly. "I... I can't really do anything if I don't know who they are and what happened to them."

Well, he knew what had happened to them, but there was no way he would ever admit that... But since he could feign not knowing what had happened to them, he knew someone who would appreciate the chance to examine them... Not only that, he knew how to get these bodies to her.

"Obviously one was shot, and two were stabbed!" the duke erupted anew.

"Have you considered letting the coroner take a look at them?" he asked as innocently as he possibly could.

"This is an internal matter!" the duke spat at him.

"Were these... were they your men?"

The duke paused mid-pace, and stared at Richard. In the meanwhile, Richard could see the gears turning in his mind, those eyes darkening as if they were a device attempting to magnify an image. The depths of scrutiny focused on him made Richard stiffen even more than his constrictive clothing had already done.

"These men were in my employ, yes..." the duke slowly crossed the room toward Richard, but there was something in the way he walked that put Richard on edge.

It was the languid, deliberate tapping of the toes of his shoes first followed by a rhythmic letdown of his heel, and the way his body moved sinuously, rather like a leopard on the prowl.

"And... so you want me to discover who murdered your agents, sir?" Richard asked. He could hardly admit that he knew the answer, but he knew the duke was waiting for him to slip somehow.

Had he guessed that Richard himself was one of the culprits? There couldn't be a stain on him, he'd changed his clothes, and everything...

"I have suspicions... but none of them are so easily confirmed."

Richard stood as still as he possibly could, his every muscle stained to painful lengths.

"Do you know something I should?" the duke asked in a low crackle, the sort one would hear from embers about to roar to life with just a simple puff from a bellows.

Richard held in his breath, afraid to stoke that fire. "I don't understand..." he said weakly, and did his best to swallow the awkward fear in his throat and force it into the depths of his stomach where he could hide it.

"What don't you understand?" the duke asked, his voice rising as if Richard had failed to stop that fire behind his eyes from stoking up.

"Why would someone attack *your* agents?" Other than being surprise attacked by them in the dark with no explanation... "Do we have a rebellion in our midst? They could be my friends or neighbors!" he shivered, but he was glad the falsehood he had spun could easily account for it.

The duke's eerie gaze lingered on Richard a moment longer. Then, by some blessed mercy, the duke swept away from Richard. Had the deception truly been successful?

Richard did not dare to relax. He still stood stiff as a corpse. This served him well as the duke whipped back around to apply his harsh scrutiny once more.

Feigning ignorance, Richard took a step back, and asked, "Your grace? Do you have any more evidence to share?"

The duke paused a moment longer, but he responded, saying, "No. My agents were returned to me in this state early this very morning... it was such a shame that you were absent from your home this morning, or you could have been here sooner..."

Richard considered asking how the duke *knew* he hadn't been home, but decided to let the matter rest for his sanity's sake.

"If I were a suspicious man, I may begin to draw a conclusion or two from the fact that you were mysteriously absent from your home so early in the morning, directly after this... *tragic* incident occurred."

Richard needed an alibi. He had examined countless alibis during his time at law school... he had to be careful. "I was taking a morning constitutional," he said evenly. This morning was the first time I thought it would be a good idea... I don't think it's such a good idea, after all, since it's ever so foggy of a morning... Perhaps I'll try again when spring arrives. It's good to stay spry."

The duke watched him a moment longer, but there was no evidence of what he sought in Richard's words. "Well, perhaps you're right. The coroner will need to see these men. Present these to him, once my servants have prepared them for burial. I will personally notify their families, but *you* will be responsible for preparing the official statement for the reports once the coroner has drawn all of his conclusions."

Did the duke not even know who the new Raven was? Richard found that somewhat startling, but at least he'd been given an excuse to stop discussing this with the duke and he was *probably* no longer under suspicion.

At least one good thing had come of this: Now Raven could continue her investigation.

Chapter 20: Necropolis

It really was a shame that Moretta had taken so long to explore the cemetery, but there was no time like the present. Since she had already lit her red lantern, which filtered a little better through the mist than she thought a lantern had any right to do, and was already in the cemetery, all she had to do was start walking.

She wended her way through the grave markers, taking in the distinctive differences in their shapes, and noting the family plots. Since she had changed back into the same dress she'd worn the previous night, she felt the stack of papers she had purloined thud against her thigh.

This reoccurred enough times that she finally gave in and curled up on a monumental stone bench, beside a weeping angel, and began to flip through them.

However, she quickly stowed them away again, when once she read a familiar name, and needed to calm her nerves.

Nearer the lake she could see the mausoleums, and decided she ought to test each of her keys on them in order to learn which worked where.

There was peculiar comfort to be found surrounded by this multitude of strangers. Not one of them could point at Moretta and condemn her for some act of criminality, of which she was indeed innocent. They knew which culprits had buried them, but they did not know Moretta had replaced them.

Indeed, had they occasion to arise from their graves, Moretta told herself they would be pleased to meet her. She had just been appraising the peace and tranquility which attended the grounds when she heard a bell of sorts, or perhaps it was a chime distorted by distance... Was that the chime by her door?

In any event, it had originated up on the hill, and having discerned this, Moretta lifted the hem of her skirts and trotted back up the hill to the gate. She was loath to travel back through the hidden door to the hideous basement room she would have needed to enter the house by, otherwise.

At the side of the house, she hung up the lantern and extinguished its light.

Along the side path to the house, Moretta saw three stretchers upon which cadaverous shapes were shrouded with uncertainty. Among the men who attended these stretchers she recognized the tense profile of Richard.

Her first assumption was that he had brought her business, but the fact that there were three bodies there alarmed her. Were these the same men she and Richard had killed the previous night? Had he betrayed her into the hands of the duke to save himself from censure? Had he given her up in the name of money? Or... had he turned on her for the sake of his family?

She shoved these whispers of dark suspicion aside, and schooled her feet to walk in accordance with her determination to guard herself from suspicion.

"Salutations!" she called as she approached the visibly agitated men at her door. "How might I be of assistance to you, gentlemen?"

One of them turned to her, and as the morning mist dispersed, she saw that the fellow's features were obscured by a stark scarlet Commedia mask. His two fellows formed with him a trio of *nearly* flawlessly mirror images to the three men she and Richard had defeated.

She gasped, but it was so subtle a sound, that she was more than less assured it had gone undetected.

"Call the coroner for us, girl!" ordered the fellow in the mask who had first twisted his neck in her direction.

She was so taken aback that her mouth could not but pop open.

"Are you a simpleton?" the second of these men demanded of her.

"The coroner must be away," Richard suggested, further astonishing Moretta.

Why shouldn't she be granted the full acknowledgment of a station she had striven so long to attain?

"This is his assistant," Richard continued. "My dear young lady, could you please allow us into the house and let these men rest in the examination room awaiting the return of your master?" Moretta could detect a note of urgency in Richard's voice which alerted her to some cause he may have to shield her identity.

"Yes, just let me unlock the place," she said, and pulled the chain of keys from her pocket.

Her back was aflame with uneasy suspicion as she turned it to the men, fearing they knew what she had done and would punish her summarily.

Instead, once the door was open, they merely pushed her aside to walk into the house ahead of her.

Standing in dismay against the wall of one tower of her home, Moretta watched them file past her.

Only Richard stopped, and took her hand to kiss it. With his lips still resting against her fingers, he muttered, "Forgive me for the indelicate intruders. One may expect a duke to employ only gentlemen, but the expectation can earn itself only frustration, it seems. Here, take this," he pressed a small purse into her hand. "The duke thought you a man, but the payment is still owed to you."

"Why is it necessary that he maintain that ignorance?" she asked, remembering the warnings she had given him, herself.

"I would that you had the chance to escape, Raven," he whispered in earnest, and grasped her hands both, brown intensity digging into her gray pools of thought. "I don't want you at the center of this."

"Of what?"

"Girl!" one of the masked men shouted at her.

"Adjourn to recess," she whispered, and winked before pulling away to tend to the duke's attendants.

She marked a prevailing degree of ignorance among them, beyond lacking awareness of her identity.

They stood by as she revealed their fellows' faces, and diagnosed the obvious causes of their deaths. It had been much easier to end their lives back when they were masked.

She was grateful now that she had seen only menacing masks rather than these frozen grimaces. Perhaps had she seen their faces during the attack, she would not have been sympathetic, even as she conducted their autopsies.

They were of course enemy combatants, who had threatened her life and Richard's both.

"Is this conclusive enough?" one of the living masked men asked.

"Does the coroner need to sign off on these men's documentation?" asked another.

Moretta considered. "You ought to have them here overnight, so that my master can use them when he returns," she told them in a practiced monotone.

This trio exchanged glances, but Moretta could see they were eager to have done with this business and leave.

"There are legal documents I ought to prepare for the coroner to sign," Richard said. "You may report back to the duke and tell him I have the situation under control."

Moretta internally raked together a prayer to the Almighty that these men would leave them, and by some miracle they assented.

"You must report back to the duke as soon as the coroner returns," one of the masked fellows said.

Moretta wished they would stop milling about, she couldn't keep track of who they were since hiding behind these masks, they were identical.

"I will do my duty," Richard bowed, and the men departed.

When Moretta closed the door behind them, she watched through the curtains to make certain they had truly left. When she knew they had not doubled back to spy on them, she turned to Richard.

"Here we go, again."

Chapter 21: Conjecture

Rather than go directly back to work, Richard and Raven partook in a brief lunch while he briefed her on what he had learned from the duke.

"He is growing suspicious," Richard explained at length, staring into his vaguely grayish brown tea.

"Suspicious of you?" she asked, stirring sugar into her own drink, which was a peculiar concoction of coffee and chocolate.

"Yes… he tested me, and I cannot know without a doubt that he has lost the suspicions he held against me, yet."

"You could stop helping me," she suggested between delicate bites of her cucumber sandwich. "I need to get the word out that the duke's armed secret forces wear red masks and are up to no good, but you needn't be associated with me."

"I object on a few grounds," Richard said gently, meeting her eyes firmly before continuing to say, "We cannot confirm that he is doing anything illegal, and I won't abandon you. Well, we can't prove he's doing something illegal unless of course you read something in those papers you hid from me and refuse to share what you've learned…"

She held his gaze, but did not hesitate to respond, saying, "They were keeping documentation regarding Amontillado's most prominent townspeople." She spoke in devastating earnest, her eyes never once wavering. "You may find it enlightening to know they were auditing your parents, as well... Under ordinary circumstances I may congratulate you on your affluent family, but I fear they may suffer the same fate as the Otranto's if the duke thinks he can get away with it."

He stared at her face, begging some quirk in her smile or twitch of her brow to betray a joke, a sick, cruel joke. However, there was no smile, and no twitch. Rather, her features were grim as she waited for him.

"My father is not so rich..." he said lamely, attempting to deflect the growing horror in his mind.

"But he *is* your father... When did you last visit home? I worry they may become hostages in order for the duke to control you if he thinks you may rebuff his orders."

Richard allowed those words to bring forth his own dark meditations. If he had failed to divert the duke's suspicions, he was most assuredly doomed. If he was not personally imperiled, his family would surely suffer for his shortcomings.

What horrors could be exacted on his dear, innocent parents for his simple greed? After all, had he but listened to the Raven to begin with, he would not be the duke's puppet, now! "Why didn't you tell me what you'd read before I left today?" he asked.

"I hadn't gone through it all. I was exploring the graveyard, though, and I started to read the documents over as I went."

"Just a little cheery morning reading to accompany your constitutional?" he asked, and couldn't help but snicker darkly. At least she hadn't betrayed him.

"I can see this troubles you," Raven said softly, "please allow me to present an option or two to you... firstly, you ought to ask your parents to go somewhere safer... Boezia may lend them the greatest safety."

"My father would never leave the factory behind, certainly not for as long as it would take to make him safe... Besides, my mother is devoted to her society clubs."

She shook her head as if this were really too bad but she had nothing better. "Then, my best advice is to do whatever the duke asks of you, or else help me expose his unlawful actions."

"I am under contract," he reminded her. "He can put my honor on the line."

"It is one thing to agree to a contract in good faith and another to find your trust betrayed by your employer," she told him. "You must make your choice soon before you are placed in an intolerable position."

He considered whether or not he ought to tell her what more he knew, but he fell back on her advice for he was at a loss. "Before I left, I received an invitation from the prince to a Masked Ether Frolic."

He watched her right brow rise until it was hidden in the shroud of her neat jet fringe, and her left wrinkled a pucker between her eyes. "You are not seriously thinking of *going* to such a dastardly excuse for a party, are you?"

"I do not know that I would call some harmless ether a dastardly element, it can be naught but beneficial, look what it does to surgery!"

"I was a medical student, I have read many a treatise on ether... however, because I have, I know it is not to be played with. You ought to be more responsible, as a respectable solicitor. Let the duke dangle his poor puppets on their ethereal nooses, but do not climb onto the scaffold with them."

"Why are you speaking in such dire terms?" he asked, vexed now as she appeared to be exaggerating the risk.

She snapped her fingers in his face, both her ordinarily narrowed eyes wide as if they screamed insults at him. "Will you live in ignorance forever? It is time to awaken! Why would someone who is attempting to steal his people's money invite them to a party where their senses shall be dulled? Answer me that riddle, boy!"

Richard sat back in his chair, staring at her as if she'd slashed a stark line across his face. He had to recover from this shame! "You don't think he would work such a scheme on a grand scale when he was under suspicion, do you? How foolhardy would he be?"

"Simple: have you not heard the dreadful mishaps which take place when those quack chemists trail into town with those vaporous demons in their wake? Those revels far outstrip the powers of alcohol, they put old Bacchus to shame! Accidents kill at such parties because it takes so little to kill someone!"

"You've read this... in your journals?" Richard asked.

"Of course, I have! But I have also heard these things reported in the local papers from all corners of Zibelaude!"

Richard sat in silence, and watched Raven's face, which kept screaming even after she fell silent. "Lenore will be there..." he muttered softly.

"And?" she demanded. "What is she to you?"

"She is... she is a lady for whom I feel the deepest affection... and though her behavior may not always be worthy of her, I know she will attend this party... I must make amends with her after what happened yesterday..."

"Must you?" she sat back in her chair, and broodingly stirred her coffee before downing a great deal of the cold brew in a single gulp.

"I must... she is my destiny, Raven." He watched one corner of her lips twitch.

"Destiny..." she muttered under her breath. "I've met a lawyer who believes in *destiny*..." She rolled her silvery eyes before peevishly snapping up a tea cake and eating it slightly more brutishly than was her usual habit.

Richard cleared his throat, as if their disagreement were merely an annoyance trapped in his throat, and rose to his feet. "It seems I must do some paperwork now, my dear... What shall I say?"

"Say that the coroner declares the lot of them dead," she said, wiping her hands and rising from the table and giving him a harsh look. "And that he who delivers those words is liable to join them soon."

Chapter 22: A Second Face

Moretta took no pleasure in donning the mantle of pitiful harbinger Cassandra, but there was naught else to be done. She and Richard parted on disagreeable terms, but there was no suitable remedy. Not yet, however.

She paced her newly empty home, before giving in and beginning to examine the new cadavers given her once more. Before she began the study, she sprayed perfume throughout the room to relieve her delicate sensibilities from the burden of their stench.

There was little point in further diagnosing the deaths she herself had witnessed, but there was still the chance that the duke had forgotten some evidence on their persons, and she could tap into the secrets of their conspiracy.

She was compelled despite the dictates of modesty to strip the men down to their stockings and their shirtsleeves, but found a reward for such. It came in the form of several scribbled notes, though their contents were not immediately obvious to her.

They were written in codes, in symbols which she sighed to discover were inscrutable to her. The symbolic makeup of these varied between alchemical signs and ancient runes, with a few Greek letters mixed in, but without a reference point for how many of these matched up with their widely accepted meaning left Moretta without answers.

Still… she smoothed out these notes before going about the standard process of cleaning the bodies and preparing them for burial.

Once they were all shut away in boxes owing to great personal exertion on her part, Moretta was finally left alone with her thoughts… well, except that it was at this time that Renata finally awoke from her nap.

At the first plaintive *meow*, Moretta was relieved from her thoughts as she was given another mundane task—namely feeding the cat.

As she watched the happiness with which Renata devoured her food, Moretta was again assailed with the knowledge that she must rescue Richard from the pitfalls of his own foolhardiness.

Even if he had upset her, she had to rescue him. It was imperative just as it was irritating. Her fingers were tapping out a restless rhythm on the countertop, and she gazed out her window upon the bleak winter's day with foul temper simmering in her soul.

Her fiendish opponent could not yet know who he was dealing with. He may not even remember what cause she had to defy her temperament and fume over his continued existence.

Unless of course he had been dissembling when he assumed the coroner for Amontillado was a man, to make her think he had failed to pick up her scent… She already had scant insight into what his agents knew, it had been a supreme boon that not every document she retrieved from them had been encoded… Was that just what they were willing to let someone see?

Renata leapt onto the counter and rubbed her head against Moretta's arm.

"What shall I do?" Moretta croaked as her hand automatically began to stroke along her back.

Renata *meowed* curiously, an oddity in her case as most often it was she who directed Moretta's soundest judgment.

"Richard is going to get himself murdered," Moretta sighed, scratching between Renata's ears, then along her spine.

Renata made a questioning noise.

"He's going to a party held by that fiend, Julian. I have to save him; he is my only ally, and my only friend."

Renata peered up at her.

"Aside from you, dear."

Renata flicked her tail to show she had just barely forgiven Moretta for the slight, but she had better not do it again.

"It's a risk… I could be discovered… I will require a mask…"

Renata rubbed her head against Moretta's arm again, and purred furiously to stem the tide of her anxiety.

"Will you go with me to purchase it?"

Renata made a noise Moretta chose to interpret in the affirmative, whether right or wrong.

"I'll need to attend to some other matters of import just in case I die, but after that I know just where to go."

She packed up the evidence she had gathered of the duke's foul assessments of who was richest in his dominion. Along with that she added in her explanation of the circumstances under which those had been procured.

Moretta knew she needed to keep the coded messages to herself pending her efforts to fully decode them.

Her heart pounded out a defiant rebellion against the notion that she was doomed. Even so, she was all but signing off on her last will and testament, so she could not particularly help it if she happened to be the slightest bit morbid in so doing.

Renata sat on Moretta's writing desk, flicking her tail back and forth, making it nearly impossible for Moretta to actually write.

"Is that your way of telling me to stop?" Moretta asked, brushing Renata's tail away with the back of her hand. "I still have work to do, you know, this is actually important."

Renata made an annoyed sneeze-like noise, but Moretta gave her an equally irritated look right in the eyes.

"I mean it," she said, "I can't honestly go out there without ensuring that they know what I've learned. What if I die out there, eh? Everything I know dies with me. That's why I have to get all of this sent to Aunt Monique."

Renata began to lick her paw, and went back to flicking her tail, not making it the least bit easier to write than it had been before.

Still, Moretta knew better than to fight back against the will of the cat, so she merely worked around her to the best of her ability.

At last, as she saw the light fading from the horizon, she knew she could delay no longer. "I'll get ready now," she informed her cat, somewhat peevishly.

Renata stretched, as if this had failed to impress her, but she still followed Moretta's movements to the wardrobe. She uttered a chortling *meow*, sitting behind Raven.

"Yes, I know," Moretta sighed, and rolled her eyes. "But I've already decided to obey you, isn't that good enough?"

Renata's next utterance rang with irony, so Moretta just sighed, aware she'd have to do better.

"Oh, just leave me be," Moretta sighed, "I'm going to do my job, now, and you've prodded me along enough, already."

With Renata on her shoulders, Moretta ventured out of the house, and told herself she would return soon to prepare herself for the party.

First, she paid a diligent visit to the office of the postmaster general.

A shiny new android greeted her behind the desk, and informed her in its buzzing, whirring voice, that all the humans were away, planning for the party at the duke's castle that evening.

Moretta grimaced at the contraption, and handed over the thick safely puzzle locked box she had chosen for the occasion. In her line of work, such enigma boxes were a necessity.

The android made polite commentary on it before stowing it away and promising to ship it off on the next delivery to the capitol, which would take place the very next morning.

Thusly deprived of diversions, Moretta pulled up her hood to hide Renata and her fears, and set out for Bonnie's.

Chapter 23: Pink Roses

It was more difficult to apologize to Lenore than Richard had first suspected. Due to her behavior the night before signaling how very jealous she was of his time, he had thought all he had to do was arrive at her door and ask for her to attend the party with him.

Not so.

She hardly even bothered to acknowledge that he was at her door, but he could see her on the upper floor, watching him down the bridge of her nose in disdain.

It was a good thing he had come armed! He revealed his first weapon by pulling it out from the folds of his cloak: a bouquet of pink roses which did seem to catch her interest.

Richard revealed his secret weapon, then, by tucking the bouquet under his arm and holding up a box which had been in his coat pocket. He opened the box to allow its contents to glitter up at Lenore in the light from both lanterns hanging on either side of her door.

It was a bejeweled brooch, and he knew she would not fail to notice how the flowers matched the gems set into it in a little circle around an elegant cameo. He saw her mouth fall open, and she ran from the window, causing a clamor throughout the house as she swept through it.

Richard stood shifting his stance uneasily as he attempted to anticipate which pose would be to his best advantage.

Too soon, she arrived at the door, shunting a confused maid out of the way. "Is that for me?" she asked in a twittering voice which ought to belong to a princess from a book of fairy stories.

"Of course, it is," Richard replied, holding out both of them to her. He held his breath, hoping desperately that she would not turn him down and take the expensive gifts, anyway.

Instead, she reached out and took them both, with a broad grin. She took a moment to appreciate them both, taking deep breaths to inhale the perfume from the roses and turning the brooch to admire its sparkle.

"I ask that you accompany me to the festivities this evening at Usher Abbey, so that we may both take in the ether together," Richard said while she was thus occupied and in a favorable mood.

Again, he discovered this method was successful as she squealed, hugging the gifts tightly to her. "I was hoping you would ask me!" she cried.

Gone was the previous night's outrage, along with the haughty disapproval of the last several minutes.

"Do you already have your mask and garments prepared?" Richard asked. "I shall attempt to coordinate with you."

"I'll do some coordinating of my own!" she was bubbling over with excitement which made Richard's heart swell with pride for having accomplished that. "I'll match my new brooch and arrange these roses into my hair!" she cheered, and suddenly Richard came to the uncomfortable realization of what he'd gotten himself into.

"So... I'll need a pink ascot, cummerbund and hat ribbon..." He cringed at the affront to his masculinity, but as long as he was there with Lenore, the clothing wouldn't matter... too much...

"Oh, but that's not enough!" Lenore cried. "You ought to wear pink and white pinstripes! That way we will truly be a matched set!"

Richard realized just how much money he would have to invest in preparing for this one event, even if he only chose to rent his suit and accessories...

"Is there some kind of problem?" she demanded, and Richard glanced up to see her pout gathering a dainty storm behind her eyes.

"I can't afford that..." he admitted, although he knew it was a grave sin against the sex. He simply couldn't help it.

"Well then! You should have thought about that before you even bothered coming to my door!" she snapped. "Try to make yourself presentable before you come back, and if I approve of your appearance, we will go together!" She flounced back into the house, and ordered her maid to, "Slam that door like I mean it!"

Richard stared at the door between them in bald-faced shock. That shock did not fade when the maid quietly opened the door a sliver so he could see her sheepish smile.

"Begging your pardon, sir," she whispered before closing the door a second time, but much more quietly.

Richard's ears burned with the echo of the slam, and of Raven's prophetic warning that Lenore only wanted him so long as he was rich. He would not allow himself to think as little of Lenore as the coroner appeared to, regardless.

She was possessed of good sense in most other matters, but as for Lenore, she was merely mistaken. She was new to Amontillado, and could not understand the local social niceties as well as Richard did.

Lenore was a lady of consequence, and was thusly endowed with fine tastes. It was simply Richard's responsibility to live up to the expectations which refined tastes demanded of him. It was hardly Lenore's fault if he failed!

Slowly, reluctantly, Richard trudged away from the Roget town home, back into town to secure better and worthier offerings for his lady love.

Chapter 24: La Muta

Moretta's weaknesses stood on trial in the case of masks versus willpower. Attending to the case was a well-meaning one woman jury who smiled at Moretta and offered to help her pick the perfect mask.

"What does the dress you plan to wear to the party look like?" the woman asked, and Moretta cringed.

She *had* been greeted with the two dresses she had previously ordered so it was possible to choose one of the two and wear it, even if it *were* fresh from the seamstress... But if they got into a real scuffle that could ruin it forever and she would never have the chance to wear it again...

Would wearing all black be more noticeable in this town than wearing something flamboyant? By now it must be noted that she favored a monochromatic wardrobe, so if she wished to disguise herself, she may do better to defy her conventional mode of dress.

"You know, I really don't want to stand out," Moretta admitted after mulling this over and trying to look at each mask in turn without having a panic attack.

As Moretta had expected, the saleswoman gasped. "But are you not eligible? This is the sort of party where you will be at the best advantage to secure yourself a suitor! The men there will be the best in the city all in the same place!"

"Honestly, I am not in a good place to acquire a suitor just now... I wish I were, but I don't think it would be appropriate at this juncture... is there some way I could project an aura of mystery?"

That would get her point across, wouldn't it?

"Ah," a smile spread across the woman's lips. "You want *la muta*! It drives men wild!"

Sure, it was missing the point, and she was now looking at a mask the saleswoman proposed that she ought to put on her own face, but Moretta smiled, anyway. This was a black velvet affair, with a placid face molded in, and gilded with baroque patterns around the edges. Pearls surrounded the eyes, and altogether, in a purely artistic sense, Moretta could not deny it was lovely.

"Oh, and it comes with a veil!" the saleswoman produced a lacy veil which had a series of pearls stitched into it.

For the veil alone, Moretta couldn't help but buy the set. She'd received a quick tutorial by the time she walked out of the shop, so that she knew how to fit the little black pearl into her mouth to hold the mask steady on her face.

When she returned home, she released Renata from her hood and showed her the mask. "Do you like it? It's called *la muta* because while I'm wearing it I cannot speak… that means I cannot reveal anything I don't mean to, and nobody will recognize my voice."

"*Meow,*" said Renata flippantly.

"I thought you'd say that," she sighed, and tucked the mask back into its box. "Still, I think it's the best possible idea."

Even without Renata's approval, she was running out of time to prepare for the party. She donned one of her new dresses. It was the eggplant-colored one, since it picked up some of the accents in her mask… even if it *were* purple and a little pretentious.

She polished a full-length mirror in one of the upper floor rooms and observed the full effect on its surface. Her disguise was so complete it unnerved her.

Despite how unnerving the mask was, disguise still meant safety to her. She tried to tell herself this was just like donning an alias before a new mission began.

She had duties to attend to at Usher Abbey, and there was no room for fear in the face of duty. Everyone at that ether frolic was more or less doomed, and Richard would be there with that silly girl Lenore.

This was what had necessitated the disguise. Moretta had proven that he would not listen to her despite how true what she told him was, as long as it threatened his impression of the duke as a noble patron or Lenore as a virtuous woman.

If he wouldn't believe her as herself, she would just have to be there for him without his knowing it was her.

Still, Moretta glared at her own reflection in the dim light of the bedroom. Something was still missing. Richard had spoken to her face to face often enough that he may recognize her eyes if he were permitted to look into them…

A thought occurred to her and she dashed to her own room, never removing the mask as it was good last-minute training to keep it on.

Back in her room, among the things her aunt had sent her with, were a pair of analysis goggles. As she had suspected, all Moretta had to do was fit these goggles into the mask's eye sockets, and she could look through the analytical goggles, as well!

She toggled the settings as she placed the mask back on, and managed to set up the night vision. That would certainly help!

She was very nearly optimistic, but she couldn't bring herself to dream she would be completely successful. Perhaps with the goggles in she would stand out more than she meant to... However, she could hope that she didn't look like herself... or whoever Richard thought she was.

Renata was at the door, watching her quietly, and Moretta curtseyed to her, silent behind her mute mask. She received a tail flick in return, and Renata blinked dismissively.

Though she wanted to defend how much work had gone into this new appearance, Moretta was still wearing the mask, so she held it in. Perhaps that was a good idea in general.

She started to the door, and made her last minute preparations. Since she had only one umbrella, Moretta was disappointed to see that it had suffered more damage in the past storm than she'd thought it would be. It was sorely in need of attention, as the tiny hinges creaked cringingly in response to Moretta's insistent attempt to open it.

Her disguise would be completely ruined if she let the rain which had begun to drum down on Amontillado. She hoped spring would mean the rain would stop coming down so often, but there was a reason spring was often called the rainy season... Well, that was yet another cheery thought to warm her heart.

She stared at the disappointing umbrella, and wished she could sigh, though the mask prevented it. All she could do was hope the umbrella wouldn't give up on her before she got to the party… or after it, for that matter, the whole getup had been somewhat expensive.

As she opened the umbrella to test it, she recalled that some people believed opening umbrellas indoors was bad luck. Well, that really was too bad.

She hadn't the time to worry about petty superstitions when Richard was in trouble. If he'd only believed her in the first place, she wouldn't have to go anywhere near masks or that horrid castle of the duke's.

He had better stop being an idiot after this! It was one thing to start out as an idiot, but if he *stayed* stupid after yet another bit of evidence that she spoke the truth.

With that last bit of stalling behind her, Moretta hastened away from her new home. One more time in her life, she would face off against her arch-nemesis.

Chapter 25: Tragedia Dell'Arte

Richard forced himself to put on a happy face before arriving at Lenore's house. He was already tremendously uncomfortable due to his rented suit—which was not quite the right size for him and pinched him in the biceps—he wasn't sure the mask he'd rented would be up to Lenore's standards, either.

But he ought to be bubbling over with pride and gratitude for even having the *chance* to impress Lenore. She had exacting standards, as he'd learned, so if he actually did by some miracle live up to what she wanted from him, he could hope to maintain that status in the future.

He stepped out of the cab, and walked toward the Roget house's door. He cleared his throat before he knocked on the door, and finally brought himself to grasp the knocker and let it send echoing thuds throughout the house.

Before long, the maid opened the door for him, and pulled it all the way open with her head bowed. "Please step inside, and let the lady see you," she said in a soft, demure voice as she gestured Richard into the atrium.

Richard's shoes clicked against the tile floors, and he walked onto the compass mosaic formed by the coffee-brown and beige tiles.

A stairwell curved up three floors ahead of him, spiraling over the circular central space upon which a chandelier shone down. He was so dazzled by all of this he almost didn't see Lenore among them.

She didn't let that stand. She cleared her throat so loudly it bounced off the walls.

When Richard's eyes finally traced their way down from the chandelier to the stairwell once more, he saw Lenore posing in a bright pink confection of silk, her hair arranged in a pompadour of ringlets and roses as she glittered with diamonds.

She took his breath away. It was amazing to experience her beauty and striking grace again as if for the first time. He dropped to one knee and pressed his fist to his chest, even though the suit he wore constricted around his every joint in protest.

"My lady," he said softly, though the sound carried through the cylindrical chamber. "I may be unworthy, but I would be infinitely honored to escort you to the ether frolic."

He waited as she paused, considering his worthiness. While he hadn't exactly seen some other man lined up to take his place, that didn't mean Algernon wouldn't swoop in from stage left and take up the role of the understudy...

"I have decided you may take me," Lenore said with an imperious sniff. "Come! Escort me down the stairs!"

Richard jumped to his feet and trotted up the stairs despite the buzzing in his skull that was beginning to dizzy him. He reached up one hand to her as he gazed up at her in awe, and watched as under her half-mask which was adorned with yet *more* rose petals, her pink-painted lips curved. She placed her pink-gloved hand in his, and took the first step so he knew to lead her down with him.

He knew he ought to be pleased, even fainting with happiness, after all, Lenore Roget had said yes to *him*! His mind ought to be permeated with a cloud of champagne bubbles and diamonds...

Yet something still troubled him. Why were Raven's words still echoing in his mind? Why did he still see her silvery eyes screaming silently at him?

Why did she have to try so hard to dissuade him from attending this party? Didn't she realize what a ripe opportunity it was for him? He wasn't a hermit, the way she was, so of course their perspectives would be different.

His heart was so troubled that he nearly tripped down the stairs, but his near-collision with the tiles below pulled him out of the muck.

He cast another glance over his shoulder to Lenore, hoping the sight of her would deprogram the track of morose doubt Raven had put him on.

"Look where you're going!" Lenore cried, and he whipped his head back around, blushing.

"Forgive me, my lady... I was merely having difficulty keeping my eyes off of you."

He heard her make a preening sound behind him, and hoped that meant he had once again met with her approval. This was exhausting!

Once the maid curtseyed to them and opened the door, Richard discovered that while he'd been in the Roget home, a rainstorm had started. Perfect. Now the sky could cry for his struggles.

The cabbie seemed eager to duck back under his canopy and Richard couldn't blame him, but his main concern at the present moment was ensuring that not only did Lenore's hair and gown remain pristine, but that his own appearance did not suffer in the downpour.

"Well?" Lenore asked the moment she'd stopped fussing about the state of the umbrella the cab driver was holding up for her and the way Richard scrambled to help her into the cab.

Richard coiled one hand on the handle of the cab door, and knew beneath his glove, his knuckles were turning white as the glove, itself. What was he supposed to say? Was he supposed to do something special? His hand tightened still more as he attempted to cycle through proprieties he'd learned since his childhood.

Here was Lenore, sitting in the cab and wearing a full-length dress for the first time since he'd met her, but he had thought he'd been just formal enough…

He gulped as the fullness of his apparent ignorance opened up before him. Full-length skirts on Zibelauden women meant formal, so everything he'd been doing up until that point ought to be correct, shouldn't it?

Lenore must expect something from him, after all! Beads of sweat appeared on Richard's brow. When Lenore peered in at him from inside the carriage, he nervously scrambled in rather than stand frozen for too long on the threshold.

He expected her to allow him to sit next to her, but Lenore's pout challenged that assumption. Thus, he moved to sit across from her, instead. What a thick skull he had! What knight would presume to sit beside a lady as if he were her equal? It really was shameful that he had even considered it!

"Finally you come to your senses!" Lenore snapped.

"Sorry." Richard felt that he deserved this scolding, so he took it humbly as he closed the door and bid the driver begin the journey to Usher Abbey.

"Good." Lenore made a point of huffing as she settled herself in her seat. "In the future, remember that you should open the door for a lady *at once*."

"Yes, Miss Roget…" Richard shut his eyes tightly for a moment, searching for inner strength to survive this ordeal, and then climbed in after her.

Richard noticed as the ride went on that Lenore was peering out the window and seemed to have forgotten he was there, altogether. He supposed that was predictable. He'd long since stopped smiling. Something important was missing here.

He would have thought that after he went to all this trouble of measuring up to her standards, and after he had offered her such a wonderful evening at the Abbey, she would be abuzz with sharing her excitement with him. Wouldn't she?

He gazed out the window along with her, hoping to find something out there that he might comment on and regain her attention. Finally, as the darkened streets yielded no conversation pieces, he asked, "Are you looking for the first sign of the Abbey?"

Lenore's eyes momentarily flickered in his direction. "I wanted to see if any of my friends were also on the way. They said they would go."

Richard was grateful for the mask he wore, as it protected his features from the scrutiny which they would have earned had Lenore seen his grimace.

It was normal for a lady to seek her friends, especially at a time like this. Of course, she wanted to see them… he just wished she still wanted to look at *him*… that was more or less a selfish fantasy.

As he brooded over the topic, he caught his first sight of what Duke Julian had done with his castle to decorate it for the evening's frolic party.

Lights were aimed at the castle as if it were a stage, tinted blue red and green and orange, all changing in turn, contrasting and blending as the patterns shuffled. It didn't even matter that it was raining, now as they exited the cab, and the two of them climbed out to enter the throng which entered the castle.

No one who lived outside of Amontillado could have dreamed the expert extravagance of the Abbey that night. Women's dresses looked more like fantastical confections from the dreams of children than physical adornment. Men wore suits in colors such as lily pad green and lemon pulp yellow. Smiles were plastered to faces like moth wings, and fluttered just as much.

Richard considered the longer they walked in the utterly transformed halls how the Abbey was deceptively named. One would expect that it was a place of worship. Perhaps that was an adequate description, after all. Not that nuns or monks or any so reverent a person would deign to enter, were they forewarned. Now, despite the way it normally appeared, pleasure reigned at the Abbey.

Echoing through they Abbey's halls, the sound of locking doors alarmed no one but Richard. He was stopped in his tracks when the screams began. Cries of "Let us go!" He then saw that men just like the Red Mask Lenore was talking to had started pointing out the locked doors... he chose to lose himself in the haze, taking in the first direct puff from a large crystalline object he'd never seen before.

The ether made him giddy; and Lenore behind him exploded in a fit of titters he couldn't help mimic.

Whereas before the whole castle had already seemed beautiful and alive with a carnival atmosphere, as Richard allowed the tide of guests to lead him into a ballroom, he felt that the castle was overtaken by fairy magic.

A grin appeared on his face which was visible just below his mask as he twirled along with the other intoxicated partygoers across the ballroom floor. The wondrous gas hung thick in the air, and his heart was lightened as the whole party formed into pairs and began to dance a polka.

The steps were erratic and their laughter rose up throughout the room with more intoxicated glee than any crowd of drunken fools had ever mustered in that room.

Richard let his worries melt away as in this flood of laughter and masks, he spun Lenore around and around again. Life had never been such a dream.

Chapter 26: The Ethereal Harbinger

Moretta joined the flow of masked revelers who were filtering into the party so that she would go undetected. There was no need in her mind to follow the throng as they passed the first double column of ether-gasping machines.

She wrinkled her nose at the exclamations of glee which escaped the lot of them, and shook her head beneath her veil. Among them was Richard, she knew, but this was her one chance to explore the Abbey, and she chose to take it, first.

She suspected that Amelia was there in the darkest caverns of the Abbey, and it was her solemn duty to retrieve her. Sure the uproar from the ballroom was distracting, but as long as she could still hear it, she was sure she could find it again when the trouble started. For now, she only needed to monitor it with the least hint of suspicion and make her way down to the depths of the castle... somehow.

The castle was a labyrinthine array of halls and doorways, and she suspected not a shortage of secret doors to accompany those she could see.

It was a good thing she had received some training in discovering secret passageways, because she did not anticipate having the time to explore them at her leisure for very long.

She pressed on down the halls in search of answers, nonetheless. While attempting to make her footsteps as quiet as they could be, she noticed that the wooden archways overhead were creaking, as if groaning with the secrets they had to carry.

As disturbing as the thought of those ancient wooden arches possibly giving way to impale her was,

Moretta had to press on, nonetheless. The deeper Moretta went into the halls, the more she could feel the secrets weighing on her.

Further still from the revelry, the laughter became distorted by the distance.

Moretta paused, attempting to decide whether it may be more prudent to turn back so she could hear their sounds more clearly. If revelry turned to shrieking, how would she know?

Was discovering where Amelia had been hidden more important than saving Richard? She ducked into a side passage to contemplate.

Richard was with Lenore, most likely intoxicated. He hadn't believed her to start with, and now lacking his sobriety, why would he follow her away from all the fun?

She knew who *did* both require and desire help, though. Thus her choice was made.

There had to be some indication as to what purpose all these rooms served, or else the duke, himself, would get lost, wouldn't he?

If *she* were trying to hide some illegal and inhumane scientific practices, she would pit it all as far underground as humanly possible. Furthermore, if she knew anything about Duke Julian's proclivities, he would repurpose the ancient dungeons for just such a thing.

Grimly setting her jaw and all but biting through the threads which bound the pearl in her mouth to the body of the mask, Moretta followed what she knew of the outward anatomy of the castle toward her estimate of where she would find the tower.

There were four in total, and most castles were arranged in such a manner that the staircases spiraled through these towers... Though certainly, Duke Julian could have altered the make-up of the castle for his singular purposes.

Still, the fact that the door she identified was locked gave her some hope that it was hiding *something* important behind it.

She pulled back a panel where the handle of an ordinary door would have been. Within, she discovered a panel of gears, none of which matched up to one another, with a vial of green fluid beside a piston which she decided was meant to fuel the gear mechanism. Only one of the gears was turning, which meant the fluid drained at a slow rate, but Moretta was still not secure in that rate of drainage.

At least she could trust the complexity of this mechanism to hide something worth finding. She would just have to open it without alerting anyone.

It quickly became evident that the oddly viscous liquid beside the gears would leak out of the vial it was stored in whenever she erred in the arrangement.

There was a lever on the opposite side of the mechanism which was marked, "refill," but she knew if this were any sort of decent lock it would pull the gears back out of alignment. They were all connected to thin metal arms and when she moved them, she could feel the mechanism resisting. It would be all too easy for them to snap back out of alignment and possibly it would even raise an alarm.

She took a deep breath to steel herself and fight back against the urge to lose her temper. She could do this if she only let herself think clearly…

It took slightly longer than she would ever proudly admit, but at last all the gears lined up properly. Even though her efforts had drained all the liquid from the tube, an unseen mechanism clicked to alert her that the door was about to swing open to reveal the spiral staircase she had been seeking.

The staircase had a bluish light which emanated from the base of it and filled the whole corridor with eerie atmosphere.

Ah well, that was more or less a good sign, she decided as she took her first steps down the stairs and let the door close behind her with a resounding *click*.

Part of her wished she had brought Renata with her, as the cat's purring could have calmed her at a time like this, but she refused to put anyone else she cared about in danger. The idea of Renata safely tucked away in her house until such a time as Moretta could return did somewhat comfort her, though not as much as the cat's company might have…

She stopped abruptly as she realized that she could hear voices below. Why wasn't everyone at the party where they belonged?

Moretta crouched against the wall and all but held her breath in an effort to both hear what was happening below and remain unheard, herself.

The words were somewhat distorted, but out of what could be clearly discerned, she heard, "Why haven't the treatments been successful yet, Dr. Shade?"

Anyone with a name like that had to be on some list somewhere, right? Why couldn't Moretta remember reading about him anywhere? The League ought to have warned her about him... Was that an alias?

The voice she supposed could belong to none other than Dr. Shade replied, "Because she is being stubborn! The girl's spirit has fled several times during the process! If I only knew where it was going —"

"And why *don't* you know where it's going? Is that *not* what you're good at?" That contemptuous voice could belong only to Duke Julian after all these years... Moretta had known she may encounter him, but so soon?

"The study of phantomology is not yet that advanced, and I'm going and one cannot rush science!"

Moretta considered how much she had actually read on the study of phanotmology. All she knew was that the dead could return if they felt like it and not much beyond that... Was it really that detailed of a science?

"Try *harder!* Once the subject starts waking up in the middle of experiments it's only a matter of time before she's useless!"

Moretta traced a dagger in her belt. She needed a plan... Where could she hide? If one of them started to come up the stairs, they couldn't help but either see her or trip over her... Did she dare run back outside to find a hiding place?

How long could she afford to wait out there? Moreover, could she even afford to reopen the mechanism? How much time would that lose her?

Moretta decided to take her chances and press deeper into the spiraling dungeon. She took slow, careful steps, never making a sound, though her hand was on her gun this time, with the full knowledge that if she assassinated the duke, she would have to go into hiding for the rest of her life.

It would be so worth the price...

By some great mercy, she did not have to make that choice straightaway. At the foot of the spiral staircase she found a series of carts upon which were stored medical implements she recognized as chest spreaders and scalpels, among other things.

So this was a doctor who specialized in ghosts and yet he still dealt with the corporeal forms... If he were the polite sort he may just occasionally visit the graveyard. Moretta would have easily welcomed him in... they could have had tea!

Well, it was not to be. She climbed into one of the carts which mercifully was not so full that she could not fit her petite frame into it.

Outside the cart, she could still hear the duke arguing with the doctor, but it was on the mundane and repetitive topic of how slow the doctor's studies were, and had descended into *ad hominem*. So petty of the duke! He was just as she remembered him.

At last, though it was a mixed mercy, the duke declared that he was going to attend his party, for his guests must be eager for him to make an appearance.

While Moretta did not like the way he said that, it would at least leave her alone with the doctor and his 'patient.'

She noticed a vial in one of the racks hidden away with her in the cart, and used the night vision function of her goggles to see what it was: *letheon.*

Moretta knew one way to make a man forget she was there, not to mention take him completely out of the equation... so if only the duke would hurry... As she heard the duke's steps departing, she slowly closed her fingers around the vial.

If only the dispensing mechanism were in the cart with her! She would have to risk reaching out of it, or even climbing completely out of her hiding place, to search for a way to either inject it or forcefully cause the doctor to inhale it...

Drat.

Still, she could plainly hear the doctor's muffled muttering to himself as his own steps echoed to a further corner of the room... If only she could be sure he wasn't looking in her direction...

Hesitantly, Moretta opened the door to the cart which was nearest the wall, and would prevent the doctor from noticing straightaway. She slowly climbed out, using the other side's closed doors to shield her from view. As she had hoped, there was a device meant to pump gasses into the mouths of patients waiting in plain view atop the cart.

As swiftly as she could, Moretta snatched it off the top of the cart and retreated behind her shield again to prevent detection. With some confidence, she was able to fit the vial into the mechanism, and with that, she knew she was prepared.

The one remaining difficulty was springing upon her victim without alerting either him or the duke. She could no more afford to have him sound the alarm than escape her, so with hungry eyes she carefully peeked out from behind the cart.

The doctor's back was to her, as he fumbled with something she could not see as it was hidden behind him.

A body was stretched out within a cylindrical device on which she could see various readouts which showed the patient was in a state of stability.

Well, that was a good sign, if nothing else.

If she were not such a devoted pessimist, she may even have smiled behind her mask, risk of losing hold of the pearl or not. However, there was still the chance that something would go wrong, and so she steeled herself.

It was good that she was prepared, as the doctor turned back in her direction to attend to his patient.

From her hiding place, Moretta considered how limited the time allotted to her happened to be. If the duke planned to harm his rich guests, he was doubtless strolling off to inflict said harm. Thus Richard was in peril, and she was losing her chance to defend him.

However, even if the person in Dr. Shade's cylindrical monitoring device *weren't* Amelia, she had a duty to this person, no less than to young Miss Otranto.

It was time to get risky.

The dungeon had to get the occasional rat, didn't it?

Moretta took out a dagger, and began tapping in a way which she predicted would annoy the doctor, but which mimicked the way a rat would skitter along a floor.

Sure enough, the doctor's irritated exclamations greeted her efforts, and she couldn't help but smirk at the colorful insults he chose to offend the rat, his mother, and all of rat-kind.

She tapped again, hoping this would at last bring her prey to her, and indeed, she heard those irritated feet approach.

"Incompetent exterminators..." he muttered angrily to himself. "Next time I'll use my *own* inventions! Time to go back to experimenting on rats!"

Moretta steeled herself. Her muscles were taut with potential energy, and her hands grew tighter on each part of the apparatus, so that she certainly would not drop it. Her nerves did not vanish without a fight, but the instant she saw the doctor on the opposite side of the cart from her, she released all the tension in a flurry of action.

First, she kicked the wheeled cart so that it slammed against the doctor and threw him off kilter, then she leapt up from the floor.

While the doctor was floundering in surprise, his arms flailing all the while, Moretta forced the mouth portion of the device over his own, and switched the device on.

His eyes narrowed and he batted the device away, but she saw his eyes beginning to cloud over. "What are you doing, woman?" he demanded, and made a grab for her, but his movements were too sluggish to stop her from slamming the device's mouthpiece against his lips once more.

Though she had considered replying, the pearl in her mouth prevented it, and she decided it was better that way. He would not remember her voice, he would not remember her eyes, he probably couldn't even tell what color her hair was. When he woke, he could tell his master nothing to help him locate her one day.

When the light faded from his eyes, and he slumped back against a large cylindrical tube in sleep, Moretta switched off the device. An idea occurred to her, and lest he should rise out of the slumber she'd forced him into, she opened this tube and lifted him into it. This way, he would at least be slowed down by the necessity of having to climb out of the thing she firmly locked him into.

With that, she went to the cylinder she knew Amelia would be in, and opened it. There she lay, bound in a plain cotton dress, and Moretta knew she had some work ahead of her.

Chapter 27: The Mute Stranger

Richard had never done so much dancing in his entire life. Now he sat exhausted by the punch bowl, downing many a glassful of the vaguely ginger-tinged strawberry concoction.

Lenore had found several friends to preen herself in front of, and he was content, as he didn't much mind watching as she posed to her best advantage.

He was distracted from languidly contemplating how beautifully Lenore's golden curls had been arranged and how well her corset had molded her silhouette by a blaring fanfare blasted through trumpet-wielding android heralds. In his half-conscious state, it took a moment for Richard to comprehend what he was seeing.

During that moment, Duke Julian stepped through a balcony door wearing a fashionably gilded gas mask. "Are all of my guests enjoying their time here?" he asked in a muffled voice through a vocal amplifier which could not completely hide the fact that the mask muffled his voice.

Cheers went up from the guests, but though Richard was no less pleased with the evening, he was so sluggish he only raised his half-empty punch glass.

"Good! Because the party has only just begun!"

Doors opened out of the very walls and from each one of them stepped a man in a black cloak and red mask.

Richard's heart jumped, but he hadn't the strength to muster his limbs to any purpose, be it rising from his seat or pulling Lenore to safety near him. Not that she would be any safer near him in his current state, he noted begrudgingly to himself.

Why were these masked fellows at the party? Certainly, even if they worked for the duke, they were some kind of enforcer, weren't they? Enforcers wouldn't come out to a social function like this!

So who invited these men? What business did they have amongst Amontillado's revelers? This was the town's lifeblood, so the duke ought to know better than to let another party get violent in the same month.

Unwelcome, Raven's warning and her screaming eyes resurfaced in his troubled mind, so that he recalled every dire proclamation she had made defaming the duke. He had already known those red-masked men were the servants of the duke, but still he had persisted in denying that the duke had sinister intentions.

Not only that, but he had come to the conclusion that *Raven* may be in danger from the duke, but not him! Her accusations of foul play had been misdirected, he *knew* that! He couldn't have pinned his hopes on someone who would misuse him like that!"

"Richard?" Lenore was twittering down at him from her fairylike confection of pink.

He gazed up at her and fought the influence of the laughing gas he had inhaled with renewed determination yet no greater measure of success.

Had they struck down good men in the line of duty? No, no, he didn't even wish to *begin* quantifying the implications of *that*!

Raven had seemed utterly convinced that the duke was leading illicit actions through his men, but Richard refused even then to believe it.

The men who had been killed were doing their jobs improperly, perhaps they had been involved in a separate conspiracy! That would make sense! If they had been legitimate law enforcement they would have attempted to arrest Raven and Richard, or at the very least they would have given a warning before shooting.

He furrowed his brow as he fought to reassert his mental faculties against the ether in his system.

"Oh, *look*, Richard!" Lenore cooed, and looped her arm through his and yanked him to his wobbly feet. "The servers are here! Now we can *finally* have dinner, together!"

Why hadn't *she* been weakened by the ether? Had she built up a resistance to it? Well... she *did* have a much more robust social life than his...

"Hey!" she jostled him, and the clouds in his head went swirling around between his ears. "Are you listening to me?" she demanded. "Don't you *want* to have dinner with me?"

"Of course..." he slurred. "Can I sit down again?"

She practically dropped him into one of the seats the men in the red masks were bringing in through the secret passages, and then harrumphed down into her own across from him.

The men in red masks were bringing out tables along with covered dishes. Perhaps it was due to his addled senses, but that made some sense to him. They were servants, after all... that was all they were... Let Raven draw her wild conclusions and cling to her outlandish theories!

Richard gratefully accepted another puff of the gas, and his fears evaporated like morning mist.

The dinner provided for them was toothsome enough, but even sitting there across from Lenore, it was not nearly as savory as... No! He would not allow himself to think of it that way!

He shook himself, and having done so realized that was the first time since they had sat across from one another that Lenore had so much as looked at him. She had been glancing back and forth to toss pleasantries to everyone around them, but never at him. Part of him felt somewhat affronted by that fact...

Except that when she did, he wished she hadn't. Her eyes were harsh with scorn, and he tried his best not to squirm visibly.

"What's the matter with you?" she snapped under her breath at him, and he started. "Sit up straight!" she demanded, and whacked his knee with her fan under the table.

He blinked rapidly as he realized that his muscles had betrayed him as he slowly sank off the chair. "I'm trying not to…" he whispered apologetically.

"Everyone can *see* you!" she hissed.

"I'm sorry…" he blushed, and rallied enough strength to prop himself up on the chair with both hands firmly on the table on either side of his plate. "I'll do better, I promise… how do you like the chicken?"

"It's *dry*," she sniffed, "but have you noticed our forks? I think they're pure gold!"

"Yes… they don't taint the taste of our food in the slightest, it's lovely…" he smiled awkwardly as he thought his lips may go slack and melt off his face at any moment.

"Does your *ordinary* silverware taint the taste of your food?" she wrinkled her nose and grimaced down it at him. "I thought you weren't still *poor*!"

Having heard that word, guests from the tables surrounding them whipped their heads around to scrutinize Richard with narrowed eyes.

"I'm not poor!" he cried perhaps too defensively, but he could still be heard over the raucous music… if he were lucky, those who had heard him would not think him overly defensive. He widened his eyes to convey the importance of his next words without shrieking at her. "Please don't say things like that, they'll give people the wrong idea of me!"

"I just hope *I* haven't been getting the wrong impersonation of *you*!" she hissed. "I had better not learn that you're a *liar*, Richard Phaal, because if I do, you will regret lying to me! Mark my words," one of her long-nailed hands clamped over his and the nails dug into the back of his hand in spite of the fact that they both wore gloves.

"I would never lie to you!" Richard squeaked in a manner which shamed him, but he was so intimidated he didn't even dare correct her usage of 'impersonation.'

"Then tell me truly…" she dug her nails further into his sin, "are you a wealthy lawyer? Is that money yours? Do you rent your clothes or do you buy them?"

"I have earned all this money you see me using," he grunted through his teeth as he slowly extricated his hand from under hers. "And I assure you, this is my solemn oath —" he coughed as a cloud of smoke wafted past him. "I am not a pauper…" he couldn't help the reflexive laugh that accompanied his words, but he still made his eyes project as much earnest truth as possible.

Lenore still frowned at him with eyes full of doubt and suspicious scrutiny. Still, she laid off bothering him and picked at her chicken before the dessert course arrived.

Richard was grateful for the lull, and took the opportunity to scan the room for anything that could ease his weary heart and put him back in an appropriately Bacchic state of mind.

In this search, he noticed that one of the ornamental trees along the sides of the room looked… *different*. Somehow, through the haze, he could see that it was not as it ought to be. He squinted at it a moment longer and realized that it was moving of its own accord.

That wasn't supposed to happen… right?

How much smoke had he inhaled?

Richard shook his head and went back to shoveling spiced velvet cake into his mouth. He told himself it didn't matter, as he downed some bergamot and lemon tea, that some of the party guests had begun to fall asleep.

That was just because the party was going so well! They were all so happy and satisfied that they had slipped into dreams…

The world went black around Richard, and he felt as if he had been wrapped in a gentle blanket of clouds...

Until something jostled him out of the sky and sent him plummeting into the unpleasant realization that reality had become a confusing, head-throbbing place.

He was gazing up into a face completely obscured in a dark mask, the eyes shielded from view by glass lenses... who was this? Did he have any friends with black velvet faces and gold set into their skin?

Oh... his head throbbed a little more harshly, but he realized that indeed he was looking into a masked face.

He flailed at first, floundering for an escape, but even though her hands were gentle, he could not escape them. Silently, she shook her head, and pulled him under a delicate lace canopy.

Was this where he would get a massage? Oh! Maybe he could get a head massage for his aching... huh... no, they were at a party before... this was under a table...

Without warning, something foul was shoved just beneath his nostrils, and his mind exploded in a furious screech of sanity.

"Who...?" he croaked, and his dry mouth nearly failed him.

She shook her head, and poured a glass of wine down his throat.

The wine warmed his throat, and sent a buzzing sensation through his skull.

"Lenore?" he whispered, reaching up to the masked face with tender affection, but the woman battered his hand away, and shook her head.

He realized then that she was wearing a Moretta mask, dark and mysterious, rendering its wearer mute in favor of mystique.

"Thank you, for the wine..."

The stranger nodded, and pressed a finger to his lips. Why was he meant to be quiet? She wasn't going to put one of those masks on *him* was she?

"Hey! What are you doing with him? He's mine" Lenore hissed from close at hand.

Richard grinned and even though he knew the expression must look idiotic on him just then, he turned his face toward Lenore.

She gave him a pouting frown, and turned back to the other woman, instead. "I only took my eyes off of him for *one* moment, and —" Lenore was reaching for the mute stranger's mask to rip it off — which was terribly rude! — when suddenly they all three heard a scream.

It began as only one, but they quickly multiplied to many. Men, women, both mingled together into a chorus of fearful agony.

"What's going on?" Lenore shrieked, and received a whack from the stranger's fan against her scalp.

Richard could do nothing but cling to the stranger, who seemed to be his one salvation in this madness. "We have to go!" he whispered.

The stranger nodded, and looped his arm around her shoulders, slowly pulling him until he sat upright amid the screams.

Scuffling was going on outside, and it was loud enough that Richard knew it couldn't be a pretty sight.

"Where are you taking him?" Lenore grabbed Richard's arm with both her hands. "Give him back!"

The masked woman gave Lenore a disapproving look, and Richard could swear he actually *felt* the irritation boiling through her.

"Please, just bring her along," he whispered to the stranger, whose eyes were not focused on him, but on Lenore. Lack of trust must be at the root of all this.

The stranger slipped one finger under the chin of her mask and pulled it forward to admit her voice out.

When she spoke, she was obviously trying to push back a tremor in her voice. "Are you all right?" she asked, her voice still snapping on vowels, like breaking twigs. "We need to escape..."

"Yes, I'm fine..." Richard scrutinized her, though, with fresh eyes. How did he know her? Something about that voice was familiar... "What's your name?"

She shook her head and placed the mask back into its proper position, once again rendering herself mute. Had she done that to prevent him from recognizing her?

He didn't really have that many friends... if only he weren't so addled... the answer should have been obvious! He was finally frustrated with himself for accepting so very much ether.

"Let's get out of here." Lenore seized Richard's arm, and tugged him in the opposite direction of the stranger, who may not actually be a stranger... Good lord did his head ache! He wanted to go to bed!

Firmly, the stranger grabbed Lenore's arm and jerked her back in the direction she was planning to flee.

"We have to get out of here," Richard noted, and looked from the not-quite-mute to Lenore. "Please, let's work together. I think she has a plan, Lenore, we should trust her. She's helped us thus far."

Lenore made a distasteful face but she no longer protested. Instead, she followed the masked woman and Richard out from under the table, at the excruciatingly slow pace the stranger dictated.

Outside the peaceful oasis of the table, Richard noticed that the room had grown quite... empty... where was everyone?

"What happened to the party?" Lenore groused in a breathless squeal.

The masked stranger turned her placidly masked face in Lenore's direction, such that Lenore quickly fell silent once more.

Richard was just as curious, but as he gazed at the ghostly surroundings which had once been alive and vibrant, he couldn't help but remember how Bacchanal Hall had been equally rendered empty and lifeless.

Bizarrely enough, when the masked stranger tapped on one of the double doors they had entered the ballroom through, it opened slowly to reveal a woman dressed in a laboratory coat and a gas mask.

Was that meant to be a costume?

"Hurry!" the gas-masked doctor gestured for them all to come through the door with slow movements that made Richard think she'd put her mask on a bit late.

The four of them travelled at a sluggish pace out of the castle, as to Richard's chagrin both the mute and Lenore had to carry him away from the ghost of their party.

He saw two men in red masks with gashes against their throats, but didn't dare to ask questions as by some miracle moments later he was breathing crisp nocturnal air, and the starlight above heralded his freedom.

"I can't believe I'm alive..." the muffled voice of the woman in the gas mask said the instant before she removed the mask, so that there she stood bare-faced on the grounds of the castle.

"Amelia!" Lenore shrieked, and threw herself at the woman who stood there in oversized boots and a laboratory coat. "We've all missed you so terribly!" she cried. "We thought you were dead! What's happened to you? Why would you play such a cruel prank on your dearest friends?"

"It was no prank... I was... stolen..." Amelia returned Lenore's hug, but Richard saw that her arms were just as sluggish as her feet had been. It was as if she were a doll whose joints had been jarred out of alignment and then poorly reconfigured. "I saw such... horrible things... I want to go home..."

"I don't think that's such a great idea," Richard said. "Miss Otranto... How much do you know of —" he halted when he saw the mute hold up a hand to stop him.

That was a good point. Amelia probably didn't need to hear about the fact that her father had died and the duke had seized their property just at that particular moment.

"But you didn't tell me... What did they *do*?" Lenore asked.

"I... was a ghost... and yet not dead... Now my mind and soul and body are all together again, but I don't feel quite so together as I should..."

"What about the other people in there?" Richard asked, supposing that was the best way to divert the conversation from Amelia's dreadful experiences.

Amelia gazed quietly at the Abbey for a long moment before replying, "They'll be trapped in there. If too many people disappeared, we'd be followed..." she looked to the mute stranger, and bowed her head. "I would not have escaped if not for our friend here... Lenore, you owe her more than that."

"Who is she?" Lenore demanded, and whirled on the mute.

"That is not for us to discuss right now," Amelia said, standing up straighter and placing her gas mask back on. "We need to get the two of you home. Then after that... I will go with her. I need to go home."

"Why would you go with *her*?" Lenore demanded.

"It was pre-arranged... she can hide me, and get me home... tell our friends to cheer up. I will send you all invitations to visit me... once we're out of harm's way." She looked expectantly in the masked woman's direction, and received a nod in return.

"We'll get home on our own," Lenore huffed. "Come on, Richard! You're staying with me, take me home!"

Richard stared at the two masked women, even when Lenore tugged on his arm, nearly yanking him completely off his feet.

"Wait." Richard whispered to Lenore. "Please let me know who you are." He entreated the mute who was wavering on whether or not to leave.

Rather than remove her mask and reveal the answer to that question, the masked woman shook her head. She looped an arm through Amelia's, instead, and the two of them hurried away into the shadows.

"Wait!" Richard lurched forward, and grabbed the Moretta's arm with one desperate hand. "What just happened? What are you going to do?"

"Everything is about to change," said Amelia plainly. "Do not try to follow us. All will be revealed in due time, we promise!"

The mute lifted her mask once, though she was not facing Richard, so he did not get the advantage of knowing what lay beneath her second face. "Tonight, a series of experiments have begun, that will tear at the very fabric of humanity. Those who wish to conduct such inhumane experiments may also have taken hold of the two of you, but now they are too busy. They do not notice that the two of you escaped."

"I was to be the prototype," Amelia said, "but none of the experiments succeeded... they will be all the more eager to try desperate measures now that they have a larger sample size."

Lenore pulled Richard away before he could press the issue. He watched the mysterious girl faded into the darkness with Amelia, who ought to have been dead, and wished he could reach for her and unravel the mysteries surrounding her.

Chapter 28: Flight

Amelia's strength gave out when they were halfway across town, and Moretta halted them in a back alley to administer a hasty dose of Dr. Shade's own personal brandy.

As Amelia panted and hoarsely coughed the brandy down, Moretta slid her mask around to the side of her face so it would no longer block her mouth. "Do you think you can keep going?" Moretta pointed to her house. "There are several rooms there which are completely free for the taking, you can sleep there and then tomorrow we will smuggle you out of town."

Amelia took a deep fortifying breath, and slid her gas mask back over her face. "You've done wonderfully so far, L'Espanaye. I'd hate to waste all that effort of yours, so I'll keep going just as long as we get there before the sun comes up... I haven't moved so much in days..."

"I understand..." Moretta peeked out of the alleyway to assess how much Amontillado nightlife might interfere with their ability to get home unseen.

Thus far, the people the duo had encountered were those enthralled with some parlor or another and its intoxicating delights. Not only did that provide the two of them with an excellent series of distractions to pave their way towards freedom, it lit their way through town... even if the lights in question were of a harsh multicolored variety.

The people of Amontillado did not yet know what had become of their fellow citizens, and Moretta just hoped they wouldn't until she had successfully stowed Amelia away in the Capitol, awaiting the embraces of her loving relatives.

Her heart clenched at the idea of such a homecoming... would she ever get such relief from her travails?

"Is something the matter?" Amelia asked through the muffling mask.

"Yes, but not dangerous," Moretta replied. "I was just thinking of how to get you home. I'll have to come with you. While you rest, I'll do some packing."

"You should get some rest, as well, you've done so much," Amelia indicated as they walked through the empty, even ghostly streets of Amontillado.

The way the buildings tilted, they seemed to be bending over them to listen in on every word. Their windows revealed peeks at the abandoned day-to-day lives of those who lived within, their teacups on their writing desks, and quill pens still settled beside them… many had parlors adorned with paintings of the seaside or a garden, and one house even kept an intact stuffed bear against one wall.

Upon seeing this, at first both young ladies gasped and shrank away from the specimen's gaping jaws with its razor teeth revealed within, and those powerful paws which were raised combatively.

"It's only a stuffed bear," Moretta whispered when the first moment of shuddering horror had passed.

"That doesn't mean I have to like it!" Amelia whispered back, and scuttled further down the street until she could no longer see the monstrosity.

Moretta found she had to agree with that statement, and she guided Amelia that last spurt of distance back to the house.

"I remember being terrified of coming here when I was a little girl…" Amelia noted in a quiet voice while Moretta unlocked the front gate. "Mama and Papa took me here to get my smallpox vaccine… and every year I came back to have the Mistress poke me and pinch my arms like she was an old witch who wanted to bake me into a pie!"

"You know, I don't think witches really do that sort of thing," Moretta noted wryly. "They mostly seem to be ordinary people who have gone through very sad times in their lives… and they wouldn't call themselves witches if people didn't force them to."

"You mean witches aren't really witches?" Amelia yawned. "But there are so many stories…"

"There are stories about fairies, too. But usually when someone is called a witch it's because she lives apart from society and has more animal friends than human friends… what's really damning is if she doesn't have any love for the people in power."

Amelia considered that in silence as Moretta locked the gate firmly behind them and then led the way to the front door so that she could unlock that.

A trio of ravens swept onto the eaves of the house, all peering down at the two ladies with their wide, curious eyes. Each of them wore collars which glinted in the lights Moretta had left illuminating her home. As interesting as that was, Moretta was more interested in the fact that she could see Renata's friendly face just inside the window, and the cat was making scratching motions on the window though her claws were retracted.

Amelia laughed breathily, and Moretta worried for her sanity. "Gracious, Moretta!" Amelia chortled, then tittered, and leaned against the wall beside the window she could see Renata through. "It's as if you're setting yourself up as a witch! Ravens? A black cat? You live alone on this hill and I only know you because we met when I thought I was dead!"

Moretta finally opened the door, and gave Amelia a half-smile. "I just thought you should know… don't be so afraid of people who are labeled as witches… A so-called 'witch' may turn out to be your best friend."

Once Moretta was back inside her own home, she immediately ripped the mask and her veil off, tossing it all aside before she locked the door firmly. "Renata, dear, help me draw the curtains, please."

"I can't believe how well-trained your cat is!" Amelia cried as Renata grabbed the lacy black curtain in her mouth. "I didn't realize cats *could* be trained!"

"Oh, she hasn't been trained, she's just quite intelligent... She's more intelligent that some people I've met." Before she closed her own set of curtains, Moretta opened the door to let the ravens in.

"Close it! Close it!" Amelia squealed. "The birds are getting in!"

"Oh, I wouldn't be so worried about them," Moretta said, and knelt beside the hearth to open up the secret room for them. "They're the trained ones. Apparently my predecessors had some unusual hobbies."

"You don't know the half of it..." Amelia shuddered. "I just wish I hadn't had to come back here..."

"It's not such a horrible place," Moretta shrugged, and put some music on the phonograph, heavy on the harpsichord and violin. "Just think of it as a home that happened to inherit a few oddball things from awkward relatives. I'll show you where to rest. Tomorrow we'll decide which of my clothes fit you, and then we'll say goodbye to this place... it's possible we won't even come back..."

And then she would never see Richard, again... but of course, he wanted to be with Lenore, so perhaps that was for the best. She would just tell the League she would prefer to have a different position the next time she was given an assignment. Somewhere with an abundance of attractive men to choose from... that would be a nice touch...

"Nobody will come after us, will they?" Amelia asked uneasily, and Moretta turned to see her gazing uneasily up at her, having paused on the stairwell.

"They would have to realize you were missing first, and I believe they are already inundated with the overabundance of new victims... I assure you, though, whatever happens, it is my personal duty to keep you safe no matter the cost. You shall be reunited with your family, and then we will get some help in releasing all the others."

Amelia stood stalk still a moment longer, still gazing at Moretta with wide eyes. "But I worry... I worry that maybe... they've followed us..."

"By the time I got into that ballroom, Richard and Lenore were some of the last guests there. The men in the red masks were far too busy to even notice I'd slipped in. When I left, they had already left. I believe they will take an exceptionally long time firstly to wake up the *good* doctor, and secondly to actually process each one of those people... I don't think all of them had quite enough ether to make them perfectly compliant, either... so we have some time to prepare for our escape."

"Should we not go straightaway, then?" Amelia asked. "What if we lose our freedom tomorrow?"

"Listen... I am a coroner... I travel with human sized boxes... and how many people do you honestly think have any intention of taking a peek into one?"

This brought something akin to a smile onto Amelia's face. "I suppose that's as good a strategy as any..." she admitted.

"And I'll make sure you can breathe out of it, as well... this won't be the first time. Not to mention, they're quite comfortable, you could use it as a bed."

"Why... why would you have to do a thing like that more than once?" Amelia asked.

"I have chosen an odd sort of profession... it helps me to deal with some of the difficulties I have faced in my lifetime." She turned away and continued up the stairs before Amelia could ask any more questions.

"I think you might like this one," she said, opening the door. "I've been burning lavender incense in here for a few days, so I think the atmosphere will be rather peaceful. You ought to get some rest."

Without warning, Amelia threw herself at Moretta and hugged her tightly about the neck. "Thank you..." she whispered. "I never thought I would be so glad to be in this house... never once did I think I would leave this life behind forever, or that I'd be separated from my friends, and I never thought I'd escape... But now I'm not so afraid of any of these things... thank you... You've done so much for me and you didn't have to!"

Moretta patted Amelia's back before extricating herself as politely as she possibly could. "Get some sleep," she said gently, and waved good night before closing the door between them.

That was more than enough touching for one day. Moretta required her own space, and she most definitely required it immediately!

Before doing anything else, she washed the makeup off her face and shook out her hair, brushed it and then wetted it down so the curls wouldn't be so obnoxious. She then slipped into one of her less lacy and more practical nightgowns.

Once the phonograph ran out of music to play, she frowned gloomily onto the night-blanketed cityscape of Amontillado. There had been very few friendly faces here, and she would be lucky to leave, she told herself.

Yet... despite herself, she longed to see Richard, again. It was nonsensical and she would certainly never admit to that fact. Her mind was clouded over with thoughts of Richard, and yet she had too many things which required her attention.

Moretta spent the remaining hours of the night meticulously packing away everything she belonged, and ignoring whispers she heard on the air each time she took something which had formerly belonged to her predecessors.

"If you don't like it, you shouldn't have been criminals. Then you wouldn't have been executed, and I wouldn't be here," she scolded petulantly to the air, and put a new song on the phonograph.

If she were imagining those voices, she had an excellent imagination. There were other apparitions she caught in the shadows, almost blending into the patterns on the wallpaper.

"It isn't my fault if I cannot stay," she shrugged at them. "I can send someone else to investigate you, and I think they might do better than I did."

That was a lie. She was one of the better investigators when it came to matters of the incorporeal deceased. But she didn't have to tell *them* that.

Her limbs grew wearier, and her eyes dropped shut repeatedly despite her best efforts. She only realized she had fallen asleep when light burned into her eyes and she snapped upright on the couch.

And thus, the night had drifted into day without her paying heed. Soon she may have to leave and make an appearance somewhere… but she shook the thought of doing that out of her mind.

Though she had been firmly convinced the best course of action would be to leave immediately, the moment the opportunity had arrived, she was disinclined to do any such thing. Leave the house? With that traitorous sun overhead? How would she escape notice with that blasted sun shining down on them?

She noticed something moving slowly up her walkway. Who would do that? She had such a blackened reputation, and it was so early in the morning… only a truly desperate case would seek her help…

Was this someone else from the Abbey?

If the news had gotten out about people missing after the party, why would anyone come inquire with her about that? Most people would be in shock… But then she saw that it was Richard trudging hesitantly up to her door.

Her heart stopped. What was she going to do now? A quick glance into her mirror revealed two plum circles under her eyes. After grimacing in disgust at herself, she decided to grant Richard an appearance.

Chapter 29: Echoes of Isolation

Crickets were performing in an operatic orchestra out in the city streets as Richard and Lenore were walking through Amontillado. If Richard had been at a normal party, he would have expected to see his cab driver return, but the entire drive before the Abbey was wiped clean of all transportation services save for those left behind by the wealthy prisoners inside.

"We should take one!" Lenore whispered to Richard, shaking his arm.

"And what happens when someone sees that we *did* steal their carriage?" he demanded of her. "We'll be in prison as soon as that happens, and I don't even want to *think* about what the duke would do with us if he had a legitimate excuse!"

Lenore fell silent after that, but she took to the much more pleasant diversion of clinging to Richard and warming his side as well as bolstering him with the knowledge that she considered him worthy.

At that rate, no matter how sluggish he was, Richard didn't notice how long it took to reach Lenore's home. His feet only began to ache when they were waiting on Lenore's front steps.

"Do you have rooms *downstairs* I could sleep in?" he asked, growing utterly terrified at the thought of climbing up the stairs he'd seen before. He kept getting images of falling down the marble stairs, and the marble would harm his feet as desperately as if he were walking on glass...

"Absolutely not!" Lenore gasped. "What do you think we are? We have a *fine* home! Nobody sleeps on the first level! That would take away space from the parlor, the billiards room, the conservatory —!"

Mercifully, the door opened before her tirade could continue, and Richard lurched through the door.

"At this point, I'm so tired I could just sleep on the billiards table…" Richard yawned.

"That would *never* happen!" Lenore shrieked, and the noise echoed off the walls up and down the spiral staircase, so Richard was instantly cowed by her will.

Was this going to be his entire life? Obeying every shrieking order Lenore gave him? Hopefully she would mellow… but wasn't she supposed to mellow out when he initially denied her an outing?

That thought brought another to him, despite his headache. *Raven.*

She was the one he had taken instead of Lenore, she was the one who had warned him every step of the way that the duke was up to no good… and it was she who had come to rescue him from the ether frolic.

"Good Lord!" Richard cried, and his own voice echoed just as powerfully off of the spiral staircase.

"What?" Lenore demanded, already on her way up the stairs. "Did you see something?"

"No, I… my head hurts…" it wasn't a lie. He dropped his hat and his mask on a table beside the door, and began the arduous trek up the stairs. "Where can I sleep? I need to sleep…"

He heard her sniff from above him in disgust, and knew that she was in no mood to reply charitably.

"Elsa!" she cried, and her maid ran to open a door, which Richard eagerly stumbled through.

"Sir," the maid whispered, "would you like me to stoke the fire for you?"

Richard's face sank into the plush pillows which were piled up on the bed, and he let out a heavy groan. He wasn't sure either way, did it matter, really? He kicked off his shoes and only with slightly more care removed his jacket. Finally he rolled over and saw that the maid had begun to stoke a fire for him, regardless of what he might say, so he smiled. "That was kind of you," he yawned.

"Begging your pardon, sir, but you look absolutely awful," she said. "I'd rather you just had some fire to warm your poor bones."

He yawned again, and sank back into the pillows, subtly removing his too-tight trousers under his blanket, and choosing to wait until the maid had left the room before ejecting them from under the blanket with him…

"Oh, drat," he grunted to himself, and when he noticed that the maid had heard him and was peering at him in confusion, he explained, "I just realized I have to wear these ridiculous clothes when I go home."

The maid tittered and shook her head. "That's a terrible shame!"

"Matilda!" Lenore cried from a floor above them, making the maid jump.

"The mistress never gets my name right…" the maid sighed, and curtseyed to Richard.

Well, that was a troubling thought…How long had Lenore lived in this house with this maid? Was she simply mistaking this maid for another she'd previously had? It was still somewhat rude… And these thoughts brought yet another to his mind…

"Sleep well, m'lord," the maid said whether or not he deserved the title.

"If she never gets your name right, what is your name?" Richard asked between yawns.

"Maybe I'll tell you after you get some sleep," she said with a light smile and a shake of her head. "You had best be getting some of that, by the way." With that, she closed the door firmly behind herself.

However, he could not sleep. Not only did he hear Lenore shouting orders at the maid next door, he was troubled by another thought… Raven was a *nickname*…

Had he ever heard her actual name?

If he had heard that name, what was it?

He was supposedly her friend, but he could not recall ever addressing her by her actual name! Richard sat upright in bed, sweating with the thought of how rude he'd been to his supposed friend in the past few days… And in spite of that, she had saved his life…

Knowing that he could never address these things if he did not recover from the effects of his rough evening, Richard shut his mind off from speculation. He sat up, opening his eyes irritably — only to meet the masked brown eyes of some phantom. Richard had never been one to scream. Nor was he one to bolt out of bed and grab the nearest thing his hands could find to fight with.

In a moment, he'd done both.

But now the phantom was gone. Hadn't that phantom had a cane with him? Richard shook it off. He'd been so sure… but the phantom was just that — a phantom, a dream. His mind must still be addled by the effects of the ether in his system… he would have to set the fireplace poker down, and try to sleep off the laughing gas.

He climbed back into bed, still troubled, but now without the burst of vigor which had instantly enlivened his limbs a moment previous.

Despite the warmth of the room aided by the roaring fire, and how he had never had such a comfortable bed in his entire life, Richard's dreams were plagued by the phantom that night.

He was a masked, phantom, one who was pleased to dart around back alleys with a vicious cane, attacking those he found there and causing general mischief.

Richard could not place what his motives were, but he could plainly recognize the streets and alleys the dastardly fellow haunted. He had passed through several of them on his way to Lenore's home…

All of a sudden the images shifted and he could see the phantom caressing Lenore's hair while both of them laughed. They were wicked, malicious laughs, which sounded much more as if they fit his sister *Hyacinth* than...

And there was Hyacinth on demand, hands on hips as mice flooded the alleyway and added to the chorus, squeaking to punctuate the laughter.

Richard shot up in bed and wanted to flee, but his limbs were too weary and his skull appeared to house its own percussion section, along with far too many piccolos.

Someone was knocking at his door, rapping on it so insistently and at such a rapid pace, Richard at first thought it was from the province of his own dark plane of tormented ennui.

"Stop making all that noise or I'm coming in and I don't care if you're naked!" Lenore shouted through the door.

Richard chewed his lip, and held the blankets up over himself, even though he had chosen to sleep in his shirtsleeves and other under things, so he was not actually naked. "Sorry... I didn't know..." he said, cowed and finding his words insufficient.

"Good!" Lenore went strutting back to her room, and Richard took the opportunity to check the time.

The sun had yet to rise completely, so Richard knew he had yet to sleep through the entire night... if such a thing were even possible.

It took some fishing around in the darkness, as the embers had burned low, but he did finally locate a clock. He brought it near the dying embers as he dropped some kindling onto the fire, and read that it was only a few minutes past the fifth hour of the morning.

He longed for sleep, but doubted he could get too much of it where he was... why was it that the only woman he *wanted* to sleep under the same roof with was both inhospitable and unpleasant to be near, and yet...

Even with ghosts in the house, it had been more pleasant to share a roof with Raven... whose actual name he had forgotten... what a dreadful friend he was...

It was after he remembered her once more that Richard realized he had to know if she were well. Not only her, but she had Amelia with her!

Strength was rapidly seeping into his muscles, and he stretched them to see how far it would go. He still yawned, but he was done with that nonsense.

As distasteful as it was, Richard pulled his clothes on and resolved that before he did anything else, he would visit his own home and pick up clothes of his own... The sooner he was rid of this ridiculous suit, the better!

He wrote up a hasty card to explain himself, and left it on Lenore's door before slipping out of the house.

The crisp morning air was heavy laden with fog, as was the norm, and for once Richard was grateful for it. At least the fog would make it more difficult for people to see what he was wearing...

More than likely, he wouldn't come across someone he knew that early in the morning, but—

"Great glistening gears!" Richard heard from the opposite side of the street. There, as the only other person on the street, was none other than Braxton Coy. "Is that you, Richard?"

Richard blushed as if he had been caught nicking sweets from a jar in an apothecary. "Yes... hello, Braxton... it's been a few days since we last spoke... er... what's in the box?"

"Ah!" Braxton lit up as if someone had just lit up a gas lamp in his skull. "The Royal Academy of Engineers has asked me to give a presentation there on my inventions! I'm leaving this morning so I can be in Boezia by tea!"

Richard's ears burned as he gazed at the fellow he'd held in such low regard for years had achieved actual success on his own efforts. "That's amazing..." he said, loath to cross the street even though his apartment was so very close. "Congratulations..."

"Well, I haven't gotten my patents yet," Braxton shrugged. "I'm more interested in your sudden change of tastes... I thought you liked brown, what are you doing in pink? Have you just changed overnight?"

"No, it was... for a party... haven't you heard anything about it?"

"You don't seem to know who I am," Braxton barked out a laugh. "I *never* hear about parties! Much too busy! And now I'm about to become even more busy! I'll write you, then you'll know how well this goes... Actually, if you don't hear from me, it means I went over about as well as a badger on a canoe!"

Richard laughed in spite of his shame. "My prayers will go with you, friend!" he said, and when Braxton waved at him rather than contradict the sentiment, he was all the more ashamed.

After a quick change of clothes, Richard hurried to Raven's home. Once he had arrived, Richard shifted uncomfortably on Raven's front step.

He was usually able to talk to Raven about just about anything. But after yesterday, when she'd so vehemently refused to come to the party with him... even though now he knew that she'd been telling him the truth from the beginning...

The door creaked open.

"Good morning." Raven croaked in a small voice.

Richard's words fell from his lips in a flood the moment she had finished speaking. First he apologized for not believing her, then told her how things had turned out with the party, and then about the girl who hadn't told him who she was. "I just wondered... when I saw her for the first time... why did she choose me?" What was so special about me? There were so many people there who had families richer than mine… Well-bred, well-connected… more valuable to society…"

"Who knows?" Raven turned her eyes toward the sky, poorly concealing that she was not actually looking at the sky. "Maybe you never will know who she is…" she appeared quite troubled at the prospect.

He hadn't helped with his constantly calling her by the wrong name… "But I have to!" he pressed, "I owe her my freedom!" *And probably my sanity*, he finished in his mind. "She has been… such a heroine…"

Raven considered. "Maybe someday you'll find her. I suppose she must have been off doing good deeds yesterday and thought you a worthy recipient."

Richard frowned, as she was still hiding in spite of his best efforts to show she could freely reveal the truth. Why would she hide from him? "I don't think so. It's like she knew me, and wanted to help me in particular… oh, and Lenore."

Raven's ears perked up at the way Richard said Lenore. She detected disappointment. Stowing away her glee, Raven opened the door wider. "Care to come in? Renata is still waiting for a petting session from you."

Richard smirked. "I'll come in and visit with your cat, then," he said.

Raven hid her answering smirk and motioned for Richard to join her indoors.

A wave of calm enveloped Richard as he entered, which he could not explain. This was a haunted house, and he had just been on the much more affluent side of time, much more ill-at-ease…

"Renata!" Raven called, some of her confidence returning as she focused on the cat, and momentarily Renata looked up from Raven's faded purple chaise.

"Say hello to Richard," Raven said, gesturing from Renata to Richard.

Renata looked at Richard for a moment with wide, thoughtful eyes, just like her mistress's save for the fact that hers were green and Raven's were gray. Then she threw her head back and released a gurgling, whiny meow, her tongue flicking out of her mouth and nearly touching her nose.

Amusing as spending time with Renata was Richard's eyes flitted over to Raven, who was bustling about preparing tea he hadn't asked for. "I never really learned your actual name, did I?" he asked her in earnest.

Her eyes flickered over to his as she came back from the kitchen, and she paused where she was. "No... I told you what it was, but... I suppose the nickname was apt..." she gestured to a pair of ravens which were on a false tree against the wall.

"How long have you been keeping them there?" he asked her.

"Well, really, they already lived here... I just let them back in here," she shrugged. "But do you really want to know my name?"

"Please tell me," Richard got to his feet, despite the fact they started to ache with the effort.

She opened her mouth to speak, but she sighed, and shook her head. "I lied to you, before... I didn't tell you my real name... and actually, I might be leaving forever, today, so... My name is Moretta. I'm pleased to meet you." She dropped a gentle curtsey.

"You... why didn't you tell me your name?"

"The same reason I wore a mask when I saved your life... because it was for my own safety and to prevent anything from jeopardizing my mission."

He stared at her, lost in a series of questions he couldn't bring himself to ask. Finally, he peered around the room for inspiration that might put coherent words in his mouth, and found a row of suitcases waiting there just as they had been arranged the day she arrived.

"Why…. Why would you leave?" he croaked, even if he had no right to expect she would stay.

"Because I have a duty to protect Amelia Otranto, and I have a duty to report to my superiors. I shouldn't say more, since you have a similar duty."

"But… why should you have to go?"

"I'm more curious about why you want me to stay."

"Is it not enough that we are friends?"

"I don't think it is… after all, I abhor this town. You are the only friend I've made here, and to be quite perfectly honest, I could pass my time better elsewhere."

Richard could stand it no more. He rushed over to Raven — no, *Moretta* — and seized her hands. "I can' t…" Why would his words fail him at a time like this?

"What?" she asked, her eyes wide silvery wells of confusion, which were steadily moistening as he watched. "Please tell me, why would you want me to stay here?"

"Because… I honestly believe you're the best thing that ever happened to this town… and I wish you wouldn't leave and take the light from it…"

Moretta stared at him, and her lips wobbled. "I… Actually, I can't believe you were actually thinking something like that…"

"Neither can I," he replied, and pulled her into a hug. It was the first time he could actually remember hugging someone in a long while, though perhaps he'd merely forgotten in the haze of ether. "But here we are."

"I can't just… stay… there's work to be done…"

"But you can come back, can't you?" Richard asked, and gave her hands a squeeze. "You won't just go and leave me with… well, without a friend…"

"I thought you had friends… someone like you ought to have friends…"

"I thought someone like you would, too, but here we are… Don't go, I don't know what I'll do if I don't have you talking sense to me! You're the one who always warns me, but now that I've finally realized I should have been listening to you the whole time... Who else will give me advice like you do?"

"Well... perhaps you could simply learn to think like I would... or you could send me telegraphs to ask me what would be best, if that's really what lawyers do when they can't figure something out. I thought you were supposed to be the detective here."

"True," he blushed, but paused. "Are you a detective?"

"Not in such plain terms," she shrugged, and took her hands back from him. "But that is among my capabilities."

"I don't think I've known you in the slightest since you got here..."

"You know, I think that could make it easier for you to let me go."

"Not when you just got leagues more interesting..." he shook his head.

She gave him a small smile. "You know, I have to get out of town in less than an hour. Would it trouble you to lend me your aid?"

"No... How about you leave some of your things here? That way... you have to come back at least once, don't you?"

She gave him a slightly broader smile than before. "Yes, I suppose I would. I'll go wake up Amelia... Can you please start moving things to the door?"

"I would be honored, my lady," he said as he watched her climb up the stairs. "Just don't forget who helped you when you go..."

Chapter 30: The Unseen Exit

It was fortunate, Moretta decided, that she and Amelia were of a similar size. Though it had been tailored especially for her, the green dress she had bought from Bonnie's fit Amelia acceptably well, at least enough that she did not complain.

Richard did all he could to ease their way out of town, working with such dogged eagerness Moretta had to ask him to sit down a moment so that he wouldn't make her so dizzy.

"Sorry!" he sat on the couch with a resounding thud, and grinned sheepishly at her.

Amelia sat beside him, casting sidelong glances at him that Moretta noticed whenever she allowed herself a moment to think amidst her own flurry of activity. Was Amelia seeking to steal Richard right out from under Lenore's thumb? Well, she couldn't but think Amelia would be a far more amiable alternative...

"Are you going to come along with us?" Amelia asked Richard shyly, which seemed to confirm Moretta's hypothesis.

"No, I..." Richard broke off with a heavy, burdensome sigh. "I fear I must attend the wants of the duke, and soon... my duties will keep me here, especially since if the duke notices I have vanished, he may do something... *anything*... to keep me quiet... And I fear what he may choose."

"I still cannot believe it was the duke who did this to me..." Amelia confessed, and wrapped the cloak Moretta had loaned her more closely about her shoulders. "Why would anyone...?"

"Money, and prestige," Moretta sighed, but gave Richard a calculated glance. "I'm afraid I cannot explain it in great detail, but he is working with a doctor of phantomology in order to push the science forward. I worry that... his experiments are meant to treat the living as if they were the dead... That is why Amelia was able to visit me. Not to mention, as long as everyone believed Amelia dead, the Otranto property was his for the taking."

"What will you do now that you know all of this?" Richard asked, and she saw him give her a look which was just as calculated as the one she had given him. He was still a lawyer, after all, and his client's business was at stake.

"I have to let people know about this," she shook her head. "You must know this, it is quite obvious to us both that lives are at stake, and unspeakable torment has been visited on them. Those who do not escape from the duke's clutches will be... well, their ghosts may be an entirely new breed of ghosts... more aware of their state and more capable of utilizing their incorporeal powers."

Richard and Amelia both shuddered, but her audience did not revolt against her theories. She had wished they would, and that somehow it may grow easier for Moretta herself to deny the horrors.

"We have to stop it..." Amelia said softly at length, her lips barely moving as if she had not spoken, and the words had merely appeared from the ether. "We cannot allow him to continue doing what he did to me and harming more people!"

"And you can be my star witness, if you feel you can," Moretta said.

"What?" Richard shot to his feet. "Do you realize that if you take the duke to court, I will be forced to appear as his lawyer?"

"It will be the crime of the century," Moretta told him quietly, seeing the true horror in his features. "You will be widely known throughout the land."

"But I will be known as a supreme *villain*! What if my efforts absolve him? I would have to do my uttermost to offer his defense, Moretta, don't you see my plight?"

It was utterly endearing to hear her own name on his lips, but even as she smiled, Moretta shook her head. "My dear Richard… please do not mistake me. I would never seek to besmirch your name. I ask only that you grant legitimacy to the case I must put against the duke… and what if he were to hire a corrupt replacement for you? Then the likelihood that he shall be absolved would rise all the higher!"

"Don't forget his wicked doctor…" Amelia said, inching closer to Richard's side of the couch. "He did such dreadful things to me… I can't imagine letting him go free, Richard, *please* don't let him go free! He could *find* me again!"

Richard turned a compassionate gaze upon Amelia, and Moretta turned away to preserve the intimacy of their shared gaze. Though she was not watching, the gravity of the words Richard spoke next resounded with the very core of her psyche. "My dear young lady," he said gently, "I will defend the duke with my words, but in my heart, I shall carry a poisoned dagger, for him should I succeed, and for myself should I fail."

When such words had been spoken, all others seemed inadequate to follow. The trio departed from the house communicating mostly in weighty looks.

Renata made herself comfortable on Moretta's shoulders, and Moretta was deeply grateful for her friendly, furry presence.

Armed with the warmth of her best friend's presence, Moretta led the way, holding tightly to her luggage and keeping her umbrella low over her head.

Several nonchalant paces behind her, Richard and Amelia huddled together, the latter wearing a veil over her face as if she were simply that fashionable, and had nothing whatever to hide.

Moretta had wired for a cab come for her during the previous night's frenzy, and she found the cab bedecked in black, as if for mourners.

"Madam," the driver hopped down from his perch and doffed his cap to her. "I am so sorry for your loss… Please, come with me." He ushered her, and then Amelia into the cab, but Richard stopped just outside it, wringing his hands.

"I know I haven't known you for very long," he began, giving her the most earnest of glances in spite of his faltering courage, "but… I do hope you will return to Amontillado when you can… This place needs a great deal of fixing, and I cannot do it on my own, by any means."

"I would not wish to abandon you to so arduous a task," Moretta returned, and while she closed the door, she reached out to give him her hand, which he kissed. "When the time comes, I shall return, and I shall bring with me a grand reckoning!" She watched his face as they parted, and her heart ached.

She must return, indeed, but to what heartache?

"Did you love him?" Amelia asked quietly, cutting into Moretta's troubled thoughts.

"One cannot truly love someone who they do not properly know..." Moretta hedged, and gave Amelia a curious glance. "But didn't you find him agreeable? Would you not want him for yourself?"

"Oh!" Amelia turned her face away with bashful mannerisms which hinted to Moretta that if only she could lift the veil she would find a blush. "His features were most charming, do you not think? Anyhow, I fear I am quite willing to find any man my stalwart champion given the slightest provocation, at least in this state... But anyhow... Perhaps I shall find a willing man waiting for me after the tale I shall tell."

"I wouldn't doubt it," Moretta arranged herself in a corner of the cab with Renata now on her lap and her heels propped on the opposite seat.

Could she have been more assertive with Richard had she not assumed he and Amelia were fated for one another?

She ought not be so ridiculous! There were duties awaiting her in Boezia, and she would do well to rest herself before they rose up to claw at her. She allowed herself to be lulled to sleep by the combination of the rocking carriage and Renata's gentle purring.

Chapter 31: Return to the Rat Nest

Watching Raven—no, *Moretta*, he reminded himself once again—leave Amontillado, Richard seemed to be watching hopeful light fade into the mists. With Moretta went her ability to cut through the confusion and show the way, like the beacon atop a lighthouse tower.

Without that beacon, Amontillado had become unbearably bleak... Richard had never disliked his hometown to a greater extreme than he did now that he saw for a fact how very menacing and treacherous it had always been beneath the surface.

Anyone could die in his new understanding of the world—which he hoped would prove untrue—at the slightest infraction or for none, at all.

Bereft of his sensible confidant, and without the option of the absent Braxton to discuss these issues with, Richard yearned for his family, instead... That is to say, he yearned for *most* of his family.

It had been almost a year, by his recollections, since he had visited his parents. Ordinarily, it was a small sacrifice to avoid Hyacinth, but at a time such as this, he simply needed proof that his parents were still living.

If he were lucky, Hyacinth had not infused their food or drink with cyanide. In his gloom, he wondered whether the letters he had supposedly exchanged with his parents had actually come from *her*. He had taken comfort in hearing quaint stories from his mother about what she and his father were doing day to day, but... what if it had all been a forgery?

Richard no longer expected to be lucky. He crossed the town with reluctant feet.

Every step which brought him closer to Hyacinth was one he wished he had not taken, and yet on he walked.

Too quickly, he found himself standing before his old home. They had maintained it well, by all appearances, at least externally.

None of the shingles had fallen off, and none of the windows had been cracked, or broken open. He stood on the very doorstep he'd walked off of long ago when he'd been his new life.

It should have been comforting, but instead, he shivered with the sensation that someone was watching him from the shadows. He lifted the knocker with one shaking hand and summoned footsteps to the door which he could not identify to his satisfaction.

Once the door had actually opened, he was relieved beyond his expectations at the sight of his very own mother. He wished he could swing the aging woman up into his arms, but she had yet to open the door completely, and he simply couldn't shove it open to do so.

"Mother..." he reached through the crack between the door and the frame to cup her cheek. "It's been too long..."

Her lips were wobbling as she threw the door open and rushed into his arms. "My son... You've finally returned... Why were you gone for so long this time?"

"I... I needed to build up my life... and —"

"How much of a failure are you this time?" the high-pitched voice of Hyacinth brought Richard's eyes toward her, as she stood in the center of the hall with gloved hands on hips.

"Actually... I've made a name for myself," Richard said, only barely fighting back his urge to take his mother and run from the house and from Hyacinth. "I am Duke Julian's personal lawyer."

"That's one of the first things I'll have to fix when I speak with him, then," Hyacinth said, tying her wide-brimmed hat onto her head with a ribbon knotted at the side of her chin.

"And when do you plan to speak with him?" Richard asked sourly, giving her a narrow-eyed glare so she knew he wasn't intimidated by her. At least, he wasn't intimidated *too* much by her.

She threw back her head and cackled, so that the wide brim of her hat reverberated as her layers of pale green muslin skirts all rippled about her legs. "Why today, of course! Didn't you hear how much he loves me, brother dear? How close can you really be to the duke when you don't even know who he's courting?"

Richard stared at her, and genuinely had to ponder that question. How long had his mother been keeping this arrangement a secret from him? He looked down at the tired woman, whose soft arms were still firmly encircling him. She had lived with Hyacinth for so long he could not imagine how severe this fate had been for her.

"It's true," his mother said gently. "We have such great hopes for her, and now we know we can give you both our blessings… our family has been chosen despite our station for greater things… I am so proud of my sweet ducklings."

For once, Richard did not bridle at the endearment. He had selfishly left his poor parents with his sister, and if his mother wanted to say something sweet, it was her right.

"Mother, may I come inside?" he asked. "I wish I'd come sooner so I could speak with you face to face, but…" his eyes drifted to Hyacinth, who was preening herself in the mirror.

His mother gave his hand an understanding squeeze, and she pulled him into the parlor, which smelled strongly of the roses which filled every vase set up in the room. There was never less than two feet between each bouquet, and the perfume was nigh overwhelming from it.

"I'm off, Mother," Hyacinth said, and flounced out of the house, slamming the door behind herself.

A carriage rolled up for her just as she stepped out, and Richard watched her as she was handed up into it with a smug smile on her face.

"I can't believe she still lives here," Richard said only when he was sure she was gone.

"She is not married, yet, it's only proper that she lives with us until her wedding day."

"And when that day comes… would you move outside the city?" Richard asked.

"But why? Your father and I are getting on in years, you know… Living in the city gives us access to things without needing to go far, and besides, all of our friends are here."

Richard grimaced as he realized that as true, and he could hardly ask his parents to undertake the arduous task of relocation without some plan or incentive in mind. Perhaps all it would take was removing the duke from power, and thus making the city easier to live in…

They could even be safe if the duke wanted to ensure he had in-laws… unless of course, Hyacinth told him to exterminate them… To do a thing like that, she would have to be ungrateful and capricious, and unfortunately for her family, Richard had no doubt she was both of those things.

"What is troubling you, my boy?" his mother asked, patting his arm gently.

"The trouble is, I'm terrified of what Hyacinth is capable of, but you aren't."

"I don't understand why you're so suspicious of her, dear. She's never done anything to you," his mother chided in her gentle way.

Richard gave her a compassionate look, taking her hand. "Mother, I never told you because I wanted to protect you. When I was small, Hyacinth would lock me in her closet. That was back when I had a nursemaid, and Hyacinth had her convinced I was reading quietly in my room and was not to be disturbed. She'd have me locked up in there as long as you two were out visiting, and every time I tried to fight back or tell her I'd warn someone, she said if I did that it meant I was a little baby."

His mother simply gaped at him in dismay, and he could see her trying to piece it all together with no success.

"Once I was finally big enough, I fought back, but before that… she just kept telling to be a good boy and obey quietly. I wasn't even allowed to cry, she told me you were testing me to see if I was brave."

His mother's eyes were glazing over as she slowly shook her head with the same expression as a grazing ewe.

"She kept mice and rats in that closet," Richard continued in a gentle monotone. "They were in cages, but there wasn't much room in that little closet for even a tiny boy with all those mice. She has a wicked streak you know. That's why I always avoid her if I can. Can you see why I don't want her near you?"

Tears were in his mother's eyes, and she gave him a desperate hug. "How did this happen if I was ever a good mother to you?"

"If I'd ever gotten up the courage to tell you, I know you would have put a stop to it. But I thought if I told you it meant I was weak and cowardly, and ironically enough that was my greatest fear. Maybe I was more afraid of your coming to my defense and making me feel like a baby who was still in his skirts… I thought I should just learn to handle it without someone's help doing that."

"You were such a brave boy, I always knew it, but this should prove it to you!" She cupped his cheeks affectionately, and he could still see tears in her eyes.

"I should have brought you along visiting with us. I always thought you preferred your books and didn't want to paddle about town visiting a bunch of ladies your mother's age and hearing all of our nonsense gossip…

That nursemaid of yours ought to have been fired rather than let go when you outgrew her!"

"No, no, don't be harsh to the poor woman." Richard brought out the half smile his mother had always liked to see him wear, and added, "she was just as afraid of Hyacinth falsifying some terrible story about her and ruining her entire life with it."

"I thought I was giving you time without your sister bothering you… and instead…" her lip wobbled and she hugged him tightly as her sobs ripped through her.

Richard gathered her into his arms and patted her back. "So did my nurse, Mother, please don't cry, it's unbearable to see you cry!"

His heart nearly exploded when he noticed that there was a *bestia* horse pulling a moderately attractive coach behind it. *Was that Hyacinth?* Already back?

Instead, his father's driver helped him out of the coach, cane and all, and the tired old fellow paid him a little extra before entering the house. At the sight of Richard and Mrs. Phaal, the latter in tears, Mr. Phaal stood staring in the doorway to the parlor.

"What are you doing?" Mr. Phaal asked. "Son, what did you do to your mother?"

"He's just told me that Hyacinth mistreated him as a boy!" Mrs. Phaal exclaimed amid the sobs Richard was still working to soothe away.

"She what?" Mr. Phaal's cane arm wobbled as he clenched his trembling jaw.

"It's not such a tremendous problem, anymore," Richard waved his hands as if to stifle a flame. "I was only informing Mother of why she ought not be trusted… I don't want her to live with you, anymore, especially because she's courting the duke… and actually I think maybe you should move out of Amontillado, altogether."

"You come into my house and tell me to run away?" Mr. Phaal asked. "Boy, you've been gone for a year, you shouldn't be giving us any orders!"

"They aren't orders, I'm giving you advice!" Richard was at his feet and shaking, constantly throwing his gaze through the parlor window to the street, wondering and fearing when Hyacinth would return.

"And what makes you think your advice is worth more than a few half *calchi*? I could cut copper pieces in half and they would still be more valuable than your advice! What? Do you want me to give up everything to appease some childhood fear of yours?"

"No, *no*, Father! I'm not talking about childhood fears here, this is about what I fear *now*! You have to get away from her before she turns around to destroy you! I don't want to learn she's poisoned your food for your money! She may even get away with it if she tried, since the duke is corrupt as any ancient emperor!"

"How could you say such a thing?" Mr. Phaal demanded. "The duke has been nothing but generous to us! In fact, business has never been better since he began to court Hyacinth! You ought to watch your tongue you've no idea what you're talking about!"

"Richard," Mrs. Phaal grabbed his hand and tugged on it for his attention just as if it had been a rope hanging from a bell. "Why don't you go upstairs? There are still some of your things there, you may wish to take them home while Hyacinth is away. I'll speak with your father." Her imploring look made Richard bow both to her and then to his father before slipping up the stairs.

These stairs still creaked, and they sang the same melody they had when he was a child beneath his feet, not a single note failing, just as a fine-tuned pianoforte. He paused to peer out the hall window on the second floor to assess how much time he would have for a brief investigation.

A few shop owners were still milling about getting their shops closed down. Richard's parents were engaged in contentious muttering below him in the parlor.

He pictured his mother with needle and thread and his father carving something idly, the way they had when he was a child, but this was a different time. There were strange noises coming from Hyacinth's room, and this was what absorbed his attention. They sounded like mice... mice that were...

He couldn't even imagine. If it were anything like what he'd seen in those cages so long ago... His mind had long ago chosen to defend him from the squeaking, screeching horror of it by making his mental images too fuzzy to interpret clearly. At least, he could not properly visualize them as long as he was *awake*...

Richard shivered. It was undeniable that these sounds were the same he'd heard when he was a child, and the same ones which echoed in his dreams. He turned over again.

How were his parents ignoring this? How had they *always* ignored this? With a shake of his head, Richard tried Hyacinth's door, and found it locked. It was really too bad he had no respect for her privacy. So long as she was courting the duke, she was likely the key to some evidence of his foul dealings.

After all his bumbling, he owed it to Amontillado and to Moretta to discover all he could and clear the path for convicting the duke. He didn't hope for evidence specifically in the Otranto case, but there had to be something!

First he went into his old room, which was more nursery than young man's room. There was his old hobby-horse, and his sailboat, and that painting of a knight fighting a dragon that he'd stared at in the gaslight from the street for hours after he was meant to be sleeping. That was something he ought to bring home, he decided, and though it pained him to alter the familiar tableau, he took it off its hook and tucked it under his arm.

There were his dear old books, as well, in the two-tiered shelf beneath his window and spreading along most of the wall, besides. He picked up the ones which seemed least childish first, but then decided he wanted them all, in case he was lucky enough to become a father, one day.

At last, having chosen a sufficiently thin but durable piece of a puzzle, Richard returned to the door for Hyacinth's room and slipped it between the lock and the doorjamb. He only realized part of him had been wishing it wouldn't open when in fact it did.

The perfume hit him first, and it was so thick he coughed on notes of orchid and vanilla. Was it so thick to cover the scent of her rodent prisoners? Why did he have to think that?

He stepped further into the room, though he had to pause in order to dab his eyes with a handkerchief in order to combat the tears which fell from them at the potent scent.

A pile of letters had been affixed to her writing desk by the point of a letter opener, which stuck out like an assassin's stiletto, brass blade and wooden handle both elegantly shaped so as to give off the air of sophistication. How many sophisticated people stabbed their mail, Richard couldn't rightly guess.

Still… he began to leaf through these letters. Envelope after envelope was addressed to Hyacinth from the desk of the duke, so as much as the perfume disgusted him, and as much as the squeaking from the closet unnerved him, Richard sat on her bed to do some light reading.

Chapter 32: Marching Orders

Hypothetically, Moretta was meant to be happy that she was no longer in Amontillado. Her mission was done, and she had successfully rescued at least three people… Even if statistically that was a laughable comparison to the victor's success.

She stood before the League of Inquirers, hands folded neatly at her back, and her head held high. For her appearance before the League, she had chosen to wear black, once more, even though her unexpected moniker of "Raven" seemed all the more fitting having chosen it.

"You have to realize how dire your accusations are, Miss L'Espanaye," one of the half-masked members said in a low voice and a feigned accent.

"I know that, but I also know what I saw with my own eyes," she said, and gestured to the easel on which pictures had been developed of Amelia's wounds. "My witness has also given her word as to the validity of my evidence… I have some photographs from the laboratory, itself, as well…" she moved Amelia's portrait out of the way to reveal the laboratory, instead. "They were taken with my goggles, so they are of lesser quality, I'm afraid."

"And this is the best you could offer us?" asked another member of the masked council. "We have to send a representative to Amontillado to demand the duke stand trial, and this is all you can give us?"

"In my opinion, this should be enough," Moretta said, grinding her teeth. "I have already detailed to you what happened to Count Otranto and his daughter, why should any more of what I've said leave you in dismay? The duke seized their property, after specifically targeting them. Are we not meant to look to he who benefits best from the killing? We thought Amelia dead for some time, and yet, she lives, due to phantomology."

"It's all so very exciting!" piped in the voice of a woman Moretta knew well, and her aunt's voice made her smile. "I rather think this is the sort of story we ought to prove correct! Imagine the scandal!" Perhaps she couldn't be perfect, but she was still her dear aunt.

"Yes, well, *exciting* as it may be, we cannot verify it," another masked member of the League said.

"I say we bring our concerns to the duke and let him answer for it," said yet another of the thirteen. "If he is innocent of these charges, it should be easily proven. However, if he is *not* innocent…"

"Then we shall have a bonfire and dance on his ashes!" Monique L'Espanaye cheered as she lightly but rapidly clapped her hands together beside her ear.

"Something like that," Moretta muttered under her breath. "Who shall be sent back to Amontillado to present my evidence?" she asked. "I'll have to brief whoever you choose."

"Why, I thought you would do it, dear!" Monique cried in surprise. "Don't you want to be the one who strikes him down after what he's done?"

"I was hoping never to meet him face to face again…" Moretta coughed.

"That's easily remedied: you could wear a mask!"

Moretta shivered, wishing she had been capable of confiding her terror of masks to her aunt, even once.

"The fact is, we cannot ask someone who has not seen what you have to stand against the duke as well as you could," one of the masked men said.

Moretta knew it was true, but she bowed her head. Yet, she knew what she would have to face should she be the one they sent back to confront the duke. It would not only be him, but Richard as well… could she truly bring herself to argue against Richard?

"While I was there, I became acquainted with the young man I know the duke will utilize as his legal defense," she said. "I fear our acquaintance with one another may put my prosecution in jeopardy, and thus I recuse myself of the position on the grounds that I could not adequately present the evidence as I normally would… Though, I will consent to appearing as the star witness for our side."

"We shall take your opinion on the matter into consideration," said Monique, holding the gavel poised aloft before letting it drop. "I hereby declare this meeting of the League of Inquirers adjourned!"

Chapter 33: Maladroit Malcontents

Richard had hoped that at least if he were forced to appear once more before the duke, he would not have to do it in the presence of Hyacinth, but this fond hope was swiftly dashed upon the rocks of despair. He stood fidgeting in the duke's office, wishing that he could be back in his apartment, arranging his reclaimed belongings and making his best approximation of the nursery he had once grown up in.

Instead, he'd had hours to spend listening to his father's ranting about how he had no right to waltz back home one day and demand that everything change to suit him, interspersed with his mother's tears. Then a mysterious telegraph had arrived at the duke's office, and a hideous rat-like *bestia* had been sent across town to fetch Richard.

Now he stood staring at Hyacinth's smug grin as she whispered into the livid duke's ear.

"My dear Hyacinth has told me you are indeed the best man for the job."

"What job is that?" Richard asked warily, glancing uneasily at his snickering sister.

The duke held up the telegraph which sat between them on his desk, and waved it in front of Richard. It was unclear how Richard was supposed to read the gold-tinged paper when it was waving about like that, but he sat patiently, unwilling to antagonize his superior.

"I've just received this missive from a group of busybodies, and apparently one of their spies thinks I need to be reined in and investigated!"

Richard raised a brow. Moretta the Raven did swift work! Just as he had suspected, however, he was on the wrong side of the issue. "In that case, what is to be done?" he asked, steeling himself as he did.

That poison dagger he'd promised to Amelia he would utilize seemed to be sharpening itself in his mind, preparing to stab him in the back. Appropriate enough, he supposed.

"When will this trial be, your grace?" Richard asked. "Part of preparing for this is about knowing how long I'll have to do it in."

"You'd better not procrastinate!" Hyacinth snapped at him. "Darling, tell him what he gets if he does well!"

"Do you mean besides his life, dearest?" he asked, and the two of them began to laugh in the most obnoxious manner Richard had ever been privy to in his lifetime. Still, the sound was beyond grating—he knew his life was now in jeopardy.

"Tell me what it is I need to know," he said, his voice trembling along with his knees. As hard as he tried, he couldn't hide either from them, and he saw their smugness written across both of their faces.

"If you are successful in defending me, I will turn over the Otranto estate to you, and you will be knighted as the first Knight of the Scarlet Order. I hear from Hyacinth it has been your lifelong wish to attain knighthood, and sadly if I do not maintain my position, there will be no order of knights for you to join..." the duke grinned broadly, yet still maliciously as he showed his every tooth. "...It would be a shame if you weren't given the chance to become a knight, when you're *so very honorable*, now wouldn't it?"

His gaze fell on Hyacinth again, and he knew she was the true primary manipulator. She knew all of his darkest secrets, and this was meant to entice him into betraying his principles in the name of earning the recognition of those same principles. If he were a lesser man, and he hoped he had judged himself well enough, he would have taken it.

"That sounds quite generous," he said, "but this is a task for a man who is much better seasoned than I."

He saw the cold smugness in the duke's and his sister's eyes shift into rage, and knew he'd said the wrong thing.

In a moment of inspiration, he dropped to his knee. "So make me something greater than I am, and I shall be capable of the task you have required of me."

Richard didn't dare look up to see their faces in the wake of this suggestion, but he could hear their hushed confidences, and knew that his fate rested in their hands.

"I shall acquiesce to your request," said the duke. "Before the court meets this evening, I will create you a knight, before the representatives from Boezia. Then they shall know I am a leader who takes pride in his citizens!"

Richard wished the duke could take pride in his citizens without taking any of them prisoner, but what did his preferences matter?

"I want some champagne before the *festivities* begin," Hyacinth said, leaning on the duke's chair before giving him a kiss to his cheek. "Please get rid of my little brother, won't you darling?"

The duke waved a dismissive hand at Richard. "Don't go far, boy, you'll be needed soon."

Richard bowed, all too eager to leave.

Once he was out in the halls, he realized he could not relax as he had expected. Sure, he could no longer see his sister or her lover, but he could not be sure they weren't still watching *him*.

Could they have cutouts in one of the portraits? That would explain why he felt so many eyes on him... He could hear Hyacinth's laughter despite the door closed between them, and he shivered at the horror of *knowing* his life was in her hands.

Any foul word from her could tell her *darling* Duke Julian to destroy him and send him into the bowels of that basement laboratory Moretta had described to him...

Which made him wonder, was it his duty to delve into that place to save its prisoners? What would he do with them if he did? There was no conceivable diversion which could rescue them, and where would he put them? They would surely all be caught!

As he was agonizing over all these things, a door opened down a hall he had been passing by. A trail of sleepy-eyed nobles wearing masquerade finery but with their masks tied around their arms were led by red-masked men in a dazed parade. They looked as if a carnival had just swept through the night before to leave them all drained.

"Move aside!" the slightly muffled voice of a man in a red mask snapped Richard out of his dismayed trance. "These are witnesses for the duke's trial!"

"Witnesses?" Richard repeated, pressing back against the wall in order to stay out of the way. "But… can they even speak?"

"That does not concern you!" one of the scarlet-masked individuals snapped at him.

"But I'm his lawyer…" Richard pressed a hand to his brow.

How was he supposed to put up a serviceable defense if he couldn't even gather preliminary information? It made a disappointing degree of sense that the duke wanted him to invent a story out of nothing, but he had been holding onto a single fiber of hope in humanity, which he now had to relinquish.

Standing aside as he'd been ordered, Richard noticed that he recognized two of the people who were being led up out of the darkness, and his pulse was arrested behind his ribs.

"Hans!" he gasped, and grabbed his cousin's arm, yanking both him and his dear Charlotte out of the doleful parade.

He gazed into his cousin's eyes, and saw that same glazed over cast to them as he had seen in every other eye.

Charlotte leaned on Hans's shoulder, and yawned, clinging to him as if he were her one anchor to reality.

Richard knew he could not leave them as they were, so he ushered their shambling bodies down yet another hall, diverting them out of the herd without drawing attention to their disappearance by some miracle. "What's the matter with you?" he demanded of them. "What were they doing to you?"

The two of them slumped against the wall, and it seemed the only thing about them that clung to reality was the way they held one another. It broke Richard's heart to see that his cousin and his sweetheart were so in love and yet so in peril. Would he and Lenore have stood like that after such an ordeal? No, he could not believe they would have.

This was genuine affection… of a desperate sort. He had never pitied his cousin before, but now, he did. It was a strange sensation in his heart when he realized that it was no longer Hans who should be pitied.

But what was he to do with the two of them? He certainly *would not* allow them to remain in the duke's custody! Would they be missed?

He checked their belongings, and found tags hanging from both their cloaks, hidden in the folds of fabric. Each of them had a subject number, and they were classified by their social stratum, both marked as the upper middling sort.

Their names, or at least abbreviations thereof, had been placed at the top of the cards, and Richard was amazed to see that somehow, an inventory of their households had been made, itemized by whether they owned any expensive works of art: paintings, sculptures, vases, miscellaneous…

Had the duke done this first with Count Otranto? Had he taken similar notes regarding the lady Amelia? This was a great bit of evidence, and Richard wished he could be on the accusing side… What could he possibly do that would save his neck as well as Amontillado?

He knew the answer: he had to be the sacrifice.

Chapter 34: Counterpart Counterpoint

Moretta was not the prosecutor, but she felt as if she'd just been handed Richard Phaal's death warrant and been asked to sign it. She sat behind a veil in the regal courthouse of Amontillado, which was thankfully merely adjacent to the grounds of the duke's castle. She was still within his realm of influence, but not within his very home.

It was much easier to walk into the courthouse with a retinue surrounding her, and her thick mourning veil hid her identity while allowing her a covert look at all those around her. It was the closest thing she could get to listening to live updates from her own cozy parlor far away from all this madness, so it was a comfort she clung to.

She sat within a wooden box on the leftward wing of the courthouse, where the benches had been cushioned in red velvet and she was able to lean against a similarly cushioned backboard.

If she could but close her eyes, she could be at her mother's dinner party years ago, when she was a precocious girl who was not really old enough for such things.

Yet, the courtroom gossip brought her back to the present, despite her wishes.

"They say the duke hired a corrupt lawyer just for this trial!" someone near her was whispering, and her heart skipped a beat with worry. Could this be Richard they spoke of?

"Oh, but this lawyer has been working for him for too long, he's not new, at all! This is his personal crony!"

Yes, they were discussing Richard. Moretta considered coming to his defense, but that may force her to identify herself, and she was in no mood to do a thing like that.

It was more enlightening to hear what gossip reported, she decided, and the facts of the upcoming trial would unveil the truths and falsehoods… At least that was her hope.

Her uneasiness was not calmed in the least when she noticed that the prosecution and jury had arrived, as well as several citizens of Amontillado, and yet there was no sign of Richard.

Had something dreadful happened to him since she left? Was the corrupt lawyer people were discussing someone else, entirely? Had Richard only been a useful pawn who was subsequently disposed of when he outlived his usefulness?

She fanned herself so furiously her veil whipped up in front of her face and nearly revealed her to the world. Had she abandoned her one true—*friend*—to his death? She would never forgive herself!

The duke appeared in a flourish of fanfare and banners appearing as they suddenly unfurled at the behest of some unseen mechanism between each window. The arms of Amontillado as well as the duke's personal crowned red dragon on black were displayed to add to the majesty of the duke's entrance.

He strode in wearing polished black boots and a red cape, with a woman on his arm dressed in matching black and scarlet, her blonde hair piled atop her head, *hatless*, and with bare shoulders as if evening attire were appropriate for the event.

Who *was* this impertinent lady?

Moretta would very much like to see someone teach her some respect for the sanctity of the court, as it was not her place to do so. Still, she was able to turn her eyes away from this woman and instead focus on the duke as he sat in the defendant's seat, and doffed his cap with a flourish.

He really ought to be much more uneasy due to his lack of a lawyer, but perhaps it was part of his game to pretend he was not afraid.

Still Moretta checked the courtroom for any sign of Richard she had missed. A fellow in a red carnival mask led a large group of men and women wearing ball gowns and motley into the audience's seating area, and Moretta quickly brought out her opera glasses for a closer look.

None of their faces looked as if they belonged to reasoning individuals… each of them looked as if they had just left an ether frolic… in fact… as far as they were concerned, it appeared they *had*… This was what the duke chose to do with the citizens he had kidnapped? What was his game?

The judge arrived, and all in attendance rose to respect the office of the honorable Judge Maximian Proust. He sat beneath his powdered wig, and gave his audience a dispassionate glance-over. "We seem to be short a member of the defense camp," he drawled.

"Yes," said the duke, "but I know my boy will come. Whatever business has will soon be concluded."

Moretta noticed the woman who had accompanied the duke into the courtroom fidgeting uneasily, and then she noticed how similar she looked to Richard. Odd. Perhaps it was down to the local attributes making the residents look similar.

"I have arrived!" came Richard's voice from the entrance to the courthouse, and all eyes turned in his direction, except for those of the duke.

His eyes remained firmly on his cuticles, as if nothing of importance had taken place.

"Where were you that was so important you could not be bothered to fulfill your solemn duty to the people of Amontillado and greater Zibelaude?"

Richard stood in the clear space between the gallery and the desks where the defense and the prosecution. His shoulders were squared off as if he were bravely standing against an onslaught, and he said, "Your honor, I found a relative of mine and his sweetheart in distress within his grace, Julian the Duke of Amontillado's home, and I secured safe passage for them, as well as someone to care for them."

"What was your relative doing in the duke's home in such a sorry state?" the judge asked.

"Well," Richard gestured to the sector of the gallery taken up by the intoxicated people who had been escorted in by the man in the red mask. "I'm afraid it is the same with them. They are all the subjects of brutal experiments in phantomology."

The sector of the gallery which was *not* made up of dazed evening-wear clad individuals peered at the sector which was, as did the jury.

"Phantomology?" the judge repeated in dismay. "That is a discredited school of thought! Lad, what are you trying to tell us?"

"I am trying to tell you I'm not a scientist of any sort, but these people have been kidnapped and tampered with to the extreme. It's inhumane, and whatever else happens today, we need to ensure that we prevent further injuries against humanity."

Judging by the set of the duke's shoulders, he had no contingency plan for a rogue Richard.

"We'll have to arrange that separately," the judge said, and gestured for the bailiff so that he could whisper something to him. "Mr. Phaal, please take your seat, the proceedings shall begin straightaway."

Richard bowed hastily and then he seated himself beside the duke, folding his hands in a tense manner that made Moretta pity him. If he got the chance, the duke would more than likely stab him.

"So it seems to me that the controversy before us today is whether or not the Duke of Amontillado has used his position as the duke to steal the assets of the Otranto family, as well as assassinate the Count, and kidnap his daughter. How does the defendant plead?"

"Not guilty," the duke said before Richard could say a single word.

It appeared that Richard would have liked to contest that argument, by the way he tilted his body away from the duke as if he smelled, but it was too late for any of that.

"Very well, the two parties shall now present their arguments," the judge said.

Both Richard and the prosecuting attorney got to their feet, and Richard cleared his throat. "I would like to allow my counterpart to speak first, should the court allow it."

The judge nodded and gestured to the prosecuting attorney. "The court recognizes the prosecution from Boezia."

The prosecuting attorney rose from her seat, and Moretta finally saw enough of her face that she could recognize her from her academy days. Adelaide Montressor was a member of an ancient family. While they were in confidence in the academy's grand library, Adelaide had once confided that she was only planning to attend law school because she knew how high the expectations her family had for her were. She couldn't stand to let down the family name.

Now, there she stood in a formal gray gown lined with black chord, and she utterly looked the part of a professional. Moretta wished she could applaud, except for the fact that it would be inappropriate.

"The prosecution contends that the accused has placed all those seen within the courtroom, as well as our witness and those who were retrieved by my esteemed counterpart in a dreadful state utilizing the *illegal* practice of phantomology. Not to mention, he is responsible for the death of a nobleman only to seize his property. However, some of this information is new, and I request that the court prolong these proceedings in order to fully examine those who have undergone this torment."

With all of that stacked against him, Moretta could only imagine what Richard planned to do.

Chapter 35: En Garde!

Richard's pulse was so rapid he thought a blood vessel was about to pop out of his wrist and he'd have to awkwardly push it back into place as if his trousers had fallen and he had to reclaim his dignity.

The duke was not actually looking at him, but he could still feel cold scorn on him. He was absolutely *doomed* once they got out of there.

Certainly, he had promised to die if it came down to that, but it was yet another thing to actually face that fate. Did he have to die immediately? He would rather prefer to hold on a little longer!

Why weren't the desks they were sitting at any longer? Why did he have to sit elbow to elbow with the duke? If everyone turned away, Duke Julian might reach over and strangle him!

He thought he could see Moretta sitting in the gallery, but it could just as easily be an actual widow, and not just a young lady who preferred black.

Was she here to come to his rescue? Ah, but that was a stupid thought. He was on his own.

"I *thought* you were going to *defend* me, not hand me over to my enemies!" the duke hissed.

"You didn't give me enough time to prepare, and I still don't know what sort of plea we're supposed to make with so many witnesses!"

The duke had been carrying a cane, Richard realized as the point of it pressed down on his foot. With a frozen, malicious smile, the duke continued to grind Richard's toes beneath the cane. "*You had better think of something!*" he whispered.

And he had better, indeed, because the judge's eyes had fallen on him and he was waiting expectantly for Richard's introduction.

He rose, though the duke did not remove the tip of his cane from Richard's toe. As he stood there, he did all he could to hide how much pain he was in.

"Your honor, I have been considering the evidence, and I believe there is another criminal who has yet to face any charges, but is no less deserving." He paused for effect, which lasted several agonizing moments longer than he meant it to.

The gallery and the jury were all leaning forward to stare at him, but they were muttering amongst themselves at such a fever pitch he knew they would not hear anything he said.

At last, they quieted enough for Richard to raise his somewhat higher-pitched voice and say, "The man who did this to these people is the one who ought to face this trial! I say we find him, and try him first. We haven't got all the evidence just yet, so no case against Duke Julian can be fully carried out."

The tip of the cane moved off of his foot, and he whistled out a desperate little noise he wasn't proud of.

"Is this all the defense has to say?" asked the judge, and Richard felt every eye on him.

Why did he have to disappoint everyone?

"Did your witnesses name the man who did this to them?" the judge asked the prosecutor.

"All we know is that he is a doctor, and that his surname is 'Shade,'" the woman said, "and we believe he is of foreign extraction."

"Our first priority shall be finding him, then," the judge said, and slammed his gavel down on his desk. "Court is adjourned until Dr. Shade can be apprehended for questioning!"

Richard's knees nearly buckled out from under him, but he somehow succeeded in standing until the judge had left the courtroom. Once he had the chance, he dropped into the seat.

The duke gripped his shoulder, and pushed him down on the chair, glaring at him as he hissed, "Next time you will do better! You will *not* shame me again!"

With that, he stalked out of the courtroom, grabbing Hyacinth by the arm as he went.

Richard sat still a moment longer until he was certain he had not soiled himself. He glanced into the gallery to check on the woman he thought could be Moretta, but she was gone.

He hoped he'd done the right thing, but how could he be certain?

Chapter 36: To Fight Again

They'd almost *had* him! The duke had almost paid for at least *some* of his crimes, and he was now free for just that bit longer! Who knew how many people he could harm as long as he had that freedom?

Moretta stood outside the courthouse with Renata furiously purring in her arms as tears streamed down her face. They were shrouded in the shadow of the courthouse in the lane where the carriages were meant to drive up out of the carriage house.

Yes, Richard had meant to apprehend the duke later, hadn't he? All they needed was more evidence… but would they ever get it?

How long could Dr. Shade remain in hiding, now that the duke knew his own freedom to do as he pleased was contingent on the man's remaining out of sight? She held Renata tightly against her chest as she wept bitterly over how very *stupid* Richard had been.

"Moretta? Is that you?" Richard's voice was coming from somewhere so near she knew she had to be imagining it. She didn't look up until a hand was on her shoulder.

"I've never seen you cry before…"

She didn't look up, and she was grateful for her veil. "You haven't known me very long, I *do* that," she pulled away and huddled with Renata deeper in the shadows.

"Why? I know I didn't handle that as perfectly as I could have, but, what—"

"You let him go! The investigation is suspended, and nobody will stop him from doing whatever he wants in the meantime!"

"No… no, I'll be—"

"As effective as you have been today?" she demanded, ashamed that she'd ever believed in him. "Any time he murders someone from here on out, the blood is on your hands!" She knew he had been struck silent without looking at him, and she sank into the corner between the carriage house door and the wall.

"I know it looks bad…" Richard knelt before her, and reached for her, but was thwarted by Renata hissing at him and taking a swipe with one paw. "I know it *is* bad…" Richard sighed. "But I also know something else… I know this is bigger than just this case we had set up, and I didn't have nearly enough preparation time to do the best job I could have."

"Why are you just giving me excuses?"

"Because that's all I have… but you can count on me, despite it all. We just need to work closer in the future… I'll need to know more of your secrets. I know there has to be a great deal you aren't telling me, but you could be my greatest ally… I need you, Moretta." So quickly that Renata could not stop him, he flipped her veil up to reveal her face and gaze directly into her eyes. "Are you going to stay in Amontillado? Do I need your address for someplace abroad?"

"I'm moving right back into the Raven house," she admitted. "My work here isn't done, yet."

"I'm glad!" he grinned genuinely and leaned closer to kiss her forehead, though she didn't feel it through the shield of fringe which covered her brow.

She honestly had no reply to that, but as they heard mechanical hooves on the carriage house floor directly behind the door they sat beside, she didn't have time to think.

Richard grabbed her hand and it was all she could do to hold onto Renata as Richard dragged the two of them rapidly out of the covered path back to the front of the courthouse.

As she gasped for breath, Richard pulled her veil down and they watched the carriage pass them by. The driver rolled his eyes at them, but the windows were shaded over.

From within the coach, they could hear an argument going on, between a man and a woman. The words were muffled, but the poison was not.

Only when the coach had passed them did Richard take Moretta's hand.

"I want to take you home, help you get settled back in," he said softly. "I know it must be dreadful to come back, and you did it out of duty, but you could still stand to enjoy some of it."

"I don't think it would be good for the two of us to be seen together," she said, though she had not the will to extricate her hand from his.

"You're wearing a veil," he pointed out. "Come, Raven, I won't reveal your name to anyone... I'm merely a gentleman escorting a lady back to her home... I need to have this time to discuss matters with someone who knows all that I do... and perhaps we have things we can share, already... please?"

Moretta pursed her lips, but she, too, longed to be with him, so she nodded, letting Renata climb onto her shoulders as she would. "So you'll just keep serving the duke? What happens when he turns on you?"

"I'll need a contingency plan for that," he sighed. "Right then wasn't the best time to reveal myself… I'm sorry if I failed you somehow."

"I think if what you say is true it's a shame we rushed into it," she shrugged. "All those people are free now, and we're going to put some investigation into whatever the duke's friends are doing… but you should know, he's going to be watching you very closely now. He can't rely on you to stay in your place."

"I don't so much know that I *have* a place," Richard admitted, and she checked his face. He seemed more optimistic than she'd expected, and that was a good sign, right?

"Well, I could always use an assistant for my own work," she offered. "Someone to batter around legal jargon with would be welcome, since I'm something of an investigator."

"Are you now? I know you were expecting to be a witness before I thoroughly dashed the case to bits."

"I was… Frankly the postponing of this case will make it all the more dire when the shoe drops, but… I would worry more about you. It is possible people who attended today's proceedings will have quite the wrong impression of you, as I did."

Richard flinched. "At least… people know not to trust the duke…" he gave her a grimace and she knew he was reaching out for her to give him hope.

Alas, she was not adept at such things.

"I'm sure you're going to face your challenges, but we all will. The duke has yet to fall, so we have no time to languish in fear."

"Right…" he cleared his throat, and before she was aware of it, Moretta realized they were at her doorstep. "I ought to… collect my thoughts… is there anything I can do for you?"

"No, I've already had my things delivered here… but thank you… it's time I went to sleep… but I shall see you tomorrow. I wish you well in your endeavors." She unlocked the door and opened it, then stepped into the shadowed house. "Tomorrow, dear sir, we shall see one another again."

He bowed to her, then tipped his hat. "Farewell, dear young lady… I am glad you will keep the light burning in this town."

She could not quite understand what he meant, but she allowed him to go without explaining himself.

As Richard walked away from her, she watched the gas lamps in the streets slowly buzzing on to light his path, as if he were walking along the path to Heaven's very gates.

"Not yet," Moretta whispered to him, "stay down here a little longer."

Renata rubbed her head against Moretta's cheek, popping her thoughts firmly back into the realm of reality.

"Yes, I know, we're back," Moretta sighed to Renata as she flicked on the gaslights.

In the sudden illumination she saw the parlor filled with specters, all staring expectantly at her.

She flicked the lights back off. "I'll deal with all of you tomorrow," she yawned and walked up the stairs, remembering well enough where to go.

Getting any sleep at all would be important—there was no telling what trials the dawn may bring.

Chapter 37: X

Ordinarily, Richard might have gone home, but he had the sneaking suspicion that if he went there, he would find an assassin or even a bomb awaiting him. Yet, he had to go somewhere and clear his mind.

That need gave birth to the realization that his mind had never been clearer than when he'd had a run-in with the green fairy.

His feet led him eagerly toward Bonnie's, his mouth watering at the thought of all the potions available at their absinthe bar.

The shop was quiet, but soft orchestral waltzes were still to be heard playing on the second floor. Richard seated himself at the bar and called for the barmaid's attention, as she was in a back room.

She came bustling back in and gave him a quick curtsey. "What can I get for you, my dear?" she asked.

"I'd like a Hearthfire Fairy, if you please," he smiled softly as he felt his exhaustion begin to overtake him. Perhaps it would be for the best if he slept in the shop and was unable to return home.

He was quickly treated to a cinnamon spiced drink which burned its way down his throat even as his mind was unlocked by the sweet magic of the absinth.

"Why are you here alone so late at night?" the woman asked. "Business is terrible when the center of town is abuzz with gossip."

"I know more about what they're talking about than any of them, so I see no real reason to be there," he shrugged, and eagerly drank still more. "Besides…

I had some part in it. I just don't know how I can make it better," Richard sighed, crossing his arms and leaning his brow on them. "Here I am, the idiot… unmasked to the world… and I'm nothing but filth."

"You know…" the bartended patted his hand. "Every day at Bonnie's, we unmask our wares and we make a grand showing of what we've got to sell… and then every night, we put our masks on and Bonnie's looks like a completely different place."

"I know, that's part of the place's charm," Richard smiled in spite of looking down at the counter and not revealing how the woman's words had distracted him from his shame.

"And, you know… when we take the masks off, we have another personality than when the masks are on… like in a Commedia or an opera. We play different roles, and the people who visit us have different feelings about us each time…"

Richard's eyes widened, and he looked up at the woman, but he could barely see her eyes behind the false lashes which created a star like outline around her eye holes. Still… he could see her smirk. "Everyone knows who I am…" he said weakly.

"Yes, and that is unfortunate," she returned, and he watched her smirk twitch. What wasn't he understanding, yet? He glanced about the room as if to see if she'd gotten an idea from something she could see in the room… But when he looked back at her, she was gone.

Instead, he saw a mask on the counter, a white Commedia mask… Pedrollino. The naïve fool… always believing people who lied to him and blaming himself for events which had either never happened, or which were out of his control.

"Fitting…" he huffed to himself, and slowly raised the mask to his face. That was fitting, as well.

Perhaps it would suit him, this new face.

One day, he could take it off in daylight, but beneath the moon, he would atone for what he had done, and none would know his name.